Wolfsbane
WINTER

Visit us at www.boldstrokesbooks.com

What Reviewers Say About Jane Fletcher's Celaeno Series

"...captivating, well-written stories in the fantasy genre that are built around women's struggles against themselves, one another, society, and nature."—*WomanSpace* Magazine

"In *Rangers at Roadsend* Fletcher not only gives us powerful characters, but she surprises us with an unexpected ending to the murder conspiracy plot, pushing the story in one direction only to have that direction reversed more than once. This is one thrill ride the reader will not want to get off."—*Independent Gay Writer*

"*The Walls of Westernfort* is not only a highly engaging and fast-paced adventure novel, it provides the reader with an interesting framework for examining the same questions of loyalty, faith, family and love."—*Midwest Book Review*

"*The Walls of Westernfort* is…a true delight. Bold, well-developed characters hold your interest from the beginning and keep you turning the pages. The main plot twists and turns until the very end. The subplot involves likeable women who seem destined not to be together."—*MegaScene*

What Reviewers Say About
The Lyremouth Chronicles

"Jane Fletcher once again has written an exciting fantasy story for everyone. Though she sets her stories in foreign worlds where the traditional role of women are reversed, her characters (are) all too familiar in their inner lives and thoughts. Unlike the Celaeno series (which I highly recommend) where there are no men, this series incorporates male characters that help round out the story nicely...Fletcher has a way of balancing the fantasy with the human drama in a precise way. She never gets caught up in the minor details of the environment and forgets to tell the story, which happens too often in fantasy fiction...With Fletcher writing such strong work, readers of fantasy will continue to grow."—*Lambda Book Report*

"*The Exile and the Sorcerer* is a mesmerizing read, a tour-de-force packed with adventure, ordeals, complex twists and turns, and the internal introspection of appealing characters. The author writes effortlessly, handling the size and scope of the book with ease. Not since the fantasy works of Elizabeth Moon and Lynn Flewelling have I been so thoroughly engrossed in a tale. This is knockout fiction, tantalizingly told, and beautifully packaged."—*Midwest Book Review*

By the Author

Wolfsbane Winter

THE LYREMOUTH CHRONICLES

The Exile and the Sorceror

The Traitor and the Chalice

The Empress and the Acolyte

The High Priest and the Idol

THE CELAENO SERIES

The Temple at Landfall

The Walls of Westernfort

Rangers at Roadsend

Dynasty of Rogues

Shadow of the Knife

Wolfsbane
WINTER

by

Jane Fletcher

2010

ISBN 10: 1-60282-158-5
ISBN 13: 978-1-60282-158-3

This Trade Paperback Original Is Published By
Bold Strokes Books, Inc.
P.O. Box 249
Valley Falls, NY 12185

First Edition: July 2010

Credits
Editor: Stacia Seaman
Production Design: Stacia Seaman
Cover Design By Sheri (graphicartist2020@hotmail.com)

Acknowledgments

To Joanie, Ruth, and Jo for reading the first draft and making helpful suggestions.

To Sheri for the cover.

To Stacia, Cindy, and everyone else at Bold Strokes for being so wonderful to work with.

To Rad for making it all possible.

Dedication

To Joanie

A mining camp, 60 miles east of Oakan
8th year of the reign of King Alvarro II
Late summer, setiembre 5, midday

Deryn pulled back the bowstring and locked her hand under her chin. She squinted, lining up the bow with the target, and then carefully relaxed her fingers, letting the string roll off the archer's tab. Her arrow thudded into the tree, a bare inch from the center of the chalked cross she had been aiming at. Smiling in satisfaction, she reached over her shoulder for her quiver.

Without warning, a fury of hoofbeats erupted, charging toward her. She barely had time to react before the rider thundered past, crossing so close behind that the horse's tail flicked her arm. A bowstring twanged and a second arrow struck the tree, this one a hand's width from the cross.

Deryn's heart pounded, in part due to the jolt of surprise and in part due to the sight of Shea, moving as if she and the horse were one, a single fluid entity. At the edge of the clearing, Shea turned in an impossibly tight circle for someone controlling her horse purely by pressure from her knees, and galloped back. Already she had another arrow on the string, ready for her second shot. This one went wider of the mark, clipping the edge of the tree. Shea wheeled around again, her horse slowing.

A chorus of good-natured catcalls came from the group of Iron Wolf mercenaries who were eating lunch at the other side of the campsite. Shea responded with a laugh and an obscene gesture as she jumped down from her horse before it had stopped completely.

Shea gave the tree a long, critical stare and then grinned at Deryn. "Okay. Your arrow was nearer, but you were standing still. Do you want to try on horseback and see if you can beat me?"

"Ah, no. I know I um…couldn't, it's…" Deryn stopped trying to talk and settled for a smile that she hoped was not too sickly.

Shea gave a loud laugh. "It's all right. You did pretty well, for a scout."

"Oh. Thanks."

"Nobody is gonna expect anything much in the way of fighting from you. That's the job of us warriors."

"Uh. Yeah."

Deryn could not believe how lame she was sounding. Not a single intelligent thought was in her head. Her palms started sweating. She tried to wipe them surreptitiously on the legs of her pants, while praying her body would not betray her in even worse ways, such as by blushing. Shea had joined the band of mercenaries at the mine six days before, and this was the first time they had exchanged more than a one-word greeting, although Deryn had dreamed about it.

Shea patted Deryn's shoulder and then strolled to the tree. "Scouts are there just so you know where you're going, but I tell you, the scout in my last party was a fucking useless waste of space."

Deryn's stomach had catapulted through a loop at the pat and her knees were unsteady. Yet somehow, she managed to follow Shea, who carried on talking.

"D'you know, the jerk led us right into the middle of a windigo nest. First thing we knew about it, I was staring at teeth the size of my fingers"—Shea held up her left hand to illustrate, then raised the other one, leaving a scant yard between her palms—"this far from my face. I tell you, I was…" She shook her head ruefully and dropped her voice to a confidential whisper, even though nobody else was near enough to hear. "I was shitting myself."

Deryn wished she could make a casual, offhand quip, as one Iron Wolf to another, expressing solidarity for the hazards of their profession, but she had never seen a live windigo, let alone fought one. She reached the tree and pulled her arrow out, which gave her a few more seconds to think, but the best she could come up with was, "That must have been…um…nasty."

"It sure was. Luckily, Hagan and Raul were sharp about it. They got the beast's attention long enough for me to get out of biting range. Then the three of us polished it off."

"Good you had comrades on hand you could rely on." At last she had managed to string a proper sentence together.

"Too true. It's more than I can say for that damned scout. Useless fool. I mean, the windigo was twenty feet long, we'd marched bang into the heart of its territory, and the idiot claimed he hadn't seen any sign of it. What was the point of having him on the team?"

"Was that when you got injured? I heard you'd been hurt riding the Trail, so you couldn't complete the journey. Someone mentioned it to me, kind of in passing." Deryn did not want to give the idea that she had been actively hunting down gossip about the new arrival, even though it would be true.

"No. That was a completely separate cock-up on his part. The jerk picked a dumb-ass place to ford a river and my knee got wrenched."

"That's too bad."

"Yeah. I couldn't ride for a couple of weeks, and the traders couldn't hang around if they were to get to Sluey and back before winter. Luckily we were near a fortified way-house, where they could leave me. When I was fit to ride, I tagged on with a group heading back to Oakan. But I'd only gotten paid for the part of the journey I'd done. That's why I needed to fill in for a month with this job here." Shea glanced around dismissively. "It's not what I'd have chosen. Way too dull. But you've been here some time, right?"

"Yes. Brise and me came with the miners, when they started, in spring."

"Why?"

"The miners wanted protection. We've had a few hungry bears and a cougar sniffing round."

Shea threw back her head and laughed. "Yeah, bears. That's about what I'd expect. Hardly needs Iron Wolves to handle it. But what I meant was, why did Brise accept a piddly, god-awful job like this? She doesn't strike me as a total waster. She's not scared to tackle the Misery Trail, is she?"

Even though Shea was the one saying it, and she had been smiling while she spoke, Deryn felt a kick of irritation. She glanced across to where Brise stood with a couple of miners, one foot on the log they were using as a seat, chatting to them while they finished lunch. A casual pose. Yet always Brise had the air of a cat about her, senses alert to everything and a lithe muscled body, ready to react in an instant.

"Brise is a really good scout, and she's ridden the Trail, loads of times."

Deryn's tone must have registered. Shea held up her hands. "Hey,

I didn't mean no disrespect. She's your mother, right? And like I said, she strikes me as being way more useful than most scouts you meet on the Trail. That's why I'm surprised she'd spend a whole season here, playing nursemaid to miners. If she used to ride the Trail, what made her stop?"

"She adopted me, a few years ago. She reckoned I was too young for the Trail then, so we've been..." Deryn shrugged rather than finish the sentence, hoping the admission would not make her seem too much like a child in Shea's eyes.

"Is she gonna do the Trail again?"

"She said she would, once I'm old enough. Just another year or two and I can join the Iron Wolves."

"You want to?"

"Yes."

"You'll be a scout, like her?"

"Of course." Deryn raised her eyes and met Shea's level gaze. A whole second passed before Shea looked away. Deryn swallowed and her stomach formed a tight knot. How much eye contact counted as significant?

"I've been a Wolf for two years. You really should talk your mother into doing the Misery Trail next year. That's a real job for an Iron Wolf. Beats any crap mining camp." Shea smiled and ran her eyes over Deryn. "You're adopted, you said?"

"Yes, five years ago."

"Right. That explains it."

"What?"

"That you don't look much like her. I mean, you've both got the scout-type build, like you could do with an extra meal or two. Anyone can see you don't have the muscles to be a warrior."

Deryn let the comment pass, even though she felt she was plenty strong enough.

Shea continued. "You're a lot paler than Brise—your skin, straw-colored hair, and your eyes. Are they blue or green?"

"I've been told it depends on the light."

"Right." Shea smiled, and her voice dropped. "You know, I'd noticed them before now. They're really nice."

Deryn's heart jumped a beat while her palms again grew sticky. "Um...thanks...I—"

"Deryn. You finished practicing your archery?" A shout from Brise rang across the camp.

"Ah, yeah." Deryn spun away from the tree, holding out her bow in a pointless gesture. Brise would be quite well aware that she had been chatting for the last five minutes, rather than doing what she was supposed to.

"We ought to run a sweep. Come on."

Deryn glanced at Shea. "Maybe we'll talk some more when I get back."

"Sure. I'm not going anywhere." Again Shea held the eye contact for a moment longer than normal.

Deryn turned and trotted away, her heart thumping against her ribs.

"We'll start out east and swing by the lake." Brise set off without waiting for a reply, vanishing into the trees.

Deryn took two steps but then stopped for a last look around the clearing. The mining camp in the valley was as close to idyllic as could be expected after a dozen miners had spent six months there, digging for gold. A dense forest of pine trees blanketed the flanks of the mountains on either side. A gurgling river ran along the bottom, glinting in the warm sunlight. Birdsong rippled down from the treetops, overlying the shushing of a breeze through the branches.

Shea had wandered over to join the remaining four Iron Wolves and had lain down, her tall frame stretched on the grass, with her hands behind her head as a pillow. The pose emphasized the width of Shea's shoulders and the firm muscles of her stomach and thighs. Deryn could not stop herself staring, taking in every detail, as she had been doing since Shea arrived at the camp.

Initially, the miners had needed guards only for wild animals, but now their store of gold had grown and human predators also presented a risk. The most dangerous time would be when they broke camp, in another month or so, and carted their entire season's cache to Oakan. Hence, the miners had employed Shea and the two other Iron Wolves who had arrived with the last supply wagon.

Immediately, the young female warrior had caught Deryn's attention. Never before had she seen anyone ride in the way Shea could. When added to her athletic body, her relaxed self-assurance, and the scant few years separating them, Shea presented an irresistible lure.

Roughly a fifth of Iron Wolves were women, most of them scouts or trackers, like Brise. Warriors such as Shea were rare. The raw muscle power required for fighting put women at a disadvantage. Even with her height, Shea could not hope to match a man in strength, but she more than made up for it with her skill on horseback. Deryn felt her skin warm with the memory of Shea shooting at the tree.

"Hey, Deryn. Where are you?"

"Coming." Deryn hurried to catch up with her foster mother and mentor.

No breeze permeated the dense matting of branches as she and Brise climbed the hillside. The warm air surrounded Deryn like a cocoon. Sounds were muted, colors dimmed. Brise drifted through the gloom, silent as a ghost. Deryn tried her best to copy the stealthy footsteps, while at the same time taking in as many details as she could. Brise would be sure to quiz her later about anything significant they had passed.

After a mile of climbing, they reached a rocky outcrop, where a recent landslip had stripped away the tree cover below. The spot was a favorite lookout point, providing a view down the valley.

Brise settled on a convenient boulder, her eyes fixed on the distance. "You and Shea were having a good chat."

"Ah…yeah." This was not the topic Deryn had expected, and she needed a moment to adjust her thoughts.

"You shouldn't take what she says too seriously."

"What do you mean?"

"She doesn't know quite as much as she thinks she does."

Deryn was confused. What did Brise think they had been talking about? "She was telling me about the Misery Trail. She said we ought to do it next year."

"That proves my point. The Trail is no place for children."

"I'm sixteen."

"Just barely."

Deryn tried not to pout. "Shea's only a bit older than me, and she's done it."

"I'd put her three or four years older. And she got hurt."

"It was an accident."

"Yup. Accidents are what kill you, and they mostly happen to people who are young and inexperienced."

"It wasn't her fault."

"She told you that?"

Deryn nodded.

"How many things that have gone wrong in her life were her fault?" Brise looked skeptical. "Believe me. I know the sort. Nothing is ever her fault or happens because she isn't good enough."

"Shea helped kill a windigo that attacked her party. If I'm gonna become a scout, I'll need to know how to deal with things like that."

Brise laughed. "Most windigos are hulking great things that leave footprints so deep you could follow them blindfolded, without getting off your horse. Believe me, after tracking something the size of a rabbit, windigos will be a piece of piss."

"There has to be something I—"

Brise did not move, except maybe the lines around her eyes hardened, but Deryn knew her well enough to tell that the experienced scout had spotted something.

Damn. Deryn had gotten too caught up in what they were saying and had let her attention slip. The lapse was not the sort of thing Brise would overlook, nor would it help win the argument over the Misery Trail. She turned and scanned the valley below.

Two miles distant, a flock of sparrows had risen and were swirling around. The small birds skimmed low over the treetops, settling for a second, only to rise again. Whatever was upsetting them lay below rather than above.

"Do you think it might be bears or wolves?" Brise asked.

"Of course not. The sparrows would ignore them."

"Something in the trees? A snake?"

This was a trickier question. Deryn hesitated. "No. The locus is moving. It's gone about fifty feet while we've been watching. That's walking pace. It has to be people, and they're making enough noise to upset the sparrows. Nobody from the camp is gonna be over there, so it's someone new in the area, but I don't know who."

Brise gave a soft laugh and patted Deryn's shoulder. "No. That would be a bit of a hard question to answer from here—even for me."

The miners' campsite was in the wilderness, with no proper road leading to it, but over the course of the year the supply wagon had left a trail that would be easy to follow, except this was not the route the strangers were taking.

Deryn frowned. "They're heading south of the mine. If they keep on that path, they'll bypass it altogether."

"That's what I was thinking."

"So have they got no interest in the mine?"

"That's another question that's a bit hard to answer from up here, but I suspect..."

"What?"

Brise shook her head. "There's no point guessing. Let's go find out."

She set off, moving more directly and faster than on her ascent of the hillside, but making no more noise.

Deryn kept close behind, stepping in Brise's footsteps. All her senses were on such a keen edge it felt as if they were outside her skin, yet it was hard to hear anything over her heartbeat booming in her ears. For the second time in an hour Deryn's stomach tightened in a knot, but in a very different way and for a very different reason. She was good in the wilderness. She knew it. Otherwise Brise would not have taken her as foster daughter and apprentice. Deryn just hoped, when it came to a crisis point, she would be good enough.

Brise motioned for them to stop in the cover of a dense clump of undergrowth. The spot overlooked a shallow gully, with a stream cascading over a rocky bed. Deryn had barely slipped into place beside her foster mother when she caught the sound of horses, getting closer. She quickly checked to ensure that the bush was concealing all of her and then peered through a gap in the leaves.

In single file, nine horsemen rode by, following the line of the stream. The riders were dirty and disheveled. Clearly they had been on the road for a while. Their clothes and gear were old and of poor quality, except for their weapons, which were in prominent display. There was no mistaking where the group had spent whatever money they had scraped together. The arsenal was quite excessive for any threat from wild animals, and the leader was not wearing the badge of the marshal's men, which left only one conclusion.

Deryn waited until the sound of horses had faded before speaking. "Outlaws."

"I fear so."

"Do you think they're here to steal the miners' gold?"

"It's hard to see what else they'd be after."

"How'd they know where the mine is?"

"Maybe we'll get the chance to ask them."

Deryn chewed her lip. "There's only nine of them. We outnumber them, if you add in the miners."

"The miners have paid us to defend them. They shouldn't have to defend themselves."

"They will, though, won't they, rather than lose their gold?"

"That's not the point." Brise pursed her lips. "And anyway, this gang might be on their way to hook up with others." She stared thoughtfully at the point where the riders had vanished into the forest. "Go back to the camp. Tell Faren what we've seen and get the camp organized for defense. I'm going to track the gang and see if I can find out anything more."

Deryn ducked her head to hide her disappointment and irritation. *She's treating me like a kid again, sending me out of danger's way.* The thought rankled, but any temptation to plead her case was immediately countered by knowledge that Brise was right. The other Iron Wolves needed to be made aware of what was happening, and acting like a sulking toddler would not be a good way to impress Brise with her maturity.

Deryn nodded sharply. "Right. I'll see you back at camp."

❖

Deryn peered over the top of the hastily erected barricade. The logs had been cut ready for use as mine supports, and it had been the work of minutes to turn them into a very solid wall around the entrance to the main shaft. To her left, a couple of miners were whispering to each other as they also stood watch. Deryn ignored them, keeping her attention fixed on the deserted scene before her.

Virtually nothing of the camp remained in view. They had dismantled everything they could and carried it into the mine. One of the miners was currently leading the horses far away up the mountain, in the hope that the outlaws would not think them worth pursuing. Only the supply wagon was left. Its loss would be a nuisance for the miners, but it would not present much in the way of spoils, should the outlaws settle for looting what they could under cover of night and then leaving.

The stretch of grass looked peaceful in the sunlight. At the far edge of the clearing, the river looped around the base of a rock face before disappearing into the woods. The only movements were branches, swaying in the breeze, and the water, cascading over rocks. On either side, the precipitous valley walls were impassable on horseback, but it was unsafe to assume that any attack would come along the rough track beside the river. The outlaws could easily scramble down the hillside. The trees would conceal their approach, although the broken slopes would not offer a promising start for a coordinated attempt at storming the barricade.

Abruptly, the background chatter of birdsong faltered and was replaced by scattered chirps of alarm. Someone was approaching. Deryn scoured the valley for the first sign as to who. A flash of white showed between the branches at a height of about eight feet, which was right for a mounted rider. However, the motion was wrong, swaying from side to side, and Deryn was not surprised that the figure who eventually stepped clear of the trees was on foot. The white cloth was a grubby shirt, tied to the end of a stick.

The man holding it was tall and powerfully built. Corded muscle bunched in his arm as he waved the makeshift flag above his head. His heavy jaw was covered in black stubble. A broken nose and a studded leather jerkin completed the look of a fighter, but was he a warrior or a street brawler? At his side was a second figure, smaller and paler in complexion, a woman with the sharp eyes and light tread of a scout.

"Faren. Someone's here. They want to parley," Deryn called.

The two miners broke off their muttered conversation. Presumably, they had been too busy talking to keep watch and had not spotted the outlaws' arrival.

Faren emerged from the darkness of the mine, his arms folded across his broad chest. He was fifty or so, easily the oldest of the Iron Wolves. His age explained why he no longer rode the Misery Trail, but he was still tough and his experience made him the unquestioned leader of the mercenary guards. Deryn trusted him totally. Even so, she would have been happier if Brise were there. Deryn caught her lip in her teeth. Why had Brise not yet returned? Surely nothing could have gone wrong.

A knot of miners clustered behind Faren. Their faces revealed nervousness, contrasting markedly with the impassive confidence of the senior mercenary.

"What do you want?" Faren shouted the challenge.

The tall man planted his feet square on the ground and smiled. "Don't be silly. We want your gold, of course."

"At the risk of sounding even sillier, I'd point out that we're a well-armed band of Iron Wolves, and we're in a strong defensive position. The miners are just as keen as us to stop you getting their gold. I'm sure they'll lend a hand, or a pickaxe, if needed. So unless you've got a good-sized army to call on, I don't rate your chances."

"I don't need an army. I've got something better."

The man handed his flag to his companion, then reached over his shoulder and pulled a black tube from the pack on his back. The tube was the length of his arm and three or so inches across. A bar protruded from a collar at the midway point. The man cradled the tube in his arms while gripping the bar.

"Let me introduce myself. My name is Martez. And I'm an Iron Wolf too." He paused and tugged on his ear. "Except I've sorta retired, ever since last year when I rode the Trail with the worst bunch of useless assholes I've ever had the bad luck to meet. Their own mothers must have been glad to see the back of them. As for the journey, you name it, and it went wrong. We were way overdue on the way back. Luckily, the weather held out for us, and I thought we were gonna make it. And then, four days from Oakan, a blizzard popped up on the horizon. I was about ready to stick my head between my legs and kiss my ass good-bye." Martez laughed loudly, but little humor underlay his tone.

"No fucking clue where we were. The scout had gotten us lost. Then we saw some ruins. I'd never seen them before, and I've done the Trail enough times. Everyone else was too scared to go in. But the sky was turning black and there was a shitload of snow coming. I reckoned nothing in the ruins could kill me any worse than the blizzard. So I gave the rest of the party a one-finger farewell and hightailed it in."

Deryn glanced at Faren. The senior mercenary had his lips set in a firm line, clearly waiting for Martez to finish his story before responding.

"It must have been a nice little town for the Ancients, back in the Age of Wonders, but the demons had hit it hard, and there weren't much left to see. I didn't wander in too far. Didn't want to bang into a windigo nest. I just dived down the first set of stairs I found, into a cellar. Then the storm hit and the snow started to follow me in. I left my horse by the entrance and moved further along. That's when it got creepy. The ceiling lit up and the place warmed a tad. I just found a little corner where nothing could sneak up behind me and settled down to wait out the storm. I had supplies. I was snug. My horse would get hungry, but there was nothing I could do about it. The rest of the party—they had no chance. No big loss." Martez shrugged.

"The storm lasted three days. After the first day, I got bored and since nothing had tried to hurt me, I poked around a bit. That's where I found this." Martez gestured with the black tube. "And I guess you're wondering what it is. Let me show you."

At one side of the clearing, a lone tree stood a short way clear of the surrounding forest. The young pine was little more than a sapling, too slender to be of use for mine supports and not enough of an obstacle to justify the effort of cutting it down. Martez held his black tube at shoulder height and pointed one end at the tree. Deryn did not see what else he did, but suddenly, a beam of blue light shot from the tube, accompanied by a rush of air. For an instant, the tree appeared to swell, as if from absorbing the light, and then it burst into flames.

Several miners yelled in panic. Deryn felt her guts turn to ice as she watched fire engulf the sapling. Heat washed over her face, carrying black ash and glowing red sparks.

Still, Faren showed no reaction. His voice was impassive when he spoke. "You've got one of the demon's magic wands from the Age of Chaos."

Martez lowered the tube. "Yup. That's what I've got, and now I want your gold as well. But I'm a reasonable man. I'm going to give you tonight to think it over. When I come back at noon tomorrow, I want every one of you waiting for me out here, with all your weapons and your gold lying on the ground. We'll take the gold and check round to make sure you haven't missed any. You can pick up your weapons after we've gone." He took a step back and smiled. "See you tomorrow." Martez turned and sauntered away, with his silent companion at his heel.

The miners immediately erupted in barrage of curses, but Faren waited until the two outlaws were out of sight before saying calmly, "I don't think so, sonny-jim."

To Deryn's relief, Brise slipped from the cover of the forest and vaulted over the barricade.

"You caught all that?" Faren asked her.

"Yup."

"Anything else you can tell us?"

"They've set up camp about a mile and a half away, to the east."

"How many?"

"Just the nine."

"Just!" The miner's voice was a high-pitched shriek. "With that wand, what else do they need?"

"Shit." Another miner chimed in. "After all our work here, they're gonna take…" Her voice faded in despair.

"No, they're not," Faren said decisively. "Well, you can hand over your gold if you want. But there's no way we Wolves are laying down our weapons."

"But you saw it. He can burn us all. I don't want to be—"

"Most likely he can't." Faren interrupted the miner's rant. "I've seen these demon wands before. They can be nasty, or they can be all show. Martez has had the wand for a year. He'll have worked out how to make it seem more dangerous than it really is. You can bet we've seen the very worst it can do."

"How much worse does it need to be?" Dace barged his way to the front. He was the most assertive of the miners and always ready to appoint himself spokesman.

"The only thing we know is that it can set fire to trees. It might have no effect on living flesh."

"Is that likely?"

"Who knows what sort of magic is in the wand? One thing you can be sure of, though, if that thing could burn us all, he'd have done it. He wouldn't have mucked about telling us stories first."

"We can't risk it." Dace was now standing toe-to-toe with Faren.

"The risk is in doing what he said. If the wand was as powerful as he's trying to make out, he wouldn't need us to lay down our weapons. The only reason he told us to do it is because we outnumber his band and he wants us defenseless so he can slit our throats."

"You don't know that."

"I'd say it was a sure bet. Either way, I'm not gonna put myself at the mercy of renegade scum like him."

"You can't—"

This time, Brise interrupted. "Faren's right. The Iron Wolves don't like renegades. Martez won't let us take our story back to Oakan. He'd be a marked man."

Dace still looked ready to argue. Faren ignored him. "Brise, you were telling us what you'd seen. What else?"

"The gang stopped the other side of that ridge, just below the skyline." Brise pointed. "The woman who was here with Martez headed off on her own. She has to be their scout. I thought about taking her out, but reckoned we needed information more, so I let her go and stayed watching the others. After a half hour she was back. I couldn't hear what she said, but they weren't happy."

"She saw we were putting up defenses, so she knew we'd spotted them."

Brise nodded. "That's my guess too. They moved their camp down to the small lake in the valley, out on one of the islands in the marsh."

"Easily defended?"

"Afraid so."

"No. It's a good sign. It means they're worried about us attacking them, which proves their magic wand doesn't make them invincible." Faren added the last point with a sideways glance at Dace.

"I guess that's the positive way of looking at it." Brise gave a rueful smile. "Once they were all sorted on the island, Martez and the scout set out again. He was clearly the gang leader, so this time I followed. He spent a few minutes studying the camp from up on the hillside, before making the big show with his white flag, coming in to parley."

"You agree it was all bullshit about not killing us if we let him take the gold?"

"Oh yes. He wouldn't have admitted being a renegade if he'd any intention of us living long enough to tell the rest of the Wolves." Brise frowned. "A bit stupid on his part, because it lets us know for sure that he's bluffing."

"He couldn't keep it a secret." The speaker was Shea. "I recognized him. He was in Oakan at the same time as me, hanging out in the Wolves' Den. He claimed he was looking for work too. I guess he was just looking for tips on where to find miners he could rob."

Faren rubbed his chin thoughtfully. "I wonder if that explains how he knew where we are. Any idea who he talked to?"

There was no need for Shea to answer. One miner's face held an expression of unease bordering on nausea, far too blatant for anyone to miss.

"You spoke to him?" Faren challenged.

The miner licked his lips. "Yeah. A bit. Like Shea said, he was in Oakan, making out like he was an Iron Wolf looking for work. We just chatted." He glared around defensively. "I was supposed to be hiring more guards. How could I do that without talking to them?"

"What did you tell him?"

"I don't remember it all. We just chatted one evening in the tavern. Talking about all sorts. He seemed friendly. Bought me a drink."

"Only the one?"

"Well…" The miner swallowed and stared at the ground.

Faren gave a sigh of exasperation. "Fucking fantastic. So Martez knows how many Wolves are here, how our supplies stand, and probably what your granny's name is too."

"If it's so obvious he's going to kill us, why did he waste his breath talking?" Dace still wanted to argue.

Brise shrugged. "An excuse to study our defenses close up, I'd guess. Maybe buying himself time as well. He's hoping we'll wait to see what happens at noon tomorrow before we make our own plans. And that's one thing we don't want to do. I've got one more thing to report. That wand of his, Martez made a big thing of laying it out in the sun as soon as they'd made camp."

Judging by the smile on Brise's face, this was good news. The significance was lost on Deryn and the miners, but not Faren. He clenched his hand in a fist and punched the air. "Yes!"

"What?"

"Does it matter?" Several voices muttered questions.

Faren answered. "A lot of the demons' magic draws on the power of the sun. This wand must do the same. Martez had to let the wand soak up sunrays until it held enough power for his display. I bet he couldn't have set fire to a second tree. He didn't turn the wand on the barricade, and us standing behind it, because the hour the wand had gotten didn't capture enough sunrays to burn through heavy timber."

Deryn looked at the burning tree. Already the flames were dying, and now that she was over the initial shock, she could see the wand had set fire to the pine needles and a few twigs, but it had not touched the trunk of the young tree. Nor had the flames spread to others nearby.

Brise frowned at the sky. "There's another three hours before dusk. We don't know how many sunrays the wand needs before it can set fire to the barricade. Maybe it never could. And Martez wants to slow things down. That looks good for us."

Faren took a deep breath. "Okay. Here's how I read it. Martez led his band out here, hoping to hide up in the woods, wait until all of us were in the same spot and then kill as many of us as he could with a single fireball. But we were lucky and caught wind of them. So he's gone to his fallback plan. They've moved to a defensible spot for tonight. He'll spend tomorrow morning trapping sunrays in his wand. They'll come over at noon, just in case we've been stupid enough to hand over our weapons. When he sees we haven't, he'll use the wand to do as much damage as he can, then go back to his camp and repeat the whole cycle again the day after, until there's none of us left. He knows time and numbers are on his side."

Brise agreed. "That's how my guess goes."

"And if you're wrong?" Dace sounded less surly than before, as if he was finally convinced of the logic. This did not mean that he was happy.

Faren shrugged. "Doesn't matter too much. Regardless of what his plans are, we need to disrupt them. And the surest way to stop him calling the shots is for us to get our attack in first."

❖

The image of the burning tree kept running through Deryn's head. She tried to push the thought aside, but the other, older memories that replaced it were worse. Briefly, she let her face sink into her hand, covering her eyes, but she was not a young child anymore and she had a job do to. Deryn raised her head.

Her position, halfway up the hillside, was a good vantage point to watch the entire lake, while the bush she was lying under provided dense cover. A few straggling leaves danced before her face, tickling her nose. Deryn carefully pushed them aside, giving herself a clearer view of the outlaws' camp below.

On three sides, the rocky islet was bounded by a lacework of oily black pools and reeds. Only the corner farthest from the bank jutted out into the open waters of the lake. The islet could be reached on foot, but that meant wading through fifty yards of thick mud, where an attacker would be a slow-moving target, out in the open. Even on horseback, the distance could not be covered quickly enough to evade arrows or fireballs, especially since the outlaws had embedded defensive rows of sharpened stakes in the mud.

The lake itself was small, no more than an eighth of a mile across. A boulder-strewn beach lined the opposite shore. Swimming to the island would be quite feasible, as long as the swimmers were not encumbered by metal or clad in heavy leather, and that was the problem. The Iron Wolves were outnumbered as it was. Arriving on the island without weapons or armor was not going to work in their favor.

The sun was setting and the pine-clad hills overlooking the lake were fading into the dusk. Deryn chewed her lip. Creeping across when it was dark looked to be the best bet, and the outlaws had apparently reached the same conclusion. While she had been watching, they had collected a sizeable woodpile, sufficient to keep a bonfire going through the darkest hours of the night.

The picture of the burning tree again slipped into Deryn's head, taunting her. How many sunrays had the demon wand been able to trap that afternoon? Could it hold them prisoner until morning, and how much damage could they do when unleashed? How much would being struck by a fireball hurt?

A branch snapped uphill, some way behind her, accompanied by the rustle of leaves. Someone was approaching, although they were still a good thirty feet away, too far to stand any chance of spotting her, hidden in the bushes. Then a hand landed on her shoulder. Deryn's heart leapt, even as she recognized the touch. But who else could have gotten so close without her noticing?

Brise crouched beside her. "How's it going?"

"Okay." Deryn hoped her voice did not give away how startled she had been.

"Any sign of them getting ready for an attack on the mine?"

"No. They've had supper and settled down for the night, except the two on watch."

"Two." Brise repeated the number as if it was significant and the corners of her mouth twitched down in a fleeting grimace.

"What is it? Does it affect our plans?"

"No. We couldn't have risked me going alone anyway."

"Wha…" Deryn swallowed the question. Brise had already slipped away. Not that it mattered. As an apprentice scout, Deryn would be told what she needed to know, when she needed to know it. Brise would decide on the when and what without being asked.

A few seconds later, Deryn again heard the sound of someone approaching—someone who was very definitely not any sort of scout. Judging by the noise, a couple of oxen might be heading her way.

Brise ducked back under the bush, with one of the miners at her side. "Paz is going to take over here." She turned to the miner. "You're sure you know what to do?"

Paz looked nervous but determined. "If I spot the outlaws moving, I run like fuck until I'm near enough for you to hear when I blow this whistle."

"That'll do." Brise patted his shoulder and then nodded at Deryn. "You come with me."

A crease formed the shape of a V between Brise's eyebrows and her lower lip protruded slightly. Both were signs that she was not happy. Deryn kept her own mouth tightly sealed. Disguising her own excitement would be impossible if she said anything, and it was never wise to antagonize her foster mother.

The situation was not hard to read. Deryn knew the senior Iron Wolves had been working out their strategy. She also knew Brise would have wanted to keep her well away from any danger. This was surely the main reason why she had been dumped on lookout duty, with the original instructions that she would be there until midnight. The change in plan implied that the desperate situation had not allowed Brise the option of shielding Deryn from an active part in the battle.

The day was fading fast. The forest was in its evening transition as the daytime animals sought their nests and burrows while the nocturnal ones stirred. Scents and sounds changed along with the light. Deryn tried to copy Brise's silent movements, keeping all her senses alert to her surroundings. It would be stupid to worry so much about the outlaws that they walked slap into a bear.

The entrance to the mine was in sight before Brise spoke. "We're going to hit the outlaws as soon as it's light enough to see where we're sticking our swords. Hopefully it will mean we can catch them by surprise, while they're still asleep." She glanced Deryn's way. "You and me are going to swim across the lake after the moon has set and take out their sentries. Once it's clear, the others will join us."

"Okay."

"We'll leave the mine while the moon can still light our way. So I'll have plenty of time to give you more details when we're at the lakeside."

Deryn nodded, battling to keep her expression suitably solemn.

A fire was burning at the mine entrance. Warm light flickered through the logs of the surrounding barricade, casting dancing shadows across the clearing where the miners' camp had been. Brise hailed the lookout to identify herself before crossing the open space and climbing over the wall. On the other side, a mixed group of mercenaries and miners were sprawled in the warmth of the campfire, passing around a bottle.

Brise nodded at them and then turned to Deryn. "We've got a few hours before we have to leave. Try to get some sleep. I need to talk to Faren."

"Right."

Deryn said a quick good night to everyone gathered around the fire and wandered a short distance into the mine, looking for somewhere safely out of the way to lie down. She did not want to be trampled in the dark.

"I hear you'll be taking part in the action." Shea's voice made her jump. The young warrior detached herself from a patch of darker shadow and stepped forward. Light from the fire glinted in her eyes and cast a red glow over the loose shirt she was wearing.

"Er, yes."

Shea gestured at the group by the mine entrance. "Aren't you going to join them? Have a drink?"

"Brise told me to get some sleep, but I don't know if I'm gonna be able to. I'm feeling rather…"

"Nervous?"

"No." Deryn denied the suggestion vehemently. "Excited."

"Is it the first time you've been in a real fight?"

"Not quite. But the other time was…" Deryn shrugged. The topic was not one she liked talking about.

Fortunately, Shea did not pursue it. She tilted her head to one side. "So what do you want to do?"

Suddenly, knowledge of exactly what she wanted to do leapt into Deryn's head, and something in Shea's tone gave her the idea she was not alone in wanting it. But what if she was wrong? Deryn wasted no more than a moment over the doubts. She did not have the time to play around. In a few hours both she and Shea would be fighting for their lives, and if things went wrong, there would be no second chances.

Deryn moved in closer and rested her hand on Shea's hip. The last awkward jitters in her gut vanished when Shea did not move, except for the grin on her face getting wider.

"There's no saying what'll happen in the battle tomorrow. And if it all goes to hell—" Deryn licked her lips and took a deep breath. "I really don't want to die a virgin."

"That's one possibility we can easily rule out."

Shea's arms slid around Deryn, locking their bodies together. Shea's mouth brushed Deryn's chin before fixing on their goal. She claimed Deryn in a long, deep kiss.

Shea's lips were so good, firm and soft in perfect measure. Deryn felt her knees turning to water. She broke away from the kiss, breathing hard. The ground was wobbling under her feet. She had to sit before she fell.

Maybe Shea realized the effect she was having, but rather than easing off, she pressed Deryn back against the wall of the mine, pinning her in place. The hard contact between their bodies drove all rational thought from Deryn's mind, but at least she could no longer fall. She was seized by a raw need, a passion that escalated with each beat of the pulse between her legs. When Shea's mouth left hers and traveled down her neck Deryn could hear her own breath, sounding like the tortured gasps of a runner.

"Wait here." Shea's breath was warm on Deryn's ear.

Even if she could have depended on her knees to hold firm, Deryn was not about to go anywhere. Shea returned with a small terracotta oil lamp. The single flame danced and quivered, amplifying the tremor in Shea's arm. Deryn was pleased that she was not alone in feeling clumsy.

Shea reached down and snagged a blanket from her pile of belongings as she passed. "Come on."

Deryn paused only to grab a second blanket and a sheepskin mat.

A short way along, an exploratory side tunnel branched off from the main shaft, going no more than a dozen feet into the rock. Although it had not been dug with a view to providing a lovers' den, it would fit the requirements perfectly. Shea even found a bump on the wall, wide and flat enough to set the lamp on. She kicked a few larger rocks aside and lay the sheepskin out. Deryn dropped onto it with relief. The shaking in her legs was showing no sign of going away. Shea stretched out on her back and pulled Deryn down into another embrace. Their bodies moved together with increasing ardor.

Deryn felt Shea's hand, burrowing under her clothes. A surge of desire rushed through her. Until that moment, she had not realized quite how desperately she wanted the contact. Deryn had kissed and fumbled around with other children before, but she had experienced nothing like this. She tugged her shirt free of her waistband to allow Shea easier access.

"You'll get cold."

"How can I? I'm on fire for you."

"Me too." Shea laughed. "Even so." She sat up and reached for the blankets.

While Shea's arms were not around her, Deryn took advantage of the temporary freedom of movement to strip off her shirt and jerkin completely. Shea's eyebrows rose at the sight, but then she smiled and copied the action. When Deryn started to unbuckle her belt, this time Shea caught hold of her hand, stopping her.

"Hey, slow down. We have time."

"But I want—"

"Believe me, slow is better."

Shea cupped Deryn's breast, rolling her nipple between thumb and finger. Deryn gasped. It was as if a cord ran from her nipple to her clit, and Shea was playing the role of harper. When Shea repeated the action, using her mouth and tongue, it was more than Deryn could bear.

"Please. I need you to…"

Shea sighed. "So impatient." But she relented and loosened the buckle of Deryn's belt.

The touch of Shea's hand between her legs was the most overpowering sensation Deryn had ever felt. It struck through the core of her being. Deryn gripped Shea's shoulders tightly, wanting an anchor to hold her body in place. The movement of Shea's hand spread a slick coating over her inner thighs, cool where the faint breeze played over it.

"I'm wet."

"Uh-huh."

Shea's touch was taking control of her, igniting every nerve with pleasure. The tension built inside her, taking her ever higher and higher, more aroused than she had thought possible. Even so, her climax caught Deryn by surprise. She had not realized how close she had been.

"Well. That was easy." Shea sounded pleased.

Deryn lay, absorbing the waves of release that faded into a warm peace. She opened her eyes. The roof of the tunnel was indistinct, barely touched by the gentle lamp glow. A burst of laughter from the group at the door was muffled by the stone. Had they heard her? How much noise had she made? Abruptly, Deryn was seized by giggles. She tried to stifle them, burrowing her face into Shea's neck. Then she pulled back. The soft light washed over Shea's wonderful face, a scant inch from her own.

"How about you?"

"With you in my arms?" Shea smiled. "I think I should be pretty easy as well."

And she was.

Afterward, Deryn snuggled in close, resting her head on Shea's shoulder while tracing lazy patterns over the tight muscles of Shea's stomach. She tried to find the words she wanted, to express how she felt, but could dredge up nothing except juvenile clichés.

Shea rolled onto her side, facing Deryn. "Let's sleep."

Deryn gave up her hunt for words and also turned over, so that they lay together, spooned. Shea's lips brushed against her shoulder. With each breath, Shea's stomach and breasts pressed slightly into Deryn's back. The rhythmical movement was mesmerizing.

"Promise me that you won't forget…"

Shea's voice faded into a mumble and Deryn missed the end of it. She was about to turn her head and ask Shea to repeat it, but instead she fell asleep.

❖

A gentle tap from a boot woke Deryn. She opened her eyes. The oil lamp had burnt out, but light from the glowing branch that Brise held was just sufficient to make out the surroundings. Deryn tried to sit, but found herself pinned down by Shea's right arm and leg draped across her, and she got no farther than an elbow.

"Time to go?"

"When you're ready. I'll meet you at the front." It was too dark to read the expression on Brise's face, but Deryn was sure she picked out an amused undercurrent in her foster mother's voice.

As carefully as possible, Deryn tried to peel the arm off her. Shea resisted, squirming free from Deryn's hand, but it was the uncoordinated action of a woman still half asleep.

"Shea. I have to go."

Shea's arm tightened in a hug and then released. She rolled away, freeing Deryn's legs. "Ugh." Shea shook her head, her movements getting sharper as she became more fully awake. She half sat up. "See you at the lake. I'll be the one standing by the pile of dead outlaws. Take care."

"Yeah. You too."

Deryn started to rise, but Shea caught hold of her hand. "And how about I meet you back here, same time, tomorrow night?"

"That sounds like, um…" Deryn paused to get the urge to laugh under control. She did not want to wake everyone. "Like a good idea."

"A good idea? Now, personally, I'd rank it as more like a great idea."

"Yup. Now that I think about it, you're right."

Deryn planted a final quick kiss on Shea's lips and then hurried to the cave entrance while attempting to adjust her clothing on the way.

Brise was waiting by the barricade. "You all set?"

"Just about." Deryn crouched to tie her boots.

"Good luck," the miner on watch duty said to Brise.

"Thanks. We'll be back for breakfast."

"I'll let the cook know."

Deryn stood. "Okay."

Brise vaulted over the barricade and set off through the dark forest. Deryn followed.

Dawn was still two hours away and the breeze was chilly. The moon hung low in the sky, etching the scene in white, with blue-black shadows. After months at the mine, the terrain was very familiar and minimal light was all Deryn and Brise needed to navigate their way, fording streams and skirting dense thickets.

They reached the shore directly opposite the outlaws' island just as the moon started to slip behind the mountains. The last beams rippled like liquid silver on the lake. The island was lost in darkness, except for where the outlaws' bonfire burned. The faint sound of crackling carried cleanly across the water.

"That will make a nice target to aim for. We don't want to end up swimming in circles." Brise spoke in a whisper.

She drew Deryn back into the trees, far enough to muffle their voices, and settled on a convenient rock. "We'll wait until the moon has gone, so there's no chance of them seeing us, if they patrol the island."

"Right."

Deryn also took a seat and rested her elbows on her knees, breathing deeply. The turmoil of emotions had her whole body shaking with eagerness for the forthcoming battle, memories of Shea's body in her arms, and the prospect of another such night ahead. Deryn wished she could run around to burn off the excess energy. She knew she needed to calm down; she needed to focus; she needed to be disciplined, because this was all so very serious. But the excitement was as intoxicating as alcohol.

"Was it your idea, or Shea's?" Brise's voice was neutral of approval or censure.

"Mine mainly, I think." Deryn looked up. "It was all right, wasn't it? I know you told me to sleep, but I was so—"

Brise laughed softly. "It's all right. It might even be written in the rules somewhere as the proper way for an Iron Wolf to spend the night before a battle. And as reactions go, it's a damn sight better than lying awake worrying."

"It's not just about tomorrow. I've had my eye on Shea ever since she got here."

"I've noticed."

"Tonight it just seemed, what with not knowing how the battle would go, there was no reason not to. Maybe that was what gave me the courage to say something. But it wasn't like I hadn't been…" Deryn's disjointed sentences ended in a shrug and a lopsided smile. "Shea's amazing."

"She'd agree with you there. I can't say I'm quite so enamored of her."

"You don't like her?"

"You could do better."

"But she killed a windigo. The way she rides. She's just so—"

"Okay. You could also do worse." Brise's tone was one of surrender. "And I admit you're stuck for choices here. If nothing else, she's safe."

"Safe?"

"You won't end up pregnant, and I don't think she'll try to kill you when you tell her you've had enough of her."

"I can't see that ever happening." Deryn ran through the implications of Brise's words. "You think there are some Wolves you don't trust?"

"I know there are. This bunch are all okay, but some are"—Brise paused—"people like Martez, for example. When you're on the Trail together, you're comrades, and you depend on each other for your life. Then you hit a nasty spot. You sleep together, and suddenly you're stuck in the wastelands with a maniac and no quick way out. Getting pregnant is the least of your worries, though I'd recommend keeping an eye on the moon and sticking to women when in doubt."

"Oh, well, for what it's worth, I think I like women better anyway."

"We all have our preferences, but sometimes you just take what's on offer. Danger can be like getting drunk. In both cases you can wake up the next day wishing you hadn't done what you did." Brise gave a wry sigh. "And I'm speaking from experience."

Deryn nodded, although it was now too dark beneath the trees for Brise to see the gesture. "Your sons?"

"Yup. They're both due to tight spots when there seemed no chance of me seeing the next day out. Worrying about what would happen nine months down the road didn't get a look in. I don't—"

Brise stopped abruptly. A couple of times it sounded as if she started to speak and then changed her mind. The uncertain manner was so totally out of character that Deryn could not imagine what would come next.

At last, Brise continued. "You know what they say about being careful what you wish for, because you just might get it? Both times I got pregnant, part of me was annoyed at myself, because it meant I couldn't work for a few months, which blew my chance of riding the Trail that year. But there was another little part of me wishing for someone to follow me into the Wolves. I used to daydream about teaching my kid to hunt, and track, and shoot. I used to imagine us heading off on the Trail together." Brise gave a sharp sigh that was trying to be a laugh, and failed. "You've met my sons, so you know how that's turned out."

Again Deryn nodded, pointlessly. The two boys lived on a farm with Brise's brother. She and Brise had spent the winter before last there, passing the slack time for mercenaries. The younger son was about half Deryn's age. The older fitted somewhere between them. Both boys had Brise's wiry build and thick black hair. Neither had her agility and sharpness.

"They're sweet, hardworking lads any mother could be proud of. And they couldn't sneak up on a rock without it spotting them. They're gonna make great farmers. I know my brother's pleased with them."

Although it was too dark to see, Deryn had the sense that her foster mother had reached out to touch her, without completing the gesture. She frowned, wondering where the conversation was going.

"I remember the first time I saw you, crouching in the bushes with your little bow. When we found out your family had been murdered, and what you'd done, I just felt like it was meant to be. What I'd wished for. Not the child of my body, but you'd be the child of my heart. I didn't stop to wonder if it was right for you, or what your real parents would have wanted. I wish I could have met them, it—"

"They'd have been pleased someone was looking after me well." Deryn broke in. The old sick feeling was rolling in her stomach and she was anxious to shift the conversation. "Do you think it's dark enough for us to swim across yet?"

Brise's hand rested on Deryn's shoulder and squeezed. "I know you don't like talking about them. But what I want to say is, I'd seen you as the child to follow in my footsteps. But with each year, I've gotten less and less certain, as I've gotten to care about you more."

"I care about you too. You've been a true mother to me."

"And I'm talking as a mother now. I know you want to ride the Trail, and you think I worry too much. But you've made me realize how dangerous this life is. I no longer think it's what I want. I'm frightened for you."

"You don't have to be."

"I do. This coming fight—"

"I'll be careful."

"It's not just the risk of getting hurt. I'm worried you'll find it exciting. I've been there. When the battle's over, your heart will be pumping and your senses will be twice as sharp as normal. For a few minutes you'll feel so alive. It's addictive, but it's dangerous. Your parents were fur trappers. It's a good trade. The things you've learned with me will still be useful." Brise took a deep breath. "I don't want you to become an Iron Wolf. I want you to go back to your parents' way of life."

"It didn't keep them safe, did it?"

"The odds are still better than in the Wolves."

"Maybe." Deryn would not discuss it. "But like I said before, isn't it time for us to make a move?"

"Yes. You're right." Brise sighed. "Think about it. Promise me."

"All right. I'll think it over." The promise was easy enough to make. Two seconds was all the thinking it would take.

Deryn heard Brise get to her feet. "We need to strip off our heavy stuff here and leave it behind. We're gonna be cold while we're waiting on the island, but wet leather won't help much anyway. We'll need our knives, bows and arrows. Most important are the bowstrings. I've got them wrapped in waxed cloth. If I keep them under my cap, hopefully they won't get wet, otherwise we're dead."

"Right."

"When you're swimming, head to the right of the fire. A clump of bushes overhangs the shore near there. It'll be a good spot to hide and far enough from their horses not to disturb them. The other Wolves will be in position at first light. By then, we need to have dealt with the sentries. It's too much to hope we'll get the chance to take them out separately, but the good news is with them standing by the fire they'll make nice easy targets. We won't be able to risk talking once we're on the island, so watch for my signals. On my mark, you shoot the one standing to the left, and I'll take the other. Aim for the throat or the heart—whichever looks best. I'll make sure we both have a clear shot when I signal. And just pray we do it without waking their mates, because we won't stand a chance against all of them. Any questions?"

"I don't think so." Deryn hesitated. "Except, clothes. Do we leave them behind as well?"

"As long as you think you can swim okay in it, keep your shirt on. It's dark and won't show up as much as your skin in the firelight. Use your pants to make a backpack of the rest and tie it on using your belt. And don't leave your boots behind. Wrap them in your pants as well. I know they're heavy, but a stubbed toe can lose you a fight."

"Right."

Even though she knew it was irrational, Deryn was relieved that she would not be naked in the enemy camp. She quickly stripped off her thick cloak and heavy outer clothing. The night air was cold through her shirt, and it was going to get worse, she knew. She headed for the lake, feeling her way with her bare feet.

The moon had dropped behind the mountains. Only the outlaws' bonfire competed with the stars. Two small figures stood in the distant firelight. It was now so dark that Deryn only knew she had reached the water's edge when she felt the waves lapping over her toes.

"Ready?" Brise's voice was the softest whisper.

"Yes."

The water of the lake was even colder than Deryn had feared. By the time it reached her thighs, she could feel her skin prickling in goose bumps. She could only hope that the exertion of swimming would warm her up. Presumably Brise was already on her way, although there was no sound. Deryn sank her shoulders beneath the water and kicked off.

The high encircling mountains cut off the sky so that, while swimming, Deryn could not turn her head enough to see the stars. The cold, black water was one with the night. Only the beacon bonfire provided a reference point. Deryn knew Brise was near, and would hear her if she spoke, yet she had never felt so isolated and forsaken. Time ceased to exist. It would be easy to panic. Deryn felt as if she would be adrift in the formless, icy void forever. The bonfire taunted her with the promise of heat, always sliding farther away.

When her knee struck something solid, Deryn was caught by surprise. The rhythm of her strokes failed and her head sank beneath the water. Her right hand landed on smooth rocks, and then both knees touched down. She had reached the island. She knelt, half out of the water, while her senses attuned themselves to her surroundings.

Now she had stopped swimming, Deryn could hear the crackle of flames and soft murmuring between the outlaws on sentry duty. The firelight made a red tracery of the matted bushes, overhanging the pebble beach above where she had landed. The fire also cast its glow across the water, which meant she would be spotted, if one of the outlaws looked her way.

The urge to hurry into the shadows was strong, but making a noise was the quickest way to get the outlaws' attention. Deryn forced herself to crawl carefully out of the lake, moving with an irregular action so any splashes would mimic the random sound of the waves. Even when she had left the water, Deryn still had to go carefully, testing the placement of every hand and knee before trusting her weight to it.

At last the bank at the top of the beach rose over her, shielding her from the firelight. Deryn was starting to relax a little when her hand landed on an ankle—that moved. Brise was already in position, waiting. Working by touch alone, Deryn removed her backpack, pulled on her pants and boots, and positioned the bow and quiver conveniently to hand. Then she lay down beside her foster mother, staring up at the stars and waiting for her pulse to calm.

The swimming had indeed warmed her up, but as minutes trickled by, Deryn felt the heat seep from her body. The wet clothes clung to her arms and legs, chafing her skin raw. Water had gotten into her boots and now squelched between her toes. The soft voices of the sentries and the occasional snore reminded Deryn that she lay surrounded and hopelessly outnumbered by her foes. She had every right to be nervous, but she was too cold to care. A chill wind off the lake added to her torment. She was racked by bouts of shivering. Would she be able to shoot straight?

Deryn looked to the east, and there, behind the mountains, the sky was showing the first hint of paling. Dawn approached. Brise shifted beside her and pressed something soft into her hand. It needed a moment for Deryn to identify it as a bowstring. The time for waiting was nearly over, and abruptly, Deryn felt a sense of calm determination sweep over her. The shaking faded as anticipation tapped a well of heat, deep inside. She smiled as she slipped the dry cord over one tip of her bow and then braced the wooden shaft against her foot to complete the stringing.

The conversation between the sentries had been an indistinct mumble, with only the occasional clear word or phrase. Now one of the bandits, a woman, raised her voice, still no more than a whisper, but enough for Deryn to make out.

"Don't get lost."

"Yeah, like that's gonna happen."

The second voice was louder than the first and accompanied by footsteps, coming toward where Deryn and Brise lay. However, the outlaw was clearly unaware that they were there. He passed by without a sideways glance. The firelight showed him standing at the water's edge with his back to them and his legs spaced wide apart. The sound of the waves on the shore was overridden by a sudden burst of splashing.

Deryn looked around, trying to judge the light and reassure herself that they had nothing to worry about. She and Brise were in the shadow of the bushes. When the outlaw finished pissing and turned around, the fire would be in his face. The paling sky was not yet casting light. Surely he would not be able to see them. Then she realized that Brise was not waiting to find out. The blade of the knife in Brise's hand reflected the merest hint of firelight as she crept toward the outlaw.

Deryn remembered the words, *It's too much to hope we'll get the chance to take them out separately.* This was their chance, and Brise was taking it. She rose up behind the outlaw and wrapped her left hand around his mouth. Her other hand was also moving, a harder, quicker action across the line of his throat. The outlaw collapsed with a guttural choking and was still.

For a moment there was silence, and then a woman's voice called softly. "You okay, Mel?"

Deryn's heart leapt. Her hand tightened in reflex around the shaft of her bow, but before she could move, Brise broke out in a deep, racking cough, accompanied by much spitting, like someone trying to hack up phlegm.

The sound was loud enough to wake one of the sleepers. "Wassup?"

The outlaw by the fire laughed. "Mel's swallowed a fly."

"Tell him to keep his mouth shut."

"Mel, you hear that?"

"Yah." Brise croaked the word out, blending it with another cough. The sound was garbled enough to safely defy recognition.

Everything in the outlaw camp again went quiet, but the ploy could have gained them no more than a minute. Brise scuttled back and then Deryn felt the light tap of feathers stroke her cheek. The message was easy to decode. Deryn pulled an arrow from her quiver and nocked it on the string.

The outlaw in the firelight made a clear target, even when viewed through the straggly fringe of bushes. Deryn glanced at Brise. Shadows of leaves blotched patterns across her face, but for the first time since the moon had set, they were able to catch each others' eye. Brise pointed first to the outlaw and then tapped her own throat. Deryn nodded. Together they drew their bows and took aim.

The outlaw had been warming her hands over the fire, but now she turned and stared in their direction. She was clearly searching for her absent comrade and was not attuned to anything else. Her eyes skimmed over the bushes where Deryn and Brise were. She placed her fists on her hips while a frown deepened on her face. Concern and doubt were growing. Deryn knew they had mere seconds before she raised the alarm.

"Now." Brise whispered the word.

Deryn's aim was true. Her arrow hit the outlaw's throat at the same instant that Brise's found the outlaw's heart. The woman collapsed, making no more noise than her comrade. Deryn lowered her bow. Snores continued, unchecked.

Brise brought her mouth close to Deryn's ear. "Get her cloak and weapons, then stand by the fire as if you're her. I'll be with you in a minute."

Deryn did not need persuading. In fact, she positioned herself so close to the fire that she could see steam rising from her wet clothes. The heat soaked into her skin. It felt so good that Deryn had to pinch the sides of her mouth to stop herself giggling.

Brise strolled up to the fire, dressed in clothes from the outlaw on the beach. "It's all right. We can talk quietly. It's what the sentries were doing." She glanced at the sleepers and then prodded the dead woman with her foot. "We should get her out of the way, just in case one of the others wakes up and notices."

Together, they rolled the body off into shadow on the beach.

Brise smiled. "Help yourself to any of her stuff that's dry. Come back to the fire when you're done."

Deryn set to work. The woman's dry pants were a huge improvement. Her shirt would have been as well, except it was badly bloodstained, and unfortunately, her boots were too small. Deryn rejoined Brise. A scant few yards away, the remaining outlaws slept, wrapped in their blankets. Most were huddled in the lee of low bushes or sand banks, taking what shelter they could from the chill wind.

"We could kill some of them now—an arrow through their brains, or slit their throats while they sleep."

Brise shook her head. "We can't be sure one won't make enough noise to wake their friends. Wait until Faren and the rest get here, then if something goes wrong we'll have backup."

"Will they be ready to come over yet?"

"I don't know. We're earlier than I'd intended, but the guy taking a piss was too good a chance to miss." Brise's gaze turned in the direction of the forest. The fire cast a glow over the marsh, but it could not reach the trees lining the nearby shore, and as yet, the light in the sky was too faint to help. "I guess it's worth seeing if they're here."

Brise stuck one end of a dry branch into the fire. Once it was alight, she waved it up and down three times before dropping the whole branch back in the fire.

As the seconds slipped by, Deryn was surprised to feel her pulse rise and ice fill her stomach. It was as if, only now the end was so close, she could allow herself to be fully aware that she was surrounded by foes, isolated and hopelessly outnumbered. She had just about given up when, faintly, on the predawn breeze came the distant chink of metal. Still, Deryn could see nothing, but the sound got closer, now mingled with the soft slurp of churned mud. Five figures materialized at the edge of the firelight.

At Deryn's shoulder, Brise whispered, "Good old Faren. I should have known he wouldn't be late to a battle."

The armed warriors' progress through the marsh was slow, but in another few minutes they would arrive at the fire. Deryn turned to the seven sleeping outlaws. Very soon, the odds would be even.

Her senses were on full alert. To the east, the sky was turning gray. The breeze carried the scent of rotting vegetation. The first uncertain trill of birdsong rippled from the trees and then Deryn heard the crunch of stone underfoot and the rasp of a sword being drawn. The first of her comrades had reached the island.

Deryn was about to glance over her shoulder when the tenor of one outlaw's snores changed. The man gave a dry cough and then, "Hey! Wha…" His voice rose to a shout. "Wake up. We're—"

Faren's cry was louder. "Go. Go."

With a roar, the Iron Wolves charged past the fire. The nearest two outlaws were dead before they had gotten clear of their blankets.

The scene was in chaos. Deryn slipped an arrow onto the string and half drew her bow, waiting eagerly for a clear target, but friend and foe were a frantic, heaving mass in the firelight. Then a movement caught her eye, a little way clear of the main battle. The leader, Martez, had backed off from the fighting. He raised his arm. Deryn saw the demon wand in his hand.

She had no time to take proper aim. Deryn loosed her shot from half set. The arrow struck Martez in the arm, making him yelp and drop the wand. Deryn plucked another arrow from her quiver, but a surge in the fighting moved between them and Martez was lost from sight.

Heavy footsteps sounded just behind Deryn, to her right. Someone was charging toward her. She spun round to face the threat and saw an outlaw, almost on top of her, his sword raised, ready to strike. This time, Deryn's hasty shot missed its target completely and she did not have time for another. She leapt back as the outlaw swung his sword and the point missed her by an inch. The outlaw kept moving forward, again raising his sword. Deryn ripped her knife from the sheath on her belt, but the contest was hopelessly unbalanced. Suddenly, the outlaw's eyes opened wide in an expression of amazement. He froze for a moment before crumpling forward. His limp body hit the ground, an arrow protruding from his back. At the other side of the bonfire, Brise lowered her bow.

Deryn was still recovering from her surprise when a new sound erupted, the pounding of hooves. A rider burst into the firelight, scattering the fighters. Deryn got only a glimpse of Martez's face as she too dived aside, and then he was gone. Deryn scrambled to her feet, nocked another arrow on her bow, and raced to the edge of the island. The horse could not gallop through the thick mud, but already it was halfway to the shore. She loosed one arrow at the fleeing figure, and missed again. Before she could get another, Martez and his horse had vanished from sight.

"Always one who gets away," Faren muttered, standing at her shoulder.

Deryn turned and looked around. The frenzied action had stopped. The battle was over and the Iron Wolves had won.

At one side, Brise bent down and picked up the dropped wand. "The king pays a reward for things like this."

"Nothing like getting an unexpected bonus," Faren agreed, laughing.

Deryn also felt laughter rise inside her. She let her head fall back and stared up, marveling at the beauty of the sky, the sweet fragrance of air in her lungs, the rapture expressed in birdsong. Deryn lowered her eyes. She had to talk to Shea, to swap stories and maybe a kiss or two.

The Iron Wolves were drifting across the campsite and forming a huddle at one side. Faren also joined the group, parting them to get through to whatever was at the center. He dropped to one knee. Deryn trotted over, wondering what they had found. Her mood of elation faltered when she saw the body lying on the ground. The Wolves would not be gathering for one of the outlaws. Clearly, one of their own was injured, maybe seriously. But who?

No sooner had the question formed in Deryn's mind than a suspicion solidified as a hard lump in her chest. She angled her head for a better view, but it was not truly necessary. With a sickening sense of certainty, Deryn realized she knew who it was, even before she saw Shea's lifeless face.

❖

Deryn placed a final rock on the cairn over Shea's grave. Tears smeared the scene before her eyes. She clenched her teeth, trying by force of will to stop her face from crumpling. She did not mind if tears spilled from her eyes, a mark of grief for a fallen comrade, but she did not want to look like an infant.

"She died as a true warrior. The Iron Wolves can be proud of her." Faren patted Deryn's shoulder and turned away.

The rest of the gathering followed, Iron Wolves and miners together, leaving Deryn alone at the graveside. She dashed a hand across her eyes before realizing that not everyone had gone.

A little way off, Brise watched with concern. "Do you want me to stay or go?"

"Why would you want to stay?"

"Because I care about you. You know that."

"You didn't like her."

"Shea was too full of herself. There's self-confidence and then there's arrogance, and she fell on the wrong side of the line." Brise sighed. "Maybe it was youth speaking. Maybe she'd have grown out of it. But either way, I'm sorry she's dead. And I'm sorry for you."

"It was so pointless."

"Death is, but some good can come of it."

Deryn scowled in disbelief. "What?"

"Remember what I told you. Being an Iron Wolf is dangerous. If I hadn't gotten that outlaw who was after you, this could be your grave." Brise's voice caught. She took a couple of breaths before continuing. "I'd never forgive myself. I know I didn't get through to you before. Please, now, think about it. For the sake of Shea's memory. You can't dismiss her death as quickly as you dismissed my words. Forget the Wolves. Become a fur trapper, like your parents."

"My parents are in their grave. I buried them as well. And my brother, my sister, my grandparents, my aunts, even my dog. I've buried everyone I ever loved." Tears flowed down Deryn's face.

"It must seem like—"

Deryn no longer cared what she was saying. "I loved Shea. And I never told her it."

"That's youth speaking. You hardly knew her, and you slept with her once." Brise put her arm around Deryn's shoulders. "I know how you feel. I've been there myself, believe it or not. You'll get over her, I promise. There'll be others."

Deryn shook the arm away. "And they'll die too."

"Oh, child, I know it hurts."

"I won't let it hurt me again."

"I wish I could guarantee that for you."

"I can. What hurts is when you care about people and you lose them. I'm never going to let myself care about anyone again. Then I can't get hurt."

"It's not that simple."

"Why not?" Deryn started to walk away, but then turned and burrowed into Brise's arms like a child, letting the sobs come. "I can love you. You're safe. You know how to keep yourself alive. But I swear. I swear on Shea's grave, I'm never going to let anyone else mean anything to me again."

The court of the demon-spawn king, Ellaye, southern Galvonia
15th year of the reign of King Alvarro II
Midsummer Day, junio 21, early afternoon

Fire cascaded over the king's shoulders and rolled down his torso, clothing him in liquid light. Sparks bounced off the steel links of his clothing and landed around his feet as he passed, igniting the few errant blades of grass that sprouted between the cobblestones. Two ice-mages were in his immediate retinue to make sure the flames did not spread. The king's chief marshal, Lady Kyra Quintanilla, kept pace with him, dressed in shifting bands of lilac and silver iridescence that contrasted pleasingly with her dusky skin tone. Her head was level with the king's, but since she was somewhat shorter, it meant her feet were six inches clear of the ground. On either side, a row of uniformed guardsmen held back the cheering crowds of commoners as the procession exited the palace gates.

From a position well to the rear of the traditional Midsummer Day parade, Alana watched cynically. The king's fire was real. Her mother's levitation was an illusion. In both cases, the aim was the same—to intimidate the spectators and remind them of their proper, subordinate status. The true audience for this was, of course, the lesser nobility, people such as herself. Who cared what the commoners thought?

Alana's father, Jacian, was indulging in a similar display of gamesmanship, although rather less successfully. He was some way behind the king, dressed in golden armor and riding on a huge white bear. Alana frowned at the sight. The bear was a creature of the northern snows and was suffering in the heat. Its distress was obvious.

Her father had chosen to ride the huge bear as a demonstration of his ability to control the most ferocious of beasts, but as was often the case, what it mainly demonstrated was his poor judgment. Everyone (or at least, everyone who counted) knew that a beast-charmer's prowess was measured by the intelligence of the animal dominated, not its size or aggression. A kitten was harder to control than a wild bull. The nobles would have been even less impressed if they had known that the bear was drugged. Alana had prepared the concoction herself that morning, on her parents' orders.

The gold armor was also a sham, made of painted tin, rather than pure gold. The issue here was weight, not cost. The Quintanilla family was wealthy enough to afford the gold, but her father was middle aged, overweight, and hopelessly out of condition. Was anyone impressed by his military posturing? In the hierarchy of magical talent, beast-charmers came well below fire-mages and illusionists, and no amount of gold paint and drugged animals was going to change it.

Alana sighed. Maybe she was being over-cynical, and the sad thing was that her family would have been delighted if she could display a quarter of her father's ability. Since the day she had been born, they had watched her, hoping for some latent talent to suddenly awaken. After twenty-four years, they had finally given up. She was a member of the nobility by accident of birth alone. Her demon-spawn heritage had left no legacy of magic in her.

Ranks of ordinary people lined the street. Alana studied them as she passed. She was the same as them, but the commoners would never accept one of the demon-spawn living among them. Anger at the demon-wrought devastation had not faded, even though the Age of Chaos had ended almost two hundred and fifty years before. If Alana left the protection of the court, her life would be at risk.

Her gaze jumped from face to face until the crowd became a tableau of open mouths and eyes, a wall of noise, animated and awestruck. If you did not know better, you might read the atmosphere as one of celebration, but beneath the facade lay fear and hatred. Alana could feel it flowing in waves as if it were a physical force, pressing down on her chest. She stumbled under its weight.

"Careful." Reyna grabbed her arm, catching Alana before she fell.

"Thanks."

"Are you all right?"

"Yes. I'm fine."

Concern etched fine lines around Reyna's eyes. "It wasn't one of your dizzy attacks?"

"No. I wasn't watching where I was going. Sorry."

Reyna's expression showed that she was unconvinced, but before she could say anything, Princess Caritina set her own shoes alight, requiring that the ice-mage attend to her royal charge.

"No, no, Cari. You must be more careful."

"Didn't mean it." The toddler gave one of her most endearing, gap-toothed grins.

Over the previous few months, Caritina had been showing signs of getting her fire magic under control, much to her nursemaid's relief, but it was not surprising that the excitement of the parade had affected her. The talent for fire mastery ran strong in the descendants of Queen Jacaranda.

"Remember what happened to your bed."

"Got a new one now."

"You can't get new feet." Reyna sighed and took the girl's hand.

Alana smiled at them and then went back to brooding about the crowd and her place in the world. Did walking with Reyna and the infant princess make it all the more obvious that she did not have as much magical talent as the three-year-old? Despite her mother's status, Alana's inclusion in the Midsummer parade owed more to her role as partner to the royal nursemaid. Her own family would have been happier if she had been absent altogether.

For her part, Alana would also much rather have been somewhere else. Only Reyna's entreaties had persuaded her to take part. Increasingly, Alana found herself trying to avoid large gatherings. Her dizzy attacks were becoming a frequent reaction to crowds, and while common sense told her they were a purely psychological reaction, her body responding to the stress of the occasions, this did not give her any more power to control them. She was so much happier alone in her garden.

"You can't hide from the world behind your plants," Reyna had said repeatedly.

Alana was still waiting for her partner to add a good reason why not.

The ranks of commoners again drew her attention. How much of their hostility toward the demon-spawn nobility was due to resentment of the current inequality and injustice, and how much was due to history?

It was true that during the Age of Chaos the demons had killed untold millions, and inflicted wholesale ruin on the world, but the demon-spawn were not to blame. If anything, their ancestors had suffered the most, losing their very souls when the demons possessed them. The avatars had been mindless puppets, devoid of free will, used and discarded by the demons. They had been no more than tools, through which the demons fought their magical battles. Without exception, their lives had been short and their ends violent.

Although children conceived and born to the avatars retained some of the demons' magical powers, there was no collusion with the demons and it was unfair to hold the demon-spawn descendants to blame. Yet when the demons had left the world, at the end of the Age of Chaos, the common people had hunted down the demon-spawn and slaughtered any they could find.

Who could say how many had been murdered? The more fortunate were able to hide. Some led secret double lives, concealing their abilities. Others had fled to remote areas, such as the large family who had sought refuge in the mountains inland from Ellaye, overlooking the desert springs. This was the group who had ended the persecution of demon-spawn in the most decisive manner, when the matriarch of the family had led them in the brief battle to take control of Ellaye and subjugate the common folk.

Only after Queen Jacaranda founded the Kingdom of Galvonia had it become apparent how many of the demon-spawn had survived, passing themselves off as ordinary people and keeping their magical abilities hidden. So if her ancestors could do it, Alana reasoned, why not she? After all, it was not as if she had any ability to hide.

Her parents would object, of course. Alana wished she had the courage to confront them and demand that she be allowed to leave Ellaye. But they would not listen to her. They never did.

The head of the procession reached its destination. The central square was decorated for the occasion. Flags hung on the building fronts. The trees lining the edge were covered in glowing red and white blossoms—an illusion, but a very effective one. A platform had been erected in the middle. Since it was made of wood, King Alvarro II had to end his display of fire magic before he mounted the steps. Lady Kyra could have continued appearing to float above the ground, but it would not be prudent to outshine the king, and Lady Kyra had not reached her current rank without a shrewd grasp of politics. The third person to join them on the platform was Orrin, the king's newly appointed high counselor. Alana eyed him with surprise and suspicion. This was a departure from tradition, but Orrin had been showing signs of wanting to change things round.

Orrin cultivated a long beard, possibly in an attempt to disguise his age, and seem older and wiser than he was. Alana would have put him at nothing over thirty, but it should not be difficult to find out for certain, if she felt so motivated. Although a new arrival in Ellaye, Orrin was actually a distant cousin of hers. One of her relatives would know when he had been born.

His rise in the king's favor had been spectacular. How far did Orrin's ambitions go? Alana had heard rumors of his plans for the country, and the monarchy. The stories he was weaving seemed like nonsense to her, yet he had, apparently, convinced the king that they held some truth.

Alana's gaze hardened. Was she being fair, or was it just that she did not like mind-mages? Even if you accepted the commonly voiced belief that their so-called magical talent was nine-tenths trickery, it still left the conclusion that the remaining one-tenth involved poking around inside other people's heads.

Orrin stepped forward to address the crowd, usurping the role of herald. "Today we celebrate the founding of the glorious Kingdom of Galvonia. The day when Queen Jacaranda led her family down from the mountains, and accepted her divinely allotted mission. For one hundred and seventy-six years, she and her noble descendants have been true to their calling. For you, they have established order and security. For you, they have fought back the windigos. For you, they will lead the world onward to a new Age of Wonders." Orrin paused, dramatically. "People of Ellaye. I give you your king." His voice had been loud. Now it rose to a shout. "All hail his majesty, Alvarro II."

The watching crowd broke into a respectable imitation of a cheer. The king now claimed the front of the podium and began the traditional address.

Alana edged closer to Reyna. "Do you think he'll get the people to buy it?"

"Who?"

"Orrin."

"Buy what?"

"All the stuff about demons of light, and the king's ancestors defeating the demons of darkness."

"Why not?"

"But it's not true."

"You don't know that. He might be right."

"Reyna. Be serious."

Alana's exasperated tone only drew a carefree smile. "Anyway, what does it matter?"

Alana took a deep breath, but then stopped. The parade was not the place to have the discussion, and no matter where they were, would she ever get Reyna to understand the games of politics and power?

Perhaps if Reyna's family had been closer to the monarchy, she might have grown up knowing that everything mattered, when it came to the king's favor. But then, one of the things that drew Alana to the nursemaid was her total lack of interest in the double-dealing, maneuvering, and game-playing of court. And if Reyna had possessed more acute political instincts, would she have aligned herself with a no-hoper, devoid of magical ability?

Alana sighed and turned back to the podium. She started. Orrin was staring straight at her. The intensity of the calculating look in his eye caught her off guard. Whatever the reason for his attention, its roots lay in more than idle curiosity.

The king's high counselor was very definitely someone who knew all about politics and power. Alana was struck by the worrying idea that he was making yet more plans, and she was clearly involved in them.

❖

The blue spikes of wolfsbane were just coming into flower. In another few weeks they would be at their best. The potent drug extracted from the leaves and roots had many uses. It could save lives or take them. The beauty of the flower was a bonus. Beauty always was.

Alana touched the tip of her finger to a swelling bud, while running a quick mental inventory. Her potion jars were currently well stocked. She could afford to wait until the flowering was over before harvesting. Beauty should not be wasted.

She moved away from the damp shade of the wall and knelt beside a bed of plants, blooming in the full sun. Her dark hair absorbed the heat on the back of her head, but the rays were not so powerful as to make her go in search of a hat. The sprouting weeds she pulled up left behind miniature craters and mountains in the soil for trains of ants to scramble over. The work was relaxing, allowing her mind to wander.

The air in the Quintanilla herb garden was thick with the scent of pollen, herbs, and wet soil. Nodding heads of gold, red, and white stood out against the vibrant green and soft purple foliage. Bees hummed between the flowers. Birds trilled from branches overhead. The garden was a riot of colors and sensations. Alana could not help comparing it with the contrived spectacle of the Midsummer parade, two days before. She should never have gone.

The herb garden was one of her mother's better ideas, even if making a place of refuge for Alana had not been the goal. Lady Kyra's intention had been to provide Alana with a flimsy charade of talent. There was nothing magical about herbalism, but it felt as if there should be. Medicine and poison, life and death, adorned with the trappings of ancient knowledge. Lady Kyra had worked hard to blur the boundary between mysticism and magic, for the sake of her family's reputation.

The crunch of footsteps made Alana look up. Reyna was strolling along the gravel path.

"Hi there. Where's Cari?"

"Her mother's taken her visiting. Said she doesn't need me."

Alana smiled as she stood. The chance to spend an afternoon together was a rare luxury. She brushed the dirt off her hands and wrapped Reyna in a hug.

"So, I've got to put up with having you around."

"Afraid so." Reyna grinned. "Sorry about that."

"Let's go sit in the—"

A footman was hastening toward them. Alana sighed. She should have known it was too good to be true, but was more than five seconds alone with her lover really too much to ask of life?

She disentangled herself from Reyna's arms. "Yes?"

"My lady." The footman bowed. "Your mother and father request your presence in the main hall."

"Do you know what it's about?"

Alana's question was a trifle disingenuous. Undoubtedly, the servant would know the reason behind the summons. Servants always did. Their grapevine was frightening in its scope and effectiveness. The real question was whether he would admit to whatever information he had.

"No, my lady, but High Counselor Orrin is also there, awaiting you."

A hint was better than nothing. "Thank you. Tell them I'll be along as soon as I've changed my clothes."

The footman hurried away. Alana scowled at his retreating back, although she knew it was unfair to hold him responsible.

"Shall I come too?" Reyna asked.

"Yes. I want you there." Alana wanted all the backup she could get.

"How about what I'm wearing?"

"You'll be fine. You don't have mud on you."

No matter how keen her mother might be to promote Alana's image as a herbalist, it would not do to meet the king's high counselor looking as if she had been anywhere near a real, living garden.

The servants' grapevine was obviously working impeccably. A jug of hot water was waiting for Alana by the washbasin in her room and someone had laid a selection of her best clothes out for inspection.

"Pick something suitable. You're better at knowing what to wear than I am." Alana threw the request over her shoulder as she scrubbed dirt from under her fingernails.

"Hey. This is nice. Is it new? I haven't seen it before." Reyna held up the long green robe.

"It's one of Flor's cast-offs."

"Shame it's a little too frivolous for an afternoon meeting."

Who knew? There were time-dependent flippancy quotas for clothing. As far as Alana was concerned, if clothes fit her body contours, kept her temperature within a comfortable range, and hid everything that should be covered up in public, then they had fulfilled all the requirements made of them.

"I couldn't wear it anyway. It needs adjusting before it will fit me." Alana was both shorter and heavier boned than her older sister. She went back to cleaning her nails.

"What do you think Orrin wants with you?"

"I can't imagine. You've got more experience of making up kiddies' stories than I have."

"Stories?"

Alana sighed and reached for the towel. "All the stuff about the royal family being descended from someone possessed by Lucifer. He's made it all up."

"Didn't he read it in that book the traders found, from the Age of Wonders?"

"What I've heard is that all he's got is a couple of half-pages and a load of dust that used to be a book."

"He claims he's been able to read bits of it."

"Exactly. Bits."

"But doesn't it say Lucifer was a demon whose name means *light-bringer*? We know the demons were fighting each other. Good versus evil. Light versus dark. What else would demons fight over?"

"Maybe they just liked fighting, and maybe they weren't really fighting at all. It might have been their equivalent of a football game."

"They wouldn't have destroyed the world for a game."

"Why not?"

"Countless millions of people died."

"I know. But the records from the Age of Chaos are pretty much agreed that dead humans didn't bother the demons in the slightest." Alana picked up the outfit Reyna had selected for her, a thigh-length blue tunic and loose black pants.

"But that would be so evil." Reyna lent a hand, tightening up the lacing on the sleeves. "Doesn't it stand to reason that we're descended from the avatars of good demons? I don't feel evil."

"You aren't."

"So if a good demon like Lucifer was our ancestor, it would make sense."

"I don't think anything about the demons has to make sense."

Reyna frowned in thought. "Okay. But even if it's not totally true, if Orrin can convince the ordinary people it was the evil demons who caused all the harm, and our ancestors were on the side of good, and that they beat the evil demons and forced them to leave Earth, wouldn't that make the commoners accept us more?"

"Queen Jacaranda didn't need the commoners to accept her. All she needed was for her family to grow big enough so that she had the power to incinerate anybody who tried to stop her taking over in Ellaye. Once all the other demon-spawn had come out of hiding and joined her, whether or not commoners felt inclined to accept her was even more irrelevant than it had been before."

"Wouldn't you prefer it if the ordinary people liked us?"

Alana planted a kiss on Reyna's cheek and then bent to pull on her soft indoor ankle boots. "You're sweet."

"I was being serious."

"It's not about liking. I don't think Orrin worries about being liked by the commoners, any more than Queen Jacaranda did. It's about getting more power over people."

"Power? Why does he want more power over the commoners?"

Reyna really was so naive it was adorable. "Not over the commoners, silly. Over the rest of the nobility. You notice it's only King Alvarro who gets Lucifer as his ancestor. The rest of us might have a demon of darkness or two in our family trees. Don't you see how much more powerful it makes the monarchy? Instead of simply being the leader of a family of demon-spawn with enough firepower to take control of the region, the king becomes divinely sanctioned, and any attempt to disagree with him is"—Alana hunted for the concept she wanted—"sacrilege."

"But Orrin won't benefit from it, will he? He's doing it for the king, not himself."

"He's in the process of wrapping the king around his little finger. Take my word for it, Orrin is going to end up rather more powerful, and considerably less well liked."

Reyna looked confused. "You want people to like you, don't you? That's what I noticed about you. You're kind." She stepped closer, sliding her arms around Alana's waist. "It's what makes you different from the others in your family."

Alana rested her forehead on Reyna's shoulder. How to say that what really made her different was that she had no magical talent, and was never going to be chief marshal, or high counselor, or anyone of note? The whole game looked very different when sitting on the sidelines. And Reyna was such a gentle, loving soul, how could anyone not be kind to her? Just being in Reyna's presence made Alana feel better disposed to all around her.

"Come on. Let's go see what new fairy stories Orrin has been making up."

The Quintanilla mansion had been built using material salvaged from the ruins of ancient Ellaye. The walls and floor of the main hall were faced with slabs of pale marble. An embossed line of small arches, like a row of stylized M's, ran the length of the hall at waist height. Strange relics in primary red and yellow hung from the walls.

Alana's parents stood on the raised dais at the top of the hall. Orrin was talking to them. He turned at Alana's approach, and studied her thoughtfully. His smile, what could be seen through his beard, held more of satisfaction than welcome.

"Alana, I've been talking to your parents, and I think I might have some very good news for you."

What was the definition of *good*, Alana wondered, and for whom. She glanced at her parents. They looked happy but mystified, so presumably Orrin had not yet shared the details with them. He beckoned her closer. Alana forced her legs to obey, although she felt the sudden urge to flee. Something about his manner seemed so predatory. All her self-control was needed not to flinch when he held his hand out to her face, stopping a few inches short of cupping her cheek.

"Alana. Have you ever wondered why the daughter of two such notable mages should be without talent? Hmm?"

Alana gave a vaguely acquiescent shrug. Certainly her parents had wondered enough to make up for any lack of curiosity on her part.

"The answer, my dear, is simple. I have felt the stirrings of talent in you. It seethes below the surface of your mind. And yet it is trapped within you, held back and repressed."

"She has a talent? What?" Lady Kyra's voice crackled with excitement.

"Ahhhhhh." Orrin drew out the sound, as if to torment everyone by delaying the pronouncement. "Now that's the question, isn't it?" He raised his other hand, also holding it a few inches from the side of Alana's face, moving slowly, as if her head were a fire and he was warming his hands around it.

After a minute or more, his arms dropped. "I believe she has the same talent as myself. That is what I read in her, a kindred soul."

No kindred of yours. Alana stamped on the thought before it could show in her expression, and then wondered why she felt such immediate need to reject the idea.

Her father clearly did not share her aversion, but still needed convincing. "Why doesn't she show any sign of it?"

"Maybe in part because she's unaware that what her talent tells her is more than a simple, normal emotional reaction to the people she meets. But I think mainly it's because she's somehow blocking the full exercise of her own magic."

"Alana?" Lady Kyra's tone demanded an answer.

"I'm not. I'd know if I was."

Orrin shook his head, making his beard waggle. "Not necessarily. If you've been doing it since you were a baby, by now it may be a subconscious response in you. Something you give no more thought to than you do to breathing."

"Can you stop her doing it?"

Once more, Orrin raised his hand to Alana's head, looking thoughtful. "I think so. The barriers are strong, but they can be broken down and swept away."

"I don't think I—" Alana got no chance to raise any objections.

For the first time Orrin touched her, laying a finger on her lips. "I know it must seem strange, even frightening to you, but great times are ahead for all Galvonia, and the talent you and I share will be called on. Traitors must be found and weeded out. Doubters must be given faith. Protestors must be convinced."

With a tremor of shock, Alana realized that Orrin's lips were not moving. His words were forming directly in her head, unheard by the others in the room.

Orrin nodded slowly, and then again started speaking aloud. "Yes. These barriers must be stripped away." He removed his finger from Alana's lips and gave a small regal bow to Lady Kyra. "I'll leave now and make my preparations. They will not take long, three days at most. I'll summon your daughter once all is ready."

Alana wanted to make her own escape from the hall immediately after Orrin had left. Unfortunately, her parents had other ideas. They seemed to be under the delusion that if they asked the same questions fifteen times, Alana would spontaneously acquire more information to give them, whereas the only clear thought in her head was that she had three days to think of a way out of it.

At last she was allowed to go. With the door of her room finally closed, Alana rested her back against it and closed her eyes. Her relief turned out to be short-lived.

"Can you read minds?"

"Oh please, Reyna, not you too."

"I'm sorry."

Alana felt Reyna's hand on her arm and the calming balm of her presence.

"I'm not a mind-mage."

But even as Alana said it, doubts assailed her. She realized that she truly did feel Reyna's presence, a sensation every bit as precise as touch. Was that normal? Surely everyone drew strength and comfort from having their lover nearby. She was aware that Reyna was teetering between hope and bewilderment, but was any magical ability needed to know this?

Alana's eyes were closed, so she could not see Reyna's expression, but why should she have to? The two of them had been together for two years. How long did it take before you could predict what your lover was thinking?

In fact, could she even be sure they were Reyna's emotions that she was aware of? Maybe she was projecting her own feelings and assuming Reyna felt the same. She was certainly bewildered enough on her own account. She did not need to be bewildered for Reyna as well.

Alana opened her eyes and lurched away from the door. She slumped down on the bed. Reyna sat beside her and hesitantly took hold of her hand.

"I don't mean to upset you."

Despite her irritation, Alana could not help smiling. Reyna would never mean to upset anyone. "It's not you, darling."

"But if you don't have mind-mage powers now, do you still think Orrin might be right? That you could become one?"

"I don't know."

"You don't sound happy about it."

"I'm not."

"But don't you see what it could mean for us?"

"Pardon?" Alana stared at her lover in confusion.

"If you were a mind-mage. You could become Orrin's assistant."

The mere thought made Alana grimace. "I don't want to."

"Why not?"

"I don't trust him."

"He's the king's high counselor."

"Yes. I know that. So?"

"The king trusts him. He has to be all right."

Alana rested her forehead on her hand. How did she even begin to explain the fallacy in that line of reasoning to someone so politically innocent?

Reyna clearly took the lack of argument as a sign to continue. "Please, Alana. I know it's different for you. The Quintanillas have always been important. But coming from a minor house, like mine, especially since I'm not a very strong ice-mage, it's not easy. If you could become Orrin's deputy, then I wouldn't have to be Cari's nursemaid. We could spend more time together. I don't want to be thought of as anything special, but it would be nice if people gave us more respect."

Alana turned her head and looked at Reyna's apologetic smile in surprise. So her lover did have some ambition after all, albeit on a very modest scale, and accompanied by feelings of guilt for not being happy with what she had.

Ice-mage ranked above beast-master, but not by much, and it was true that Reyna's talent was very limited—just about adequate for stopping a three-year-old setting fire to herself. Alana was sure Reyna genuinely loved her, but was she equally sure that Reyna had not entered the relationship with one eye on the prospect of advancing her position, by allying herself with the powerful Quintanillas?

The thought was one that surfaced from time to time. Usually, Alana dismissed it as the normal sort of self-doubt that afflicted everyone, apart from the most narcissistic of egoists, but for the first time she felt genuine uncertainty. Was she picking it up from Reyna?

"Please, Alana. For me. For us. Promise that you'll try."

❖

Thick curtains covered the windows. The ceiling, walls, and floor had been painted black, diminishing the light yet further. The overall effect, when combined with the red wax candles and chalk pentagram scrawled around the silver chair in the middle of the room, merely served to reinforce Alana's opinion of Orrin. She would have been sure he was a complete charlatan were it not for the voice in her head when he had placed his finger on her lips. He was waiting for her now, wearing long white robes in counterpoint to the absurdly theatrical decor.

Orrin waved her to the chair. "Please, be seated."

Alana tried to swallow her misgivings. Her attempt met with very limited success, but it was too late to start coming up with excuses. As Orrin shut the door, she turned her head for a last glimpse of Reyna and her mother, waiting in the antechamber outside.

Orrin walked in a circle, lighting each of the red candles in turn. Once the last candle was burning, the increased illumination allowed Alana to see the previously missed small table at one side of the room, also painted black. Candlelight glinted on several metallic objects arranged on it. The only item with a function she recognized was a silver goblet.

Orrin picked it up and handed it to her. "Drink this."

Alana sniffed and took a cautious sip. "Kava?"

"Just a light concoction, to help you relax."

"If you'd said, I could have prepared my own draft."

"Oh yes, you do study herbalism, don't you? I'd forgotten." Orrin's tone was too bland to be completely credible. "Never mind. The one I've produced will be fine."

Alana swilled the kava around in the goblet and took another sniff, while toying with the idea of refusing to drink it. Was the drug really necessary? Yet Alana could hardly deny that she was tense and her choices were limited. Either she could comply with Orrin's instructions, or she could give in to her distrust of the man and go. The latter option was by far the more appealing, except that it would leave her with a lot of explaining to do to her parents. For a moment, Alana's decision hung in the balance, but then she raised the goblet to her lips and drained it.

As a herbalist, Alana was familiar with the effects of kava. Before long, the faint numbing of her lips and tongue became noticeable. She waited for the relaxed sense of well-being and clarity of thought to follow. Instead, her pulse began to race and her head spun. The tingling in her lips flowed away from her mouth, down her neck, and rippled over the entire surface of her skin.

"What else was in the potion?" Alana could hear the alarm in her own voice.

"A few minor trace elements, just to aid the process. Nothing significant."

"You should have told me what it was before giving it to me to drink."

Orrin smiled as he walked around the chair. "I'm sorry if I've been a little presumptuous, but you know I only have your best interests at heart. A great future awaits you, and I'm going to help you achieve it."

He was lying. Suddenly, Alana was quite certain of it. She was in the process of rising when a noose dropped over her shoulders, binding her to the chair. Before she could manage more than a gasp of surprise, a band of cloth was wedged between her teeth, gagging her.

Orrin reappeared by her side. "Don't be alarmed. I'm not going to hurt you."

More lies.

"This is going to be a delicate operation. If you were to move or shout at the wrong time, it might have unfortunate consequences. Please believe me. You need to be restrained for your own good."

Lying. He was lying.

Orrin pulled a fresh length of cord from his sleeve and started binding her wrists to the armrest of the chair. Alana wanted to struggle, but her limbs were shaking and her muscles were seized with cramps. The kava had been little more than a disguise for whatever else had been in Orrin's potion. Even if she were not tied, Alana did not think she would have had the strength to walk to the door. But she could have crawled. She would have done anything to get out of the room and away.

Abruptly, Orrin was standing before her, with one of the items from the table in his hands. Alana had not seen him move. Had she passed out briefly? She tried to focus on the candles, to see how far they had burned down, but her vision was distorted. Light and color were smeared. Her heartbeat thundered in her ears. Sweat trickled down her back and sides, soaking into the waistband of her pants.

Orrin came closer. Alana's eyesight cleared briefly, enough for her to see that the item he held looked like a small steel club, no more than a foot in length. One end was engraved with cross-hatching, either as decoration or to provide a secure grip. Bands of green light danced up and down a flattened surface along the other end. What sort of weapon was it?

As if in answer to her thought, Orrin spoke. "This device was brought back from the wastelands some years ago by a band of Iron Wolf mercenaries. It's lain in the king's armory since then. Nobody knew what it was. In fact, I still can't give you a name for it, but I know what its purpose is. You can think of it as a sort of lens, if you like. It sharpens up thoughts, and it's going to assist me in focusing my talent on you. It will give me the keen edge to cut through the barriers you've built around your mind."

Wielding the metal bar as if it were indeed a carving knife, Orrin sliced through the air. The flattened section swept by Alana's face, passing a scant inch from her cheek. She flinched although the device did not touch her, and despite the absence of physical contact, some part of Alana was severed. Like taking peel off an orange, a strip of the casing around her mind was cut away.

The universe flowed in. Had the gag not been in her mouth, Alana would have screamed, from shock rather than pain. An avalanche of emotion overwhelmed her. Anger, love, regret, pride, amusement, disgust. Any consciousness that she might have claimed as her own was lost in the torrent from outside.

Again the bar passed before Alana's eyes. Another gap in her head opened up and more emotions flooded in. Orrin's smug triumph. Her mother's excited hopes. Reyna's optimistic concern. The disappointment of the stable boy in the yard outside. The boredom of a guard on sentry duty. A courtier's irritation. A lover's desire. A thief's greed. A widow's grief. The whole of Ellaye was streaming into her head. Alana could not pick her own thoughts clear from the confusion.

Still Orrin sliced with his bar. How much more was there to the world? The arcane device was flaying her mind, laying her soul exposed and utterly vulnerable. She no longer knew herself. She no longer existed. The onslaught obliterated and overwrote everything that she could call Alana.

With relief, she embraced the dark jaws of unconsciousness that consumed her.

❖

For the merest instant upon waking, Alana wondered what was going on, before the tumult of the world ripped all coherent thought to shreds. Stabs of anger and dismay filled her head, filtered through a choking web of terror. Further away, the thunderous roar of love and hate seethed around nodes of other emotions. Her identity was lost amid the chaos.

Desperately, Alana clawed at her senses, trying to use whatever they could tell her as building blocks to construct some self-awareness. Soft pressure along her back revealed that she was lying on a bed or couch. The acrid bite of smelling salts defined her nose. Sunlight glowed red through her closed eyelids. Someone was whimpering softly, while other voices talked in the background.

"He ought to have known."

"But what are we going to do?"

"What can we do?"

Alana tried to concentrate on the words and ignore the way they sparked new bursts of irritation, but another emotion was strengthening. Anxious satisfaction was getting closer, and then Alana heard a door open. The bitter anger that had greeted her when she first woke flared to fresh heights.

"About time."

"I'm sorry. It wasn't where I thought it was."

At the sound of the new voice, the terror erupted, obliterating everything else. The soft whimpering became a half-scream.

"She's awake."

"Good. She needs to drink this."

Alana's eyes flew open. A barrage of faces surrounded her and nearest was Orrin's. He was holding another goblet to her lips. Alana turned her head aside, ignoring the way sharp motion made the room reel.

"Hold her head steady."

Alana tried to fight, but the panic was so strong it formed iron bands around her chest. Breathing was impossible, and with the resulting dizziness, the ability to resist left her. Honey-sweet liquid filled her mouth. She swallowed because it was less effort than spitting.

"And now this." Orrin spoke again.

Alana felt the weight of cold metal on her throat, and suddenly the monster of emotions took a half-step back. The space was just sufficient to separate herself from the world. She knew who Alana was. She realized that the terrified whimpers had been hers.

Orrin patted her hand. "There you go. Have another mouthful and then lie down. Once the potion takes effect you'll feel better."

Some small voice warned her not to obey, but Alana could not concentrate enough to work out why. The chaos in her head had eased, and she would willingly do whatever was necessary to make it calm still further. Alana stretched out again on the bed and concentrated on breathing. Slowly, the sharp definition on the emotions in the room became blurred and the roar from the city outside faded to a buzz. The relief was so great it left Alana light-headed.

Orrin was still holding her hand. "I'm so sorry, my dear."

"Na-yer-nor." Alana's tongue was too sluggish to move.

"Don't try to talk."

Alana closed her eyes. She might as well follow the advice, since nobody would understand a word she said. Orrin had done this to her. His presence made her feel ill and she wished he would stop holding her hand, but she lacked the strength to pull away. For now, all she could do was to try ignore him and concentrate on getting her head back together. When she felt better, she would be able to tell her side of things.

"You're an empath, a very powerful one, stronger in the talent than has ever been recorded before. I have to admit, I'm amazed. If I'd have known, I would never have—" Orrin broke off with a sorrowful sigh.

"But you have, haven't you? What's going to happen to her now?" The anger inside Reyna burned hotter than Alana would have imagined possible for her placid lover.

"Yes. That is the question. What next for Alana?"

"The talisman you've given her, she can keep it?" Lady Kyra was a complex knot of ambition, anxiety, and hope.

"Oh yes, of course. In fact, I insist that she does. She must have it with her at all times, but I fear it can do no more than take the edge off what she is experiencing. The potion I have given her will also help, but it is not safe, and should not be taken over a lengthy period of time. I fear this means she will not be able to continue her life in Ellaye."

Although his tone was somber, Orrin was filled to the brim with satisfaction. He took a moment to gather himself for his prepared speech and then let go of Alana's hand and moved away. "As I have said, your daughter is a very powerful empath."

"She can read minds?"

"In a way, although what she senses are basic emotions rather than exact thoughts, and it is the unfiltered nature of her talent that is the problem. I was right about the barriers she had raised around herself, blocking her talent. But what I had not realized was she'd built them for her own protection."

"Why? When?"

"As for why? Imagine what it must be like, to be bombarded by the raw emotions from everyone around you, without respite. I suspect she started shutting everyone else out when she was still a baby. An instinctive response. She probably never knew what she was doing."

"You said she had to leave Ellaye. Why? Surely she can rebuild her barriers."

"Maybe, given time." This was not the way Orrin's hopes were leaning, of that, Alana was certain. "But it won't happen quickly, and she'll need the right environment."

"What sort of environment?"

"Peace and as few people around as possible. That's why she has to get away from Ellaye." This was what Orrin was so happy about. "The farther she can be from towns, the better it will be for her."

"You want her to go live in the wastelands?" Fear shot through Reyna's outrage.

"Oh no. It needn't be than extreme. A small hamlet, on the edges of Galvonia, but still under the protection of the King's Marshals. I am sure somewhere suitable can be found."

"Would somewhere like that be able to support a proper household for her?"

"Alana won't be able to have a household."

"She'll need bodyguards and servants."

"Anyone who can project emotions will put a strain on her, and even the dullest of commoners can do that. Maybe she could have one companion, but anything more she would not be able to bear."

"But she can't go on her own. Her life will be in danger. We all know how the commoners view us."

"Does it matter? Sounds like there won't be enough people around to form a lynch mob." Her mother was bitterly cynical.

Orrin's voice was a plea for calm. "The local inhabitants need not know of her heritage. She can pass among them as one of their own. She need not be at risk."

The irony was not lost on Alana. *Be careful what you wish for, because you just might get it.*

For the first time, Alana's father spoke. "Commoners! You expect my daughter to go and live among the commoners, in some impoverished farming village, without a single servant or any of the trappings she's used to? You're suggesting she can live in squalor, like a peasant?"

"I'm afraid there's no other option. If she stays here, she'll be driven mad."

"The life of a peasant is not fitting for my daughter."

"It needn't be forever. With just a few people around, Alana might be able to regain control of her talent. If she could learn to manipulate the new barriers, so she can be selective in whose emotions she taps, why…" Orrin paused dramatically, as if a new idea had just struck him. "Can you see how valuable she could be to the king? She would be able to return to the court as one of his most senior advisers. It would be a great day, for Galvonia and the Quintanilla family."

Alana did not need to feel the sudden spark of excitement to know, with that one sentence, the argument was won. Her parents' ambition was so easy to ignite. Fighting it was not worth the effort. She closed her eyes and let drowsiness reclaim her.

❖

When Alana next awoke, night had fallen. Moonlight poured through the open window. The city was silent, its inhabitants asleep. The absence of emotional clamor was enough for Alana to think clearly, or as clearly as Orrin's drugs would allow. Alana was sure that she had been given more of whatever the second potion had been. Her body was numb and would not obey her. When she tried to move, her head fell to one side. She saw Reyna, slumped in a chair beside her bed.

"Uhh." Alana's throat was too dry for talking, even if she could control her tongue.

Reyna shook herself and sat up. "How are you, darling?"

"Wa'er." Alana pointed weakly at the jug on the dresser.

Reyna poured a glass and then helped Alana into a sitting position. The cold liquid was a blessed relief, although much of the water spilled from her slack lips and trickled down her chin. What was Orrin dosing her with?

"Thangs. What waz..." Wheezing stopped Alana from saying more.

"Don't try to speak. Orrin has got you pretty heavily drugged."

This much Alana already knew.

"It's to help you."

Considerate of him.

"You don't need to worry. It's all been sorted out. I'm taking you away from Ellaye tomorrow. I know where we're going, far to the north, a small valley. I'm going to stay there with you until you've worked out how to control your talent."

With the city hushed, picking out a single thread of emotion was easier. Fear and uncertainty were battling inside Reyna, fueled by a warm core of affection. Alana paused in doubt. Or were the fear and affection her own? The drug-induced blurring made it impossible to be certain, although the potion was affecting her body more than her mind.

"Orrin has said we need to leave as soon as possible."

And he wanted his victim unable to speak coherently until she was away from Ellaye. Yet, even if Alana could talk, what could she say? Orrin had promised to remove her mental barriers, and that was what he had done. He claimed he had not known how it would affect her. The only proof that he was lying came from this new wild talent of hers. If she challenged him, it would be the word of a nobody, manifestly suffering from devastating mental problems, against the king's high counselor. Alana did not rate her chances of winning the argument.

Plus, he had done what he could to alleviate the symptoms. The silver talisman hung on a cord around her neck. She must have grabbed hold of it subconsciously, in her sleep. Her fingers tightened, clinging to it like a lifeline. She could feel the protective sphere it cast around her. Clearly, it was some demon device from the Age of Chaos.

So why had Orrin done it, harmed then healed her? Alana suspected she would never get a full answer, but she could guess. Orrin's goal appeared to be removing her from Ellaye. Since she had been an untalented nonentity before, either it was part of a complex strategy to undermine the Quintanilla family, or Orrin had been worried that some day, she might spontaneously take control of her talent and become a power in her own right.

The high counselor was ambitious, and his plans demanded that he kept the king's ear. Orrin had said they were kindred talents. Had he been concerned at the possibility of her becoming a rival, and so had removed her from the game before she became a threat? If so, it was a bitter irony. Had he asked, Alana would have told him that she had no ambition whatsoever to play games at court. He could keep the king's ear—both of them, and his nose as well, for all she cared.

"Orrin—" Alana managed to choke out the name.

Reyna did not give her the chance to finish. "Yes. He's given me instructions on how to take care of you. And I will. I won't leave you. I promise."

Discomfort now blended with the affection, tainting and weakening it. Was Reyna unsure of her ability to fulfill that promise?

"I love you."

Yet the affection ebbed still further as Reyna took Alana's hand and squeezed it.

"I'm going to do everything I can so you learn how to cope with crowds again and we can come back to Ellaye. Maybe we'll only be gone for a few months. I'm sure it won't be long. And we'll be together, so it…"

A stream of emotions rippled through Reyna as she spoke, a weak flare of hope mingled with sexual desire, squashed by misery. Guilt that threatened to tip into resentment, if it were not for the counterbalance of affection. Alana could read it so easily.

Reyna did not want to go, would rather stay in Ellaye, yet was feeling compelled. It was all so obvious, exactly what Alana would have expected, except for the desire. Reyna's affection had been for her, but the desire had not. It had flared at the thought of returning to Ellaye, and it had been extinguished as the resentment grew. In going away from court, Reyna was leaving a lover, or someone she hoped would become a lover—but who?

Alana closed her eyes, willing sleep to return, willing the stream of information to stop. She told herself that she could put no faith in what she thought she was picking up. She refused to put any faith in it. Not only was she drugged to the point of stupor, but this new sense was untried and unfamiliar. Yet she could not block out her thoughts.

Who was Reyna hoping to see when she came back to Ellaye?

Approaching the town of Oakan, northern Galvonia
17th year of the reign of King Alvarro II
Fall, octubre 6, midafternoon

For the last few miles of the journey, the track left the riverbank and passed through dense forest. Tall pines overhung the rutted dirt road. The route climbed steadily, crossing the southern slopes of Beck Hill and cutting off a wide loop in the course of the Oakan River. The roar of the water faded away behind, replaced by the trill of birdsong.

Off to one side, Deryn spotted a flash of white rumps as deer fled deeper into the forest. The animals vanished amid the wilting yellow undergrowth. Summer was gone and the ferns were dying back. Another month or two, and there would be nothing except snow and the occasional outline of an ancient ruin beneath the pines. The road turned a bend, zigzagging on the final, steeper section of the ascent. Up ahead, a patch of sky peeked between the tree trunks.

At the crest of the hill, Deryn pulled on Tia's reins, bringing the mare to a standstill so the rest of the team could catch up. As scout for the party, her position out in front was traditional, even though nobody could possibly get lost, this close to home. While waiting, Deryn took in the view.

A ring of mountains surrounded the broad valley below. The white-capped peaks were stark against dark clouds that threatened rain. Tallest of all, Mount Oakan filled the skyline to the northeast. The river looped back into sight and meandered away, a gray band under a grayer sky.

The forest ended in a ragged line where farms cut patchwork strips between the blue-green pines. Twisted strings of smoke marked the location of farmhouses and herds of sheep and cattle grazed in fields. In the middle of the valley, the farms were tightly packed together, squeezing out the pines. In the center of it all, the town of Oakan squatted by the banks of the river. The dense jumble was so compact that the buildings appeared to be crawling over each other.

The town was too distant to make out details, but from experience, Deryn knew it was hastily tacked together and poorly maintained. Each year, the heavy winter snows took their toll. The roads were potholed and the timber-framed houses were warped and weather beaten. The settlement had grown in the wilderness, without any sort of overall plan or vision, as each new arrival had tacked on whatever construction best fit their needs and pocket. Most of the building material had come from the surrounding forest, supplemented by anything usable that could be scavenged from the ruins of Old Oakan. The clumsy blend of rough-cut timber and ancient masonry made Oakan an ugly mess of a town. Yet as ever, on her return from the wastelands, it was the most welcoming sight that Deryn could imagine.

Oakan marked the beginning and end of the Misery Trail. It provided a base for the Iron Wolves and also a hub for the miners who prospected in the mountains to the south and east. Both groups were happy to take advantage of the town's position on the borders of civilization, where the King's Law was interpreted a little more liberally than in the heartland of Galvonia. Oakan's streets held more taverns than tailors, more casinos than carpenters, and more brothels than bakers.

The depravity of Oakan was notorious and the staid farmers and tradesfolk of the region might have preferred a quieter life, were it not for the profit to be made from a stream of customers on their doorstep who were willing to pay over the odds for supplies. The King's Marshals were the only ones who actively objected to the loose morals and tried to keep a lid on the revelers' high spirits, but they were spread too thinly on the frontier to do more than make the occasional firm gesture.

Beltran stopped beside Deryn. "It's party night, tonight."

"Every night's a party night in Oakan."

"I like to make the easy calls."

Deryn grinned. Beltran did not hesitate to make the tough calls either. He had been a capable leader for the band of Iron Wolves guarding the caravan.

He patted Deryn's shoulder and then urged his horse on. "You've done well. Got us home nice and early."

"I can't take all the credit. I had help from the weather."

"You can take most of it. I've been with so-called scouts who couldn't get back much before the Night of the Lost if they'd had nothing but clear blue skies and a hot coal up their ass."

Deryn shrugged in answer. Just over three weeks remained until the festival, which had become the target date for the completion of the trade route, although in practice, anything up to a month either side was normal. Those taking much longer on the Trail were likely to get engulfed by the winter snows and never complete the journey at all.

"Best of all, you kept us safe."

"It's my job."

"I mean it. You spotted those windigos lurking in the shallows. Some scouts need their head bitten off before they think to check." Beltran nodded appreciatively. "You're a good scout."

"I had a good teacher."

"In that case, pass on my thanks."

"I will."

Just a few weeks more, and she would be able to do so. Deryn intended to spend the winter with Brise—a chance for them to catch up. They had not met for a year and a half. Brise was currently riding the desert trails, far to the south. The work was less profitable but also less strenuous than the Misery Trail. Brise claimed it was a concession to her age, even though she was still in good shape. Deryn felt her foster mother had given up too quickly. Alby, a member of her current team, was even older, and he had coped just fine, proving that experience counted for far more than speed. Maybe, when they met, she would be able to talk Brise into giving the Misery Trail one final shot.

Beltran glanced her way. "Do you think you'll ride the Trail again next year?"

"Maybe. I'll see how I feel, come spring." Her plans for the future were not something Deryn was ever happy discussing.

"I'll recommend you for any crew I'm on, if I get a say in the hiring."

"Thanks, I may take you up on that." *And I may not.*

The dismissal was nothing personal. Beltran was a capable warrior who led by example. Deryn had found him to be a shrewd judge of both people and danger. He was exactly the sort of Iron Wolf she would pick to follow on the Misery Trail, if it were not that she made it a rule never to travel on the same team with anyone twice, except for Brise.

Deryn glanced over her shoulder at the other Iron Wolves, who were following, strung out on either side of the line of wagons. For seven months they had lived together, day after day, sharing the dangers, the hard work, and the excitement of the Trail.

Rico was a loudmouth and Chay had taken too many knocks to the head. For both of them, Deryn could think of several brick walls she could have more fun talking to, but the rest of the band were okay. Nina had a wicked sense of humor. Alby was easygoing and dependable. Corbin had risked his life for her, crossing the swollen river. Saying good-bye would be hard enough, after just one season. Deryn did not intend to risk growing fonder.

In under an hour, they reached the outskirts of Oakan. Ramshackle corrals and stables clustered around the approach road. Deryn patted Tia's neck. After once again completing the Trail, the horse deserved better care than anything she was likely to receive in these cheap establishments. When the traders paid off their Iron Wolf guards there would be plenty of money to go around, and Tia had earned her share of it.

"Oats for you tonight, girl, and the best stable in town."

Tia's ears twitched back and her head bobbed, as if she was cheered by the thought.

"What will you have to reward yourself?" Beltran asked.

"Beer." Deryn paused, thinking. "And maybe a whiskey or two."

"The Lodestone?" He named a tavern, popular with Iron Wolves. "You'll be there?"

"Yes. Nina and me talked about it over breakfast. Rico liked the idea too. We'll tell the others when we stop."

Deryn nodded and said nothing. The end-of-Trail gatherings were something else that she always avoided. What was the point in dragging a celebration out of saying good-bye?

Tomorrow they would all drift apart. Like the smoke rising over a camp fire, the team would be carried away on the draft of circumstance. These people had been her comrades, but once the team was paid off she would never set eyes on most of them again. They were no longer part of her life, and it did not matter. Deryn forced the thought to the front of her mind. It did not matter. They were not friends or family. They had never been anything other than a chance grouping, brought together for a job. Now the task was over and all Deryn wanted was to go. Just take the money and turn away.

Oakan's wide Main Street was unpaved. The traffic kicked up a choking haze of dust in summer and churned it to ankle-deep mud in winter. The wooden facades of the establishments on either side were in better shape than most of Oakan, even if the buildings they were attached to were the same old decrepit shanties. Painted signs in gaudy colors hung outside, proclaiming their owners' trade or profession. Raised wooden boardwalks lined the storefronts, running beneath flimsy verandas.

The rain started as Beltran called a halt outside the Wolves' Den, the hiring post where they had started out, seven months before. Copies of their contracts would be stored inside, should any of the traders be so misguided as to want to argue.

Deryn turned up the fleece-lined collar of her jacket and looked up and down the street. Half the buildings were taverns, gambling halls, brothels, or some combination of the three. She considered each in turn: the Drunken Dog, the Lucky Strike, the Warrior's Return, and the rest. The prices they charged were even more outrageously inflated than for the rest of Oakan, relying on the inexperience of newcomers too nervous to risk the back streets. None of the Main Street taverns would be her preferred drinking spot, except that she was unlikely to run into another Iron Wolf in any of them.

The Lodestone lay on a side street. Deryn glanced at the junction that led to it, and then looked away. She was not going to join the end-of-Trail party. It was not as if she would have to drink alone, wherever she went. Most of her pay was needed to cover the costs of her trip down south to Ellaye, and to see her through winter, but this still left plenty to ensure she had company that night, and the ones thereafter. The sort of company that could be bought might be shallow and artificial, but it was readily available and even more readily disposable, no ties and no expectations.

True companionship would have to wait until she got to Brise.

Even if she went to the Lodestone with the others, what would it give her? Her ex-comrades did not know her well enough to understand her. Nobody did, apart from Brise. The sudden stab of loneliness surprised Deryn. She clenched her teeth, as if it would help clamp down on the maudlin emotions. Next year, if Brise would not ride the Misery Trail, maybe she would join her foster mother in the desert. A change in scenery would not be such a bad thing.

Beltran had dismounted to talk with the leader of the traders. The rest of the caravan were milling around. Everyone was laughing and chatting. Soon a round of hugging and back thumping would break out. Deryn stroked Tia's neck. This was the part she hated. She just wanted her money and to go, but she knew that some would try to drag things out. Deryn looked up at the sky. The rain was getting heavier and a full-fledged cloudburst was looming. With luck, it would speed up the proceedings.

Corbin nudged his horse close. "Shame the rain didn't hold off a bit longer."

"Yup."

"But we're home safe."

"Yup."

"Back in Oakan."

"Uh-huh."

Corbin was a nice young lad, if a not brilliant conversationalist. He was eighteen years old, tall and broad shouldered, with dark skin, curly black hair, and a crooked nose from an accident in his childhood. Deryn knew that he now also had a scar on his thigh from where he had fended off the broken tree, carried by the torrent—an action that had given her the time to regain her footing and complete the river crossing.

If Corbin had not been there...

Deryn pushed aside the thought. Corbin might have saved her life, but he would have done exactly the same for anyone else that the traders had chosen to employ. There had been nothing personal about it. Helping each other through the dangers was part of the job they were paid to do. The job that was over.

Corbin was going out of her life, with his strength, his cheerfulness, his love of smoked bacon, his absurd pink undershirt, his off-key whistling, the letter from his father that he held but did not read each night before going to sleep. Deryn ticked off the details in her head.

What did it count for? How well did you know someone after seven months?

"First time I've done the whole Trail."

This was also something she knew about him. "What did you think of it?"

Corbin scrunched his nose. "Wasn't as exciting as I'd expected."

"Not even having windigos on our tail?"

"Well, that bit maybe. But you got us out of it without a fight." He sounded disappointed.

"You wanted one?"

"It'd be something to tell my dad about."

"If you'd survived."

"Yeah. There is that." Corbin laughed. "Dad will have to make do with the story about the flooded river. I can show him the scar."

Deryn nodded. "I owe you. Big-time."

He shrugged. "You'd have done the same for me, but if you want, you can buy me a drink. Will you be at the Lodestone tonight?"

The one-word answer slipped out before Deryn could stop it. "Yes."

❖

The air was heavy with the combination of wood smoke, stale beer, and unwashed bodies. The tavern smell was thick enough to wrap around the patrons like a blanket, enfolding them in a warm alcohol cocoon. Yellow candlelight lapped over flushed faces, blurring them with soft shadows. Waves of rough voices rose in laughter. A fiddle scratched a tune in one corner, accompanied by a thumping of feet that bore little correlation to the rhythm.

Deryn sat on a bench in the corner, leaned her shoulders on the wall behind her, and drained her tankard. The beer had a rich malt flavor and a solid kick to it. It was definitely some of the best to be found in Oakan, and the price was below average for the town, a combination that went a long way to explain the popularity of the Lodestone among Iron Wolves.

The three pints she had downed were making Deryn comfortably mellow. She was tempted to go to the bar for another, but it was not her turn to buy the next round. Not that this was an issue. She was in a generous mood and the purse tied to her belt was heavy with coin, but there was no need to rush. She could take her time and still be sure of finishing the night dead drunk.

A loud burst of shouts and cheering claimed her attention. Even in the hubbub she recognized the voices. Rico and Corbin had joined the dancers. Judging by the wild cavorting, they were having a competition as to who could expend the most energy. The activity could be called dancing only because there was no other word that described it any better. Corbin saw her watching and waved, beckoning her over. Deryn shook her head. She had not drunk enough—not yet.

The bench shook as Alby dumped himself down beside her and propped his feet on the rungs of a nearby stool. "Another ride over."

"Yup."

Alby had undoubtedly completed more rides than most. His skin was weathered like old leather. Once his hair would have been black. What was now left was mostly gray. Yet he had more than pulled his weight on the Trail, putting many of the younger Iron Wolves to shame. He was easy company, uncomplaining and quick to laugh. Added to his vast store of knowledge about the wastelands, it had made him one of the most valued members of the team.

Alby sighed. "You know, every year I do the Trail, I tell myself it will be the last. I'm getting too old for the game."

"How many times have you done it?"

"Thirty something. I've lost count."

"Won't life be dull if you stop?"

"Ah, now there you've got it. At the moment, I'm thinking about when you're stuck between windigos and rapids, and it's way too dangerous to be fun. But after another winter, cooped up, I'll have itchy feet again. Come spring I'll just be remembering the open spaces."

"You sound sure of that."

"I am. I've tried giving it up before."

"Why?"

"Have you got family?"

Deryn was startled, and not merely because of the abrupt change in tack. Families were not something you ever talked about on the Trail. Fortunately, Alby did not wait for a reply.

"I've got three kids sitting back home, with their mother."

Home was another unfamiliar word. Deryn wondered if she should ignore it, but in the end she asked, "Are you going to see them?"

"Oh yes." Alby's expression softened and his voice dropped. "Yes. Eli runs a dairy farm just outside Sattle. She's…" Words were unnecessary. His smile said everything. "When I met her, I thought she was the one I could give up the Trail for. Two years I tried being a farmer, but it never worked out. I went back to riding the Trail, but I go clutter up the farm in the off season, getting in Eli's way and pretending I know how to make cheese. My youngest kid is twelve. I've missed seeing her grow up. I've missed all of them. Each winter when I go back, they're strangers to me. But maybe I've not left it too late to find out who they are." Alby took a long draft of his beer. "Will you be seeing your family?"

Deryn hesitated before giving a quick nod.

"You got kids?"

"No."

"How about your brothers, sisters? Will you visit them?"

Deryn shook her head.

"You don't get on with them?"

"I haven't any."

"What family have you got?"

"My foster mother. She's the one I'll be visiting. She's an Iron Wolf. Been working down in Ellaye, running the desert trails." Deryn was keen to shift the conversation. "I'm thinking I might join her next year. It would be something new. Have you seen much of the south?"

The ploy did not work. "What happened to your real parents?"

Deryn stared down at the empty tankard, dangling from her fingers. Lamplight reflected on its scratched surface, as it swung to and fro while she mustered her thoughts.

This was why she never hung out with her comrades, once the job was over. *Ex-comrades*, she reminded herself. All the rules were changed. Suddenly they wanted to talk about life outside the Trail. Why had she joined in with the farewell party, this time?

Rico appeared through the crowd. He grabbed her hand. "Come and dance."

Deryn let herself be towed into the midst of the dancers, but only as a means of escaping Alby's questions. She was not going to stay in the Lodestone any longer, but before she could disengage herself from Rico's grip, Corbin flung himself around her neck. The smell of alcohol, sweat, and wet leather swamped Deryn with nearly as much force as the weight of Corbin's heavily muscled torso, pulling her off balance. Were it not for Rico they would have ended up on the floor.

"De... Deri..." Corbin showered spittle in her ear. "I nev'r said this, but youz an fuckin good scout. An, I'll mish you."

Deryn peeled the drunken warrior off. "Yeah. I'll miss you too."

Corbin hunched down so their eyes were on a level. The feat strained his balance. He wobbled left and right before steadying. Despite his size, the young man clearly had a bad head for drink. "You actz like a fish. Cold. But ish all in there. I know. I can tell." His face crumpled in a cross-eyed smile. "Comeon, ish the las' night. Dance wi' me."

"I don't..." Deryn stopped, uncertain of what she wanted to deny. "Look, you keep dancing with Rico. He's better at it."

"Rico's a good mate, but he's not as priddy as you."

"Hey! That's not what you said before."

"Yeah, b' I've already humped you. I still gotta sweet-talk Deryn."

"You old heartbreaker, you." Rico's parody of indignation was clearly in jest. Corbin laughed until a bout of hiccups hit him.

While their attention was diverted by backslapping, Deryn ducked away, slipping between the other dancers until she reached the bar. She dug out a coin and attracted the innkeeper's attention. "This buys the next round of drinks for that group of Wolves." Deryn pointed. "I've got to go, but tell them..." Deryn frowned. What did she want to say?

"I'll tell them you bought the round." The innkeeper finished the sentence for her.

"Thanks." If it was not what she intended, it was also not worth the effort of correcting.

The daylight had faded into premature dusk, brought on by heavy clouds, but the afternoon's rain had eased off. It fell as no more than a soft misting against Deryn's face, cold after the heat of the tavern. She stopped at the junction with Main Street, and considered her options. What did she want to do?

Activity outside the various taverns was brisk but orderly. This was unlikely to last. Drunken brawls were common on Oakan streets. Most evenings would see at least one break out, although currently, the only disturbance came from the whores leaning from the upstairs windows of the Hunter's Moon Saloon. They were shouting to a group with the look of miners about them, standing below. Judging by the grins passing between the miners, some were tempted.

The breeze carried the scent of damp wood, and also that of cooking. Deryn turned her head in the direction it came from and smiled. A good idea, and far more appealing to her than the whores were. Food would soak up the alcohol in her stomach, and maybe she would not get drunk after all. She could eat and return straight to the bunkhouse where her bed was reserved. An early night would speed her departure in the morning. The journey to Ellaye would take long enough, without dawdling on the way. Deryn sighed. What she wanted to do was actually an easy question. She wanted to sit with Brise, chat and relax. It would have to wait.

"Excuse me. Do you know where the Silver Strike is?"

A young man appeared at Deryn's side. He had clearly been out in the rain for a while. His fair hair was plastered to his forehead. The hopeful expression on his face would have looked at home on the muzzle of a puppy dog. He was dressed in the rough-spun woolen clothes of a townsman, rather than the sheepskin and leather preferred by miners and Iron Wolves. Deryn was a little surprised by the faint scent of flowers about him. What line of business was he in? She doubted that even the richest households in Oakan employed a professional gardener.

"The Silver Strike?" Deryn shook her head. "Never heard of it. There's a Silver Nugget and a Lucky Strike. Are you sure it isn't one of them you want?"

"No. Neither sounds right." The man cast around, staring up and down Main Street, as if the tavern he wanted would materialize if he looked hard enough.

"What road is it supposed to be on?"

"Do you know the town well?"

"Pretty well."

The man's gaze returned to Deryn and he smiled. "I wouldn't have taken you for a farmer."

"I'm a mercenary. An Iron Wolf."

His eyes lit up. "Have you ridden the Misery Trail?"

"Got back from it this afternoon."

"Wow." He looked awestruck. "I've always wanted to see the

wastelands, but my wife won't hear of it. This is the first time I've gotten her as far as Oakan, and I'm not sure I'll ever get her out again. She's picked up a cold. I've left her in the bunkhouse, sneezing her head off. I was going to meet the friends we traveled with, but…" He shrugged and then held out his hand. "My name's Abran. I'm a trader from Sattle."

"Deryn."

"I'll be going, then. Thanks anyway." Abran turned, as if to leave, but then paused. "Say. I don't suppose if I buy you a drink, you'll tell me about the Misery Trail? It doesn't look like I'm going to find my friends and I don't want to go back and listen to my wife sneeze all evening."

"Oh, why not? Sure." What better than the company of a total stranger to pass a spare hour? One drink more would not hurt, and she could still have her early night.

Abran headed for the doors of the nearby Warrior's Return. Maybe he thought the name appropriate. Deryn hesitated for a moment before following. The tavern would have been well toward the bottom on her own list of choices. Not that the beer was bad, quite the opposite, or so she had heard, but it had the reputation of being the most expensive in town. Her new acquaintance was clearly unfamiliar with Oakan. However, he was the one paying, and at least the prices ensured no shortage of spare chairs.

Abran returned from the bar with two full tankards. "There you go."

"Thanks."

He took his seat. "Are the wastelands as dangerous as they say?"

"In places."

"What's the worst, rapids or windigos?"

Deryn took a mouthful from her tankard before answering, and fought back a grimace. The beer in the Warrior's Return did not live up to its reputation. It was overhopped, with a sour aftertaste. If she had been the one paying, she would have complained.

"Windigos. The rapids probably kill more people, but that's normally their own stupid fault. The rapids are predictable. You know where they are. The windigos can turn up at any time."

"Have you seen many windigos?"

"Hundreds."

"They're all dangerous?"

"No. Some aren't. I once met a man who had a small one as a pet."

"What did it look like?

"A six-legged squirrel with horns."

"Sounds weird."

"I've seen weirder." Deryn smiled. "Windigo is what you call anything in the wastelands that you can't think of another name for. In the forests on the other side of the mountains, there are clans of tiny green people, about the size of this tankard. They'll steal your stores and mess up your stuff, just for the fun of it, but they won't do anything worse. I've heard they can talk, though I've never spoken to one. Maybe they have a name for themselves, but nobody else knows what it is, so they're windigos."

"I've heard about huge flying lizards and men with bull's heads."

"I've heard about them too. I've never seen one."

"Nothing close to the stories?"

"Huge lizards, yes, but not flying ones."

"I guess breathing fire is out as well?"

"Yup." Deryn rubbed her nose, while trying to think what she could tell Abran in exchange for the beer. "The most frightening one I've ever seen was like a cross between an enormous cat and an eagle, with hair all round its head. That one could fly. It attacked a party I was with, but luckily it cleared off once it had gotten a couple of arrows in it."

"Have you been as far as Nawlings?"

"No. I want to, some day. But, after Sluey, the trade all goes by boat. There's not much call for a scout."

Deryn continued talking, recounting stories of life on the Trail. By the time she had finished her pint, she no longer noticed the aftertaste and did not argue when Abran brought her a second. He was an attentive listener, who showed no sign of wanting to ask personal questions, and Deryn found herself surprisingly relaxed in his company.

She moved on to anecdotes of mishaps she had heard from other Iron Wolves—or she tried to, but concentrating was becoming more of an effort. Events unraveled in her mind. She would find herself in the middle of a sentence, with no idea how she got there, or where she had planned taking the tale. At the same time, the tavern around her was vanishing into a dreamlike haze. She was powerless to stop her storytelling lurching from topic to topic in a random sequence. Yet, somehow, Abran appeared to follow what she was saying. At least, he managed to laugh in the right places. Maybe she was not doing as badly as she thought.

Once Deryn stopped and stared at her tankard. It was almost full. Surely she had drunk more than that? Was it her third pint? It all seemed very silly and Deryn was seized by giggles. Abran joined in, presumably just to be sociable. At his prompting, she continued with her stories, while the tavern dissolved into an impression of sound and movement. Only the occasional wafts of Abran's faint flower scent remained distinct.

The shock of cold air cut through Deryn's mental fog. True night had fallen and they were out on Main Street. Abran linked his arm through hers and guided her into a side alley. Deryn did not notice which one. Isolated lanterns, hanging over doorways, provided the only illumination. It was insufficient to recognize the road, but even were it broad daylight, all Deryn's attention was needed to navigate around the potholes. In fact, all of her attention was needed just to make sure her feet stayed on the ground. If she did not watch out, she might just float away. She stared down, mesmerized by the sight of each foot in turn, swinging out in front of her and striking the ground.

Abran guided her left and right. They could have been walking for five minutes or fifty. Deryn had lost all sense of time and direction. She did not have the first idea which part of town they were in. She was just pleased that someone knew where they were going. The rain started again and cleared her head a little, but thoughts still kept slipping from her mind so she could not keep a coherent sequence in focus.

They turned into a passageway too narrow to walk side by side. Abran slid his arm from hers but still held her hand and towed her along behind him. Deryn was so unsteady on her feet that her shoulders bounced off the walls with each step. When Abran stopped unexpectedly, Deryn ran into his back, barely managing to keep upright. The light was too weak to make anything out, but she heard Abran knock and a door opened. Weak lamplight flooded out, dazzling after the darkness.

Abran's smile had lost none of its friendliness as he drew her inside. "Here we are. You'll like this, I promise."

The dingy room was another tavern of sorts, and even in her drunken state, it was a sort Deryn recognized immediately. Two small tables took up most of the floor space. No other customers were currently seated, although an indistinct cluster of people gathered in the shadows of a doorway at one side.

The scent of flowers was much stronger, and Abran was no longer the main source. He obviously spent enough time here for the odor to impregnate his clothes. The sweet smell was heavy, cloying. It launched a fresh attack on Deryn's senses, blunting what little cold-induced clarity she had mustered. When Abran released her arm, she fell into the nearest chair. Abran positioned himself opposite.

A bottle and five mugs were already on the table. On cue, three figures left the doorway and joined them, two women and a man. Their clothes revealed a lot and suggested more, an impression aided by the dimness of the room. The lighting was low enough to mask details—how cheap the wine was, lacking any label; how shabby the decor; how unattractive the whores. Deryn had no doubts as to their profession.

She sat slumped in her chair and stared across the table at Abran. She should have guessed. Who had not heard about the sort of establishments where everything on sale was at five times the market rate, or about how they obtained their customers? Abran was not a trader who had lost his friends. The whole charade was a ruse to get drunken punters into his employer's brothel. She wondered how big a cut he took from the profits.

"Deryn, this is Arnie, this is Lana, this is Del."

Another pointless sham, and an insulting one. How stupid did they think she was? Deryn braced her hands on the underside of the table. She should just flip the whole thing over and walk out. But when she tried to flex her arms, they were too weak. Her legs were equally slow to obey her. Would they support her weight if she stood? And even if they did, would she be able to walk?

In an instant, her mood changed and the absurdity of the situation struck her. She began to laugh. Two whores joined in, although they could have no idea of what was so funny—but then, Deryn did not know either. The thought made her laugh even louder.

One of the women stood behind Deryn. What little lucid thought Deryn could muster was drowned in the sweet scent of flowers, now recognized as cheap perfume. The whore's fingertips lightly traced the back of Deryn's neck, and then massaged her shoulders. It felt so good. Deryn could not deny it, as the muscles in her back relaxed and any urge to resist was swept away.

The man shifted his chair closer to Deryn. He took her hand and raised it to his lips. Deryn made no attempt to stop him, but she met his eyes and slowly shook her head. A brief expression of regret crossed his face, but he released her hand and rose from the table. His place was immediately taken by the second woman.

Her hands were soft. Her lips were softer, hot and wet. She first sucked the tips of Deryn's fingers, and then flicked her tongue against them. The effect of the suggestive touch rippled down Deryn's arm, sparking a response in the pit of her stomach, and then lower. Deryn felt herself grow wet.

Why not? The question drifted through Deryn's head.

The contents of the bottle on the table would taste like hog's piss. The chances were that it was rainwater, collected from the nearest horse trough, rather than wine. Nobody would drink any, yet she would be charged as if it were the finest vintage. A similar mark-up would apply to the whores, but Deryn had a year's pay in her purse. She could afford it and she was in no fit state to go anywhere else. And was this not what she had been looking for when she left the Lodestone? Company with no questions, no ties, no risks?

And it's not as if I've never bought it before.

Deryn made no objection when she was helped to her feet and urged along the corridor. The room she entered was darker than the one they had left. When the hands released her, she stumbled and fell. She landed heavily on a straw-stuffed mattress that was drenched in scent, although the cheap perfume could not cover the other, mustier odors. Deryn was grateful she could not see the state the mattress was in.

One of the women lay beside her and stroked the hair back from Deryn's face. The whore's lips touched hers, at first a tentative brush, then returning more assertively. Deryn pulled the woman to her. She was impelled by the sudden desperate need to touch flesh. Her hand scrabbled clumsily though the whore's clothes, seeking a way inside.

The whore pulled away and then shifted over so that she sat, straddling Deryn's waist. The weight, pressing down on her, ignited a fire in Deryn's groin. Her hips began to move of their own accord, to the rhythm of her desire. She could not stop them if she wanted. She felt the whore's fingers slipping loose the buttons on her shirt.

The material fell open, letting a cooler draft of air play over her inflamed skin. Deryn grabbed the whore's hands and fastened them on her breasts. The whore trapped both nipples between thumbs and palm, squeezing and rubbing them, making Deryn groan. At the same time, other hands untied her bootlaces and slipped them off. Teeth nipped gently at her ankles.

Two whores. Double the cost. *Money well spent.*

Deryn's need to be touched, to be given release, was a monster inside her, taking control, except that lying down in the dark was working against her. Deryn's thoughts had been dissolving ever since drinking the beer in the Warrior's Return. Now the dark was seeping into her head. Her body was drifting apart.

The touch of a tongue between her legs was a flare of absolute pleasure, calling her back from sleep for an instant, but only an instant. The wave of darkness could not be held back. Deryn's thoughts floated away on a sea of flowers.

Rain splattered on Deryn's face. The droplets trickled down her cheeks and into her hair. They seeped around to the back of her neck and soaked into the collar of her shirt, so that the cold, clammy material stuck to her back and shoulders. Still asleep, Deryn twitched her head, futilely trying to avoid the unpleasant sensation until a chill gust of wind brought a sharper salvo. The sudden drenching was enough to draw Deryn back to the world. Her eyelids flew open so sharply that Deryn heard the snap.

A thin band of morning sky stretched above her, sandwiched by the dripping eaves of two roofs. Gray clouds scudded across the gap between. A mist of raindrops fell into her eyes, making her blink. Deryn raised a hand to her face, feeling her icy wet skin.

Memories returned in a stampede—soft lips and hooded eyes, masquerading desire; beer and Abran's voice, urging her to drink more; the blur of streets as she had stumbled along with her new acquaintance; hands removing her clothes; the scent of perfume and sex.

Between one heartbeat and the next, a pounding headache erupted.

Deryn clamped her hand over her forehead. Her skull felt as if it was about to crack open, but her groan owed more to despair than pain. How could she have been so stupid?

One hand she kept tightly wrapped over her head, just to be sure the top did not come off when she moved. Deryn levered herself up onto her free elbow. She was lying at the end of a blind alley. Green slime and refuse covered the ground. It stank of rotten cabbage, piss, and vomit. The rotten cabbage was nothing to do with her, but Deryn could not be so sure about the rest.

Her clothes were all in place, although disheveled in such a way as to imply that someone else had dressed her hurriedly, and with little care. Her belt and bootlaces were loose. Only two buttons on her shirt were done up, and one of those was in the wrong hole. Her pants were plastered with brown sludge that she hoped was mud.

At the far end, the alley opened onto a wider street. A solitary figure hurried by, without looking in Deryn's direction. Apart from this, the town was quiet, which Deryn took to mean that it was not long after dawn. Normally she could estimate the time from the light, but something was wrong with her vision. Even through the thick clouds, the sky was painfully bright, making Deryn squint and her eyes water. Her lips tingled numbly and nausea was now matching her headache. Her hands were shaking, and not from the cold.

She had been carried from the clip joint and dumped, without waking. Deryn knew she had not drunk enough to account for it. Taking everything together, it confirmed her suspicion that Abran had laced her drink with some other drug. Why had she not been more suspicious of the strange aftertaste to the beer in the Warrior's Return?

Carefully, Deryn rose to a sitting position and then buried her face in her hands. She needed to prepare herself before confronting the world and owning up to her ridiculous gullibility. She could not believe how dim-witted she had been. She did not know where in Oakan she had ended up the previous night and had even less idea where she was now. Apart from Abran, she would not be able to identify anyone she had seen, and it was a safe bet that he would not be showing his face around town until it was certain she had left.

Abran had hooked, drugged, and trapped her. How had she not spotted it? The con was so old that Deryn could not claim she had never been warned about it. Of all the sordid, catchpenny tricks, she had just fallen for the cheapest.

Deryn did not need to feel for her purse to know it was missing.

❖

The King's Marshals did not much care for Iron Wolves. The sentiment was mutual.

Deryn stood, glowering at the two officers on the other side of the room. "Useless, arrogant, fucking ass-kissers." She mostly kept the thought to herself, no more than muttering the words under her breath. For their part, the two men ignored her, as they had been doing for the previous half hour.

The marshal's station was a typical example of Oakan architecture, with rough-sawn, mud-plastered walls, a stone floor, and waxed cloth instead of glass in the windows. The main thing that marked it as different from any tradesman's workplace in the town was the king's standard, hanging from a rafter. The other thing was the complete absence of anything resembling work going on.

One officer was a clerk, sitting at a small writing table. He had insisted Deryn tell her story three times, doubtless for the entertainment value, before he had taken any notes. The other was a soldier, armed with a weighted net and quarterstaff, the usual weapons employed by marshals in towns for enforcing the king's laws and subduing criminals. So why was he not out in the town, stopping crime, rather than farting around in the office? His only role seemed to be sniggering at the clerk's comments and scratching himself.

From the outset, Deryn had known that making a formal report on the theft was a waste of time, but she was low on options. Without money, how would she get through winter? The only question would be whether she starved or froze first. If the marshal could not help her track down Abran and his gang of crooks, she would have to go cap in hand to the Wolves' Den and see if someone would lend her money to cover the journey south. Having to beg would be humiliating beyond enduring, but nothing compared to hearing what Brise would have to say when she got to Ellaye.

Deryn closed her eyes and leaned back against the wall, trying to restrain a groan. Maybe starving in the snow might not be so bad. The only good thing was that she had paid the stable in advance for Tia's care. Of course, her final option was to sell her horse, and Deryn was nowhere close to being desperate enough to do that. *I'll starve first.*

"Hey. You."

Deryn opened her eyes. "Yes?"

The clerk jerked his head toward the door behind his shoulder. "The marshal's free now. You can go in."

Seeing that nobody had left the room, Deryn suspected the marshal had been free ever since she arrived. The clerk had made her wait for the fun of it.

As she passed the two officers, she heard the soldier murmur to his colleague, "Like they say, fighting and fucking."

"What else can you expect from rabble?"

Their voices had been low, but they clearly intended Deryn to overhear what was said. She clenched her fists, wishing she was able to force the words back down their throats. Regardless of her chance of winning the fight, taking her anger out on someone would feel so good, but under the circumstances, the luxury was not one she could afford. The door closed behind her, cutting out another round of sneering laughter.

The King's Marshal for the district sat behind his desk, pouting disdainfully at the sheet of notes from the clerk. He was a hatchet-faced man in his mid forties, with a more businesslike manner than either of his subordinates, although this was no great feat. Deryn knew his name was Palemon, and that he was a distant cousin of the king, although allegedly out of favor, which explained his exile to the unfashionable northern fringes of Galvonia. The prior knowledge was useful, since Palemon did not bother to introduce himself.

"You claim to have had money stolen by a whore?" Palemon's tone made a question of the statement, as if its truth were in doubt.

"Yes, sir."

"But you have no idea where, and only a rough guess for when?"

"Yes, sir."

"Could you describe the whore?"

"No, sir."

"Male? Female? Or didn't you notice?"

Deryn ignored the sarcasm. "I can describe the grifter who spiked my beer and took me to the clip joint."

The marshal looked again at the notes, as if refreshing his memory. "Ah, yes. You claim you were drugged."

"I was drugged."

"I have no difficulty believing you weren't in full possession of whatever wits you own. But what's your evidence it wasn't merely that you'd had a few beers too many?"

"I'm sure."

"Can you prove it?"

"I thought at the time the beer Abran gave me had a odd aftertaste."

"I asked if you could prove it. Do you have any proof?"

Deryn sighed. "No, sir."

Palemon leaned back and steepled his fingers. "So, supposing I have all my officers ignore the rest of their responsibilities, and devote themselves solely to tracking down this brothel, though we have no information about where to look, or how to recognize the place, or anyone in it. If they should be fortunate enough to succeed, what if the whores claim you had agreed to pay them this money for their services? Could you deny it? I agree, given the state you were clearly in, it's doubtful you could have gotten value for money, but that's not their fault."

"I was drugged, not drunk. It was part of the scam they were all in on, so it fucking well was their fault. And I had a whole season's pay in my purse. For that much, I could have had every damned whore in Oakan for the week." Admittedly, this was a slight exaggeration. Even five years' pay would not stretch so far. Oakan held a vast army of prostitutes.

Palemon slapped his hand on the desk. "I don't appreciate that sort of language in my office."

Deryn dropped her eyes to the floor, fighting to keep control of her anger. This was worse than being robbed. Abran had taken her money, not her self-respect, and if ever she laid hands on him, he would not object to her swearing. He would have quite enough else to worry about. She would make sure of it.

"The fact remains that you can give us nothing to work with in tracking down these supposed thieves, and no firm evidence to hold against them if we did. I really don't see what you're hoping for me, or my officers, to do." Palemon's self-satisfied smile was the final insult.

Deryn would put up with it no longer. She turned to the door. "I'm sorry for wasting your time, sir. I hope you're equally sorry for wasting mine."

"Wait a minute."

Deryn stopped with the handle in the grip. "What?"

The smile had gone and Palemon was now giving her an appraising look. "If that was your entire year's earnings, what do you intend to do now?"

As if you give a flying fuck. Deryn swallowed her first reply. "I'll think of something."

"Because, although I can't help you with the lost money, I might have an offer you'd find useful."

"Such as?"

"A job."

Was it another game? Judging by the marshal's expression, there was more to it, but the bait was too enticing to ignore. Deryn turned back to face him. "What sort of job?"

"There's a small farming community, a few miles to the north of here. It's only a day's travel, but when the winter snows hit, it will be cut off for weeks on end. However, it's part of the Kingdom of Galvonia, and therefore it's my job to protect it. Luckily, it doesn't need much protecting—the odd pack of wolves, a half-starved bear, a lost child. At worst, a farm may get hit by an avalanche and need digging out. That's all you'll see in winter. In summer, they might have an occasional thief who makes the mistake of going there before finding out there's nothing worth stealing. The winter garrison is only three soldiers, but I'm still having trouble finding volunteers."

"Why?"

"I'll be honest with you. It doesn't pay well, and it's deadly boring. I'd prefer to have my own men stationed there, but I've employed Iron Wolves in the past when I had trouble making up the numbers. Are you interested?"

Deryn raised her eyes to the ceiling while she made a pretense of thinking it over. Instead of a winter in the southern warmth, swapping stories with Brise, she would be freezing her tits off in the ass-end of nowhere, with soldiers, snowmen, and sheep for company. But what option did she have? If nothing else, it would be an excuse to put in the letter to Brise, explaining her absence that winter.

"Okay."

The hills above Neupor,
30 miles north of Oakan, northern Galvonia
Two days later, octubre 9, dawn

Alana woke and rolled onto her back. Gray predawn light peeked through the window shutters and drew faint lines across the rafters. She yawned and stretched out her arms. Something was missing. The bed beside her was empty.

Alana closed her eyes, mentally rebuking herself. Why should it still surprise her each day? The bed had been empty for the last year. How long before she got used to it? Or was missing a warm body to hug and soft lips to kiss every morning something that only got worse with time? In which case, the future looked grim. The ribald local jokes were no longer quite so funny. *Another few years and I'll be eyeing up the sheep as well.*

The crowing cockerel broke the peace, destroying any hope of snuggling under the covers and going back to sleep. Alana took a deep breath and slipped out of bed. Chores awaited her: wood to chop, the cow to milk, eggs to gather. She pulled open the door, letting wisps of morning mist trail into the room. The air was crisp and clean, heady with the scent of pines and wet earth.

On three sides of the cottage, the forest of dark green conifers formed a high protective hedge. Her herb and vegetable garden filled the clearing in front, with the chicken coop and cow shed off to one side. Her home was sited high on the hillside, overlooking farms dotted around the glittering small lake below. From the doorway, Alana had an unimpeded view of the mountains lining the horizon on the opposite side of the valley, buttressed by sheer cliffs and topped with snow. The sky to the east was a riot of pink and gold. Dawn was close. Only the brightest stars still twinkled directly overhead. Even the ramshackle hamlet of Neupor looked quaint in the distance.

Alana sighed. The panorama that greeted her each morning was worth everything Ellaye had to offer and more. It was a shame Reyna had not thought the same.

Looking back, Alana had not been surprised when Reyna finally left. More surprising was that she stayed as long as she did. In the end, it had been the comforts of court life, not the arms of another lover, that Reyna had been unable to live without. Even so, Alana wondered who the rival had been. Reyna never offered any clues and Alana had not challenged her on the subject.

The cottage was admittedly basic, just a colorless single room. The furniture was sparse; a couple of chairs by the stone fireplace, a table under the unglazed window, a dresser against the wall facing it, and the box bed built into the corner. The thatched roof was smoke blackened. Unpainted clay plaster filled the gaps in the log walls.

Reyna had complained that the decoration lacked refinement, and it had not helped when Alana pointed this was not strictly true. There was no decoration, refined or otherwise. Everything was purely functional, simple and basic. No paintings or relics hung on the walls, no hint of gold or gems enhanced their possessions, no embroidered carpets lay on the slate floor. Alana had offered to get a sheepskin rug, but this had not made Reyna happy, although her refusal had surely cheered up a sheep somewhere no end.

The absence of anything beyond what was absolutely necessary included their clothes. Alana grabbed her outer garments off the back of the nearest chair: loose pants and a looser shirt, made from coarse, homespun cotton; thick woolen socks; and boots so chunky they had probably taken half a cow each to make. Alana's family could have afforded better—the Quintanillas' annual outlay on shoe polish alone would buy the cottage several times over—but fine linen and a mansion would rather have spoilt the pretense of being ordinary commoners.

Reyna had understood the logic of it, yet clothes had been the start of their final argument.

The stem had snapped while the carrot was stuck half out of the ground. Reyna had slipped and fallen on her butt. She squeaked as she landed and Alana had laughed.

"What's so funny?"

"Sorry." Despite the word of apology, Alana had continued laughing. Maybe that had been the biggest mistake.

Reyna scrambled to her feet and scowled over her shoulder, trying to see the coating of mud she had acquired. "It's bad enough I'm wearing rags I wouldn't give to a stable boy. Now I'm filthy and I've got to put up with you cackling. Look at the state I'm in." Disgust and shame came off Reyna in waves.

"It doesn't matter. Who's to see you?"

"Nobody." With that word, the nature of her upset shifted, from distress to anger. "Damn well nobody."

That was when Alana knew it was serious. Reyna never swore. She tried to block out her lover's anger. If she started to feed off it, they would be into another pointless argument. Alana clenched her hand around Orrin's talisman, hung on its cord at her throat, trying to summon strength. The action had become a reflex for her when faced with a bombardment of emotion.

"Reyna, I really am sorry I laughed. But I'm here, and I don't care what you wear."

"No, you don't, do you? You don't miss having nice things. But I do."

"Of course, I...er, like..." There was no point lying. Alana did not think about clothes from one week to the next, and Reyna knew it. She tried for a compromise. "I like the way clothes look good on you."

"No, you don't. You just admitted it. You said you didn't care."

Whoops. Why did lovers want you to be consistent when you were trying to butter them up? "Pretty clothes make you happy. I just want you to be happy."

"Do you know what would really make me happy?" Tears filled Reyna's eyes.

"Um..." Alana had a nasty feeling that she could guess.

"Having a meal I don't have to dig up myself and then wash the muck off before I can eat it. Not having to chop down a tree to get warm. Sitting with Jules and Nina, and chatting about fashion and... oh, I don't know—stupid things."

"Such as, who's sleeping with someone else's partner?" This had been their favorite topic, and would not have been quite so stupid if it had contained more fact and less fantasy.

"You never liked my friends, did you?"

Where had that come from? It might be true, but Alana did not see how it followed on from what she had said. "They were okay, but *they were your friends, not mine. I didn't have much in common with them."*

"And we've got so much in common with everyone around here—cows and peasants." Sarcasm was another bad sign in Reyna.

"I know you miss the life in court." Alana had put her arm around Reyna's shoulders, only to have it shaken off.

"And you don't."

"I don't miss the backstabbing and the double dealing, the hypocrisy. Remember it was different for me, because of my family."

"Because they were so important?" Reyna sneered.

"No, not that. My family live their lives in a constant fight to see who can crawl the farthest up the king's ass. And when you think about him, he's an unpleasant, stupid man who nobody would give a fish's fart about, if he wasn't king. The only noteworthy thing about him is the ability to call fire—that and the fact he's his mother's eldest child. It's true. Everyone knows it. But if I were in Ellaye, I wouldn't dare say it aloud."

"You don't want to go back."

"Yes, I do."

Reyna had stepped back, shaking her head. "No, you don't. I've just seen it. All the twaddle you've been giving about trying to rebuild your mental shields. You're not trying at all. You want to stay out here. And I don't." Reyna's voice rose. "I won't do it any longer." She ran into the cottage and slammed the door.

Alana had stood in the middle of the vegetable patch, trying to master the anger, and not merely her own. At least half of what she was feeling she was picking up from Reyna.

Maybe the bit about not wanting to return was true. She had hated all the political maneuvering when she lived in Ellaye. From a distance it was even more absurd. Out here, she had space. She had peace and sanity. She was free to do whatever she felt needed doing, without worrying about how it would reflect on her family.

However, the main thrust of the accusation was completely unjustified. More than anything, Alana wanted to regain the ability to shut other people out of her head. She wanted to be sure that what she was feeling was really her. She wanted to be sure of who she was. Yet her ability to control her talent was growing so slowly, weak and haphazard, Alana suspected she would never be able to cope with more than a dozen people nearby at once, and she would never be able to interact fully with just one person without losing part of herself.

Pain in her hand had made Alana glance down. She had been grasping the silver talisman so tightly it had dug into her fingers.

When Reyna emerged from the cottage her anger had faded. Reyna's temper never could burn hot for long. She was contrite and tearful, swamped in remorse, but she also had a bag packed with all her belongings.

"I'm sorry, Alana. I didn't mean it. I know how hard you've tried to rebuild your barriers."

"And I'm sorry I've not done better at it."

"It's not your fault. And...and it's not mine either. I've tried as well, but I can't stay here."

Alana had fought back her own tears. "I know."

"I'll write."

"Yes. Do that."

"Maybe, without me around, you'll be able to concentrate more on learning how to..."

Alana would have recognized the sop to a guilty conscience, even if she could not feel the embarrassed remorse coming off her lover—ex-lover. She nodded. "Maybe."

Reyna had hugged and kissed her one last time and then walked away down the hillside toward Neupor. Alana had watched her go. The promised letter had never arrived. Alana had not been surprised.

Alana sighed, picked up the egg basket, and headed to the chicken coop. She did not know whether she still loved Reyna, but she missed her. The loss was all the worse since there was no likelihood of finding anyone else. The company of the cow and the chickens was all she had, and all she was ever likely to have. *Perhaps I could get a dog...a puppy.*

The wonderful thing about animals was the lack of ambiguity in their emotions. Alana could tell what they were feeling, with no risk that she might confuse their reactions for her own. It was only after Reyna had gone that Alana realized the silence at night did not make her anxious. The fear had been purely Reyna's.

Once let out of the coop, the chickens scratched the ground with a simple chickenish satisfaction and hopefulness that Alana could observe without internalizing. She smiled as she collected the eggs. She was pleased that they were content, but was not unduly swayed by them. At that moment, though, she caught another blossoming of emotion, getting stronger. This one sparked a reaction inside her, expectation compounded by other unsettling sensations. Somebody was coming— somebody definitely human. She knew it before she heard the horse's hooves. Alana raised what pathetic shielding she could and backed out from the coop.

Jed, her neighbor's eldest son, rode up on a cart horse. He smiled when he saw her. "Good. You're up."

"Of course. It's morning."

"Do you think you could call by the farm? One of the calves is sick."

"Any idea what it is?"

"Ma reckons it's a touch of lungworm."

Alana nodded. Eldora was an experienced farmer who knew what she was doing and was probably correct in the diagnosis. "Hold on while I get what I need."

"You can come now?" Jed's happiness shot up another few notches. "I'll give you a ride down."

Alana did not need her talent to know the reason why Jed was so pleased at the thought of her being on the horse with him. A blind woman could have worked his intentions out from his tone. *Maybe it would be wiser to walk.*

Yet Jed was a decent, trustworthy young man, and it was not as if he could try anything with her sitting behind him. Alana accepted his hand up, and then realized her mistake. The problem was, of course, not whether Jed would try to make a move, but whether she would, and while she could say no to him, he was unlikely to give her the same answer. As soon as her arm went around his waist, the surge of sexual arousal hit her like a sledgehammer. The temptation to explore his body was so strong, it would have been overwhelming, were it not that Alana was quite certain the emotion was not her own. Jed was very definitely not her type—for starters, he was male—but that did not save Alana from being flooded by his desire.

Fantastic. Now I've got to deal with the double assault of his attraction to me combined with my own frustration after a year on my own.

"Are you all right there? Settled?"

"Yes. Sure." Alana spoke through gritted teeth.

"You can hold on with both hands."

"Right, Jed. Thanks."

Humans were so much more difficult to deal with than animals. Thankfully, the ride would be short, although bouncing around on the saddle was not going to help. To distract herself, Alana searched her surroundings, looking for anything of note that she could concentrate on, anything to blunt the edge of her sexual craving. *There's never a dance troupe around when you want one.* In fact, there was no one in sight at all, except down in the valley below, a lone rider traveling the road into Neupor.

❖

Neupor was obviously where they sent buildings deemed too decrepit to be allowed to stay in Oakan. Deryn eyed the riverside hamlet with a mixture of disbelief and horror. This was where she had to spend the next five months! The place offered neither the raw beauty of the wilderness, nor the comfort and amenities of civilization.

The collection of crude huts was too small to count as a village. A dozen hovels had been dropped haphazardly around a central patch of trampled mud. Deryn identified a smithy and a stable, but no tavern. At the outskirts were a number of smaller constructions that were presumably pigsties or hen coops, although from what Deryn could see, they did not offer significantly worse living conditions than the huts. An empty dock jutted into the river, with a small warehouse nearby. Nothing looked like barracks, which might be a good thing. The farmsteads along the road had been far more inviting. Maybe she would be billeted on one of them.

Deryn did not need to hunt out somebody to ask directions. Neupor was the sort of place where newcomers got noticed. Even before she had reined Tia to a halt, one of the villagers was homing in.

"Can I help you?"

"I'm looking for the marshal's station, and someone called Sergeant Nevin."

"Oh. Him." Judging by the woman's expression, Nevin was not one of her favorite people.

"Yes. My name's Deryn. I'm an Iron Wolf, but going to be working with the marshal's men this winter." Deryn hoped she was talking to the local busybody and gossip. With luck, if she introduced herself now, she would not need to do it again for the duration of her stay in the area.

"My name's Regan. Welcome to Neupor. I'm the elected town mayor."

Counting the votes could not have taken long. "Thanks."

"You need to go there. That's the station." Regan pointed out one of the hovels.

"Right."

"Nice to meet you."

"And you."

Deryn tipped her hat and urged Tia to amble the last few yards. The marshal's station was about thirty foot square, with log walls and an unkempt thatch where weeds and mildew grew unchecked. The door was ajar. The state of its hinges was such Deryn thought there stood little chance of it closing properly, which did not bode well for winter. In fact, now she studied the building, its state of repair was such that it achieved the almost impossible feat of lowering the tone of the neighborhood. The two nearby pigsties were in much better condition. Deryn chewed her lip. Would the pigs mind if she moved in with them instead?

Deryn jumped down from Tia and approached the door. Despite the fact that dawn was an hour past, the unmistakable rasp of snoring came from inside. The hinges seemed to be supporting the door mainly out of habit. Would they snap if she knocked hard enough to wake a heavy sleeper? Deciding not to risk it, Deryn rapped on the frame with the hilt of her dagger.

The snore turned into a gurgled cough. "What is it?"

"I'm here to talk with Sergeant Nevin."

"Why?"

"I'm reporting for duty."

"What?"

Deryn closed her eyes. The day was not getting any better. "I've volunteered to be a member of the garrison here for the winter. I need to report to Sergeant Nevin."

The thump of someone falling out of bed was followed by

shambling footsteps. The door was wrenched open. "They've sent me a girl?"

"An Iron Wolf."

"Shit."

And I love you too. "Is that a problem?"

"Aw, what the hell." He scowled at her. "I'm Sergeant Nevin."

Deryn had feared as much.

Sergeant Nevin was in his mid forties. He was wearing a loose shirt, heavily stained, that hung to his mid thigh and did nothing to disguise his bulging waistline. Both of his chins were covered with a two-day growth of stubble. His eyes were watery and bloodshot. Added to the way he was squinting in the light, Deryn suspected he was nursing a hangover. On the positive side, this meant alcohol was available in Neupor. Deryn had the feeling she was going to need a drink before the day was done.

"Nobody told me you were coming."

"It wasn't arranged in advance. I needed a job. Marshal Palemon saw a chance to fill in the post here. I've got a letter from him in my pack."

"What you doing, turning up so early in the day?"

And waking you up? "I'd planned on getting here last night, but the storm blew in. So I took shelter at a farm a few miles outside town."

"Yeah? Well, I don't want you going AWOL every time there's a few specks of rain. It's not a damned holiday camp."

"You didn't know I was coming, so you weren't waiting for me. And since I'd have got here too late to do anything useful, I thought it wasn't worth getting drenched."

"You thought? You don't get paid to think. In the future, you leave it to me to make those sort of decisions." Nevin stepped back and kicked at the bottom of the door to open it wider. "You better come inside."

The station consisted of a single room. A fireplace was in the middle of the wall facing the door, with a double bunk bed on either side. A warped table stood in front of the hearth. One small corner of the room was cordoned off by wooden bars and a gate. Presumably this was for holding prisoners who were not bothered about escaping. Deryn doubted the cell would hold any able-bodied person possessing an ounce of determination. But who knew—maybe Neupor was plagued by lawless gangs of great-grandmothers.

The military precision personified by Sergeant Nevin was also apparent in the room. Cast-off clothes littered the floor. The table was covered in the remains of at least three meals, as well as other, less readily identifiable garbage. Swords hung from pegs by the door. Even in the poor light, Deryn could see that the leather was cracked and the metal was pockmarked with rust. The hearth had not been swept for days and soot spilled out across the floor. It looked as if someone had been rolling in it—possibly Sergeant Nevin, judging by the state of his shirt.

Another man was sitting on the side of one of the beds. He was younger and less overweight than his colleague. Unfortunately, he also looked denser. His face was frozen in bland incomprehension.

Nevin nodded in his direction. "That's Ross."

"Hi, Ross."

"Uh?"

"This is"—Nevin looked at her—"What's your name?"

"Deryn."

"Right, Ross. This is Deryn."

"Uh?"

"She's going to be joining us for the winter."

"Uh?"

Deryn managed to keep from burying her face in her hands, but it was not easy. It answered one question that had been bugging her—what sort of warrior would chose to be permanently stationed in Neupor? Nevin doubtless owed his rank to being the first one from the pair who could work out an answer to the question, "Do you want to be sergeant?"

"I'm going to take my horse to the stable." Deryn needed a break to gather herself.

Nevin planted his fists on his hips, pulling his shirt tight enough to reveal the full extent of his flabby stomach. "When I tell you to."

"What?"

"And you're supposed to say, 'yes sir,' not 'what.' Get it?"

"Yes...sir."

"We belong to the King's Marshals. We're professional soldiers, not rabble for hire. While you're here, you'll live up to our standards."

Does that include letting rust grow on my sword? Deryn did not dare look around the room, in case her incredulity got the better of her.

Nevin would not last three days in the Iron Wolves. He probably would not last much longer in the marshals either, if there was anyone else at all who wanted his job.

Nevin jerked his thumb to one side. "That's your bunk there. On the bottom. Don't expect any special treatment because you're female."

As if there was the faintest possibility of anyone getting special treatment on the Misery Trail. You earned your place in the team, or you died. "No, sir."

"There's a box under the bed. You can put your things in it."

You mean I can't leave it all lying around on the floor with your stuff?

"When you've finished. Ross will show you around town."

That should take at least thirty seconds.

"Then he'll take you out and give you a feel for the area. I don't want you claiming you don't know where places are."

While you go back to sleep.

"You do what he says."

You mean he can speak?

Yet maybe Ross was not completely brain-dead after all. An expression of contempt slowly inched onto his face, directed at Nevin's back. Ross could recognize a lazy, useless, arrogant asshole when he saw one, although it was not a hard call. Presumably, Ross had also been given plenty of time to make his mind up about his superior.

The prospects for the winter were looking bleaker by the minute. Just about the only entertainment on offer was going to be working out, in precise and graphic detail, exactly what she was going to do to Abran if she ever met him again.

❖

The calf was going to be fine. The infestation would possibly clear up on its own, but the herbal supplement in its food would speed things along. The animal was mainly surprised by the cough, and not suffering any distress, as long as it could see its mother. Alana patted the calf's flank and stood.

The farmer, Eldora, was perched on a fence, watching from a suitable distance. Alana had shooed everyone else away, including the ever-optimistic Jed. Her reputation for not tolerating company while she worked was well known. However, a preference for solitude was so common among the isolated homesteads that it did not even count as an unusual quirk.

Eldora hopped down from the rail and strolled over, brushing sawdust off her pants. She was a couple of inches shorter than Alana and her skin was several shades darker. A wiry firecracker of a woman, she ran her farm and her family with a no-nonsense attitude typical of the region.

"Was it lungworm?"

"Yes. If you send someone by my way this afternoon, I'll give you a bag of the herbs it needs."

"Reckon my Jed will volunteer for that."

Alana tried to look nonchalant. "Whoever."

"I'm thinking you could find a home for some cheese."

Alana smiled. "Probably."

"I'll send a round up with Jed."

"Thank you."

In the farming community, neighbors would help each other as they could, with an informal barter system to even things out. Alana's skill as a healer had become highly regarded in the valley, and the goods she received in return ensured that she never went short of anything.

"You're a damn good animal doctor."

"Thanks."

"It's like you understand what the cows are thinking."

More than you guess. "It's mostly luck."

"Don't put yourself down, girl. I've watched you work."

"It's nice of you to say so."

Eldora nodded thoughtfully. "You know, my Jed's rather smitten with you."

"Really?" Alana could not stop herself glancing up the hillside in the direction of her cottage. Now would be a good time to sidle away.

"It's what now, over a year since your girl left you?"

"Something like that."

"It won't do to stay on your own forever."

Alana gave a smile and a shrug. There was not a lot she could say.

"I don't doubt you prefer women." Eldora gave a snort that held more wry humor than anything else. "Nothing wrong with that, and I dare say it works just fine for folks in the city, or even Iron Wolves. But out here? I don't see as it's practical. Running a farm takes a family, the bigger the better, and that means kids."

"I'm not sure how long I'm going to stay."

Eldora gave her a shrewd look. "You don't belong in the city. I could tell that the first time I saw you—unlike your girl. Now, she was like a cow up a tree from day one. Didn't fit in at all."

"Maybe."

"I know it's me sticking my nose in where it ain't needed. But if you do decide to make a real go of it here in Neupor, well, I reckon a woman could do a lot worse than my Jed."

Alana nodded in what she hoped was a thoughtful fashion. "Yes. I guess so. He's a fine young man."

Eldora patted her arm. "Anyway. You be getting on back, and think it over. I'll send Jed up with the cheese this afternoon."

"Thanks. Bye."

"Be seeing you."

Alana turned away, fighting to hold back a sigh of relief. She would have been far more tempted had it been Eldora's daughter showing the interest, but her answer would have been the same. Hiding her magical ability was hard enough as it was. Eldora's innocent comment about her understanding the cows had been uncomfortably accurate. *How could I hide, day after day, from someone I lived with?* Every emotion her lover felt would reverberate in her. In anger, in the act of making love, in an everyday grouchy mood, her lover's emotions would become her own. *How long before she suspected the truth?*

The local farmers had accepted her story of being a herbalist who had grown tired of city life. Her skill at healing both humans and animals had made her a welcome part of a community that did not normally look favorably on strangers, but if it became known that she was a member of the demon-spawn aristocracy, everything would change. Alana had a momentary vision of a pitchfork-wielding mob storming her cottage and setting fire to it with her inside. Maybe it would not go that far, but remaining in the valley would be out of the question once the truth about her was known.

Alana walked back along the track between the pastures and the trees, thinking things over, as she had done repeatedly in the months since Reyna left. Jed was not the first to show an interest in her. Alana chewed her lip, remembering Eldora's remarks about children.

Same-sex relationships were common among the aristocracy and professionals such as artists and lawyers. Iron Wolf mercenaries in particular were notorious for their indiscriminate sex lives. Yet for most ordinary people, whatever their personal preference might be, children were an economic necessity. Alana had become familiar with the attitude among local farming folk that a long-term same-sex relationship was a foppish luxury they could not afford.

So could she use it to her advantage? If Alana let it be known that she was only attracted to women, and that men held no interest for her, would this discourage the suitors who were dreaming of the patter of tiny farmer's feet? The locals would pass it off as another sign of her funny, city-born ways. The biggest advantage of spreading this story was that it would be true.

The risk was she might then become a target for every woman from miles around who felt the same way. What excuse could she use then? And saying no to them would be so much harder. Alana was aware the loneliness was starting to get to her. All it would need was an attractive woman coming on to her when she was feeling down, needy, or even drunk, and she would be in trouble.

Her cottage came into sight around a bend in the track. Alana stopped and turned around, staring across the valley at the distant mountains, while she battled with mixed feelings. Reyna had been right. She did not want to go back to Ellaye, but neither did she want to spend the rest of her life alone. If only she could learn to control her talent. Maybe she would be able to block her lover out of her head, well enough to keep her ancestry secret. But was that what she wanted? What value was there in a relationship based on deceit? *Do I just want to get laid? Am I that shallow?*

Alana let go of the talisman, only then realizing she had gripped it out of habit. She tried to work on summoning her own, inner strength. Instead, what she got was a sense of malevolence. For an instant, she was convinced that someone was watching her, with hostile intent. Alana's heartbeat surged. She was in deadly danger. She knew it. The emotion was raw, bestial.

Alana spun and faced the forest—an instinctive reaction. In that instant, the emotion vanished. Whatever it was had now gone and was no longer watching her. But what sort of animal had it been? It had lacked any anticipation of food, so that ruled out a bear, a mountain lion, or other predator big enough to pose a threat. Alana's pulse slowed and her panic faded. Maybe it had been a particularly aggressive squirrel. And maybe it had just been her imagination.

After another deep breath, Alana shook her head and continued walking back to her cottage.

**The paddock behind the Neupor Marshal's Station,
Northern Galvonia
Six days later, octubre 15, noon**

The section of log was about a foot long and a little too thick for Deryn to close her fingers around. Sun and wind had dried the wood out, leaving it too light and splintered to make an effective club. Yet the idea of putting its weapon capability to the test was so very tempting. How wrong she had been, thinking that her only source of amusement over the winter would be planning her revenge on Abran. As things were turning out, the thoughts of violence she could inflict on Sergeant Nevin were proving to be every bit as much fun.

Deryn took a moment, hefting the log in her hand and playing with the resulting image. A bigger, more solid piece of timber would make a better weapon, but she was not quite at the point of wanting to murder him. A couple of good blows to shut him up should do, and if the wood did splinter, it would be so much more effective when she completed her assault by shoving the remains up his ass. It was something to bear in mind if ever the time came to put fantasy into action.

Appealing though the image was, daydreaming about cracking Nevin over the skull was not what she was supposed to be doing. Deryn took a sharp breath and then tossed the log high over her shoulder. Immediately, she spun to the left, twisting and pulling the knife from her boot as she dived. Her shoulder hit the ground and she rolled on, up onto one knee. A dozen yards away, the log was falling. Deryn threw the knife with a sharp flick of her wrist, and watched it miss its target by an inch.

"Har, har, har. Better luck next time."

Deryn closed her eyes. Yes. Splinters would definitely be better.

The unwanted audience was sprawled on a dilapidated cart parked outside the paddock gate. Deryn did not need to look to know that Nevin's face would hold a smirk, and that Ross would be staring vacantly into the distance. To be said in Ross's favor, he had managed to wash and shave himself that morning. Nevin had done neither. Nor had the sergeant changed the shirt he had been wearing ever since she arrived, although it was now tucked into his pants, which meant his gut would be spilling over his belt.

Deryn retrieved her knife and the log target, ignoring the two men partly out of disdain, but mainly because Nevin's waistline was something she really did not need to see any more than she could help. She returned to her stance, facing the rear wall of the station with her back to the paddock, and tried to dismiss Nevin from her mind. Giving in to irritation could be fatal. Brise had taught her that. An Iron Wolf had to concentrate; had to stay focused. Deryn took a deep calming breath and again tossed the log behind her. Thinking about Brise rather than Nevin helped, and her aim was true. The point of the knife embedded in its target.

"Didn't miss that time." Ross rarely spoke, unless he was stating the obvious.

"Well, it's a stupid fucking party trick, isn't it?"

"It's a good trick."

"Yeah. But it's all the Iron Wolves are good for—playing games. Who cares if you can hit a bit of wood? If you want to chop logs you should use an axe. If you want to fight you should keep your feet on the ground, not roll around in the dirt."

And get your shirt mucky? Deryn collected the target and pulled her knife free.

Nevin was not finished. "Throwing piddly little knives? It ain't no good if you're up against someone with a sword. Take my word on it."

What did Nevin know about fighting? In fact, why go that far? What did he know about anything? Deryn would not have trusted Nevin to give a report on the weather. He would need three guesses to tell sleet from hail.

"You can't expect women to do proper fighting. That takes skill and strength."

Some day, when she was far away from Neupor, Deryn knew she was going to look back on that line and pee herself laughing. Even with her current irritation, she had to struggle to keep a straight face. The only exercise Deryn had seen Nevin take was walking to the latrine and back. He had not drawn his sword once. Possibly it was rusted into the scabbard. The only way he might win a fight was if he farted and his opponent collapsed from the stench—although this was not impossible. Despite the cold nights, Deryn was already appreciative that the station door did not close fully. If Ross had possessed the brains for it, she would have suspected him of deliberately sabotaging the hinges to ensure a supply of fresh air.

A shaggy, cream-colored horse stopped in the road beside the cart. The rider was a young woman, dressed in the loose, hard-wearing work clothes of a farmer laborer. Judging by the size of the horse, it was mainly used for plowing, rather than riding. The saddle looked decidedly unstable on its broad back. A couple of sacks were strung on either side.

Great. Another spectator. Nevin and Ross had nothing to do, and would not have been knocking themselves out doing it even if they had, but surely the farm worker had something better to occupy her time.

Deryn's mood improved marginally when it turned out that the new arrival had not stopped merely to gawp. After clearing her throat twice to attract attention, and being ignored, the woman spoke. "Sergeant Nevin?"

"Yeah?"

"Got a message for you. Finn wants you to see him at his farm."

"Why?"

"He's had trouble with a bear. It's taken some of his sheep."

"What's he expect me to do about it?"

The messenger stared blankly at Nevin, clearly confused by his indignant tone and at a loss for what to say next.

On Nevin's behalf, Deryn had to concede that the question did not have a straightforward answer. On one hand, the farm worker could point out that dealing with bears and similar problems was part of the job Nevin was paid for. On the other hand, anyone who had met Nevin would know that having any expectation of him doing something useful was foolishly optimistic.

After a lengthy pause, Nevin rubbed the side of his face and frowned, as if trawling through his memory. "Finn...his farm is round in Sprig Valley, isn't it?"

"Yes."

"How's his cider gone this year?"

Of course. Deryn should have guessed. Nevin was angling for a bribe—something that went totally against the Iron Wolf code. You quoted your price and you did the job you said you would do. But apart from personal ethics, Deryn would have intervened anyway, just for the sake of upsetting Nevin. She slipped her knife back into her boot and strolled forward.

"A bear, you say?"

The farm worker looked surprised, but then nodded. "Yes. Three of his sheep have gone."

"You come from near him?"

"Next farm over."

"And you're on your way back?"

"Yes."

"Right. Give me five minutes to saddle my horse and you can show me the way. I'll see if I can track it down."

"Hey. I give the orders around here." Nevin jumped off the cart, moving quicker than Deryn had seen him do all week.

"Sorry, sir." Deryn paused. "What do you want me to do about the bear, sir?"

"Nothing until..." Nevin's mouth kept moving after his voice had stopped. Even for him, *after I've screwed some free cider out of the farmer* was too blatant to say aloud.

"I have experience of hunting dangerous animals, sir."

"Bears?"

"Fifty-foot-long windigos, sir."

"Yeah, okay, whatever." Nevin looked sick, and he had to know that the excessive deference was an act, even though Deryn had been careful to keep any hint of mockery from her voice. He finally spat on the ground by his foot and then twitched his shoulders, like a horse trying to shift a fly. "Go over to Sprig Valley and see what you can do now."

"Yes, sir."

"And..."

Deryn could tell Nevin was trying to think of some additional order he could give, to bolster the facade of being in command. He failed. After another furious scowl, he stormed away. His attempt to slam the station door behind him also failed.

"He's angry at you." Ross's grasp of the obvious was undimmed.

"Do you really think so?"

"Uh, yes. Why…um…do you, er…"

Deryn patted his arm. "It's okay, Ross. You're probably right."

"Oh. Good…or…" His bewildered frown cleared slowly. "Do you want me to come along as well?"

"No. But thanks. I'll be fine."

The offer was the first time Deryn had heard Ross show any sort of initiative. Maybe, if she got to spend some time with him, he might reveal something resembling a personality, but the possibility was not strong enough to influence her. Deryn wanted some time on her own—space, an afternoon alone in the wild, and the chance to forget all about Neupor for a few hours. And if her memory would not cooperate, once she was alone, she would be free to draw a picture of Nevin on a tree and use that as a knife target instead.

❖

The swath of pasture was about fifty yards wide, on a slope running between the bogland bordering a stream, and the wall of trees uphill. Fifty or more sheep were grazing there, drifting slowly from one tussock of long grass to the next. The sound of their bleating formed an unrelenting cacophony, competing with the gurgle from the stream.

Deryn looked down. The ground was sodden. Water oozed from the mud into the depression caused by her boots. The soft earth would mean plenty of prints. Unfortunately, the wandering sheep had undoubtedly trampled most of them already. She might be lucky, or she might have to wait until she was in the trees before she could pick up the bear tracks.

The fence around the pasture was formed by thin stakes driven into the ground with thinner twigs woven through. The flimsy barrier would certainly not keep a bear out. Deryn was a little surprised it could keep sheep in. The same crude construction techniques characterized the other buildings. The farmhouse was identical to the buildings found in Neupor, although in the pastoral setting it looked quaint and rustic, rather than decrepit. Regrettably, the same could not be said of the owner.

Deryn glanced over her shoulder. Farmer Finn was standing a few feet behind her. Presumably, the sheep did not mind his dirt-encrusted clothes and skin, and since he lived alone, there was nobody else to complain. He was about sixty years old, with a level of personal charm and hygiene to give Nevin a run for his money, although in total contrast to the flabby sergeant, Finn was scrawny to the extent that if he took a bath, it would halve his weight. He also differed markedly from Nevin in that he was manifestly devoted to his work. The lost sheep were like a personal injury.

"Breaks my heart to think of them gone like that. My best damned sheep as well."

"I'll try to make sure it doesn't happen again."

"Huh—try." Finn did not sound impressed.

"Where did you find the sheep?"

"I didn't. That's the point. They've gone." Finn's tone made it clear he thought he was talking to an idiot.

Deryn bit back her first reply. After all, if he was used to dealing with Nevin and Ross his attitude was understandable. "I know. But you must have found the remains somewhere."

"Nope."

"Then how do you know a bear got them?"

"Because they're gone."

"It could have been a mountain lion or wolves."

"Nope. Like I keep telling you. They're gone. Takes a damn bear to knock a hole in the fence. If it'd been wolves or lions, they'd've jumped over and eaten them. I'd have found what was left of my sheep in the field."

Deryn felt that Finn was vastly overstating the strength of his enclosure, but it gave her something to work with. She looked around the pasture, trying to spot the break. "Where?"

"Where's what?"

"Where's the hole in the fence?"

"I've fixed it, haven't I? I don't want the rest of my sheep running off."

Deryn sighed. Her task was not getting any easier. "Can you show me where it was?"

Finn stared at her for a while, as if considering the reasonableness of her request. "This way. Come on."

The farmer led her to the corner of the paddock farthest from the farmhouse. At this point the pines were close enough to overhang the fence. The ground was also drier and harder, but the thick layer of pine needles ought to show tracks clearly enough. Under Finn's critical glare, Deryn crouched and started to examine the area.

There was nothing, not even scuffs where Finn had made the repairs.

After five fruitless minutes she looked up at him. "Are you sure it was here?"

"Course I'm damned well sure."

Unconvinced, Deryn studied the fence. Sure enough, a section had been repaired, but it was not as distinct as she would have expected. The newer branches were the same dark color as the rest. She stood and faced the farmer. "The new bit you did is wet."

"So?"

"It hasn't rained this morning."

"I know that."

"When did they get wet?"

"Yesterday."

"You fixed the fence yesterday?"

"No. A bit before that."

"A bit?"

"I couldn't leave it open until you decided to show up."

"I've come as soon as I got word."

"Makes a nice change."

The patronizing tone did nothing to soothe Deryn's growing anger. She took a few seconds, in an attempt to stay calm. "When did the sheep go missing?"

Finn pouted at her, for the first time seeming less sure of himself. "Five days ago."

"Five!"

"I had to wait until young Ailie was going into town for supplies to take the message."

"All the tracks will have been washed away."

"I didn't know it was going to rain."

"Like rain's such a rare occurrence. What fucking use is there in calling me out now?"

Finn shrugged. "What fucking use is there in calling out the marshal's men at any time?" He stomped away back to his farmhouse.

Deryn turned and walked in the opposite direction, giving him time to get well away and herself time to calm down. If she remained within knife-throwing range of the farmer, she could not guarantee her self-control.

The soothing influence of the wilds started to work on her. Trees rustled overhead, the boughs creaking in the breeze. A distant woodpecker hammered out staccato bursts. The air was heavy with moisture and rich with the scent the forest. Deryn stopped and rested her shoulder against a trunk.

Mainly out of habit, she scoured the ground for tracks. The dense forest had shielded the ground from the worst of the weather, but the only footmarks were human and a few sheep, no doubt from where Finn had rounded up his stray flock before mending the fence.

Deryn clenched her teeth, fighting back the fresh wave of anger. If Finn had made any attempt at an apology for wasting her time, Deryn would have done more—a rogue bear in the neighborhood ought to leave traces easy enough to spot—but she was not feeling the slightest degree of goodwill toward the farmer, especially considering that she had volunteered for the job largely to stop Nevin taking his cider.

Deryn turned her head and looked back at the farmhouse. Finn was safely out of sight. After a final cursory glance at the section of repaired fence, she went to reclaim Tia for the short ride back into Neupor.

A mile below Finn's farm Deryn passed a junction where a side trail led off, climbing the hillside to the west. She remembered it from her way out. Now she reined Tia to a stop and followed the route with her eyes until it vanished into the forest. Her gaze continued to rise higher, over the ranks of green firs to the mountain above.

The last of the morning's clouds had blown away, leaving a clear blue sky arching over Mount Pizgar. A long ridge ran down from the peak in the direction of Neupor, cut with a deep V midway along. The break was a likely looking pass, and the side trail appeared to be heading straight for it. If that was the case, the trail would surely join up with the main Neupor to Oakan road on the other side of the mountain.

Deryn smiled. Why not take the scenic route home? There was definitely nothing in Neupor worth rushing back for.

❖

A forest fire had swept through the pass some years before. Deryn emerged into the area of open grassland it had left behind. All that remained of the previous tree cover were the black fingers of charred stumps, pointing at the sky. Young trees had sprouted, but they were still too low to cut off the light, or to restrict visibility. The tall grasses and clumps of wildflowers had taken over, for the while. Deryn slipped off Tia's back and left the mare to graze. A small knoll to one side of the path provided a good vantage point to take in the scenery. The panoramic view had definitely been worth the detour.

Pine-covered mountains filled the skyline on all sides, fading into the purple distance. The air was so clear the white peaks looked as if they had been cut with a razor. A half mile ahead, the trail plunged back into the forest, descending the mountainside's rolling contours to the broad valley below, filled with a patchwork of small farms. The road to Oakan was just discernible, cutting a straight line between the fields. Deryn felt as if she stood on top of the world, that she could reach out and touch the sky.

The view was reminiscent of that from her childhood home, in the mountains way to the south of Oakan. As the comparison struck her, she pursed her lips. Normally the memory was one she would work to dismiss immediately, but she now found more comfort than grief in the raw beauty of the scene. Had time taken the edge off the pain? The mountains and open spaces were where she belonged. This was the home of her heart, the only home she would ever have and the only home she needed.

A gentle breeze pushed ripples though the lush grass and dried the sweat on Deryn's face. The day was turning out to be unseasonably warm, although a dark band of cloud lined the horizon. More rain was on the way, but it raised no immediate cause for concern. Hours would pass before it reached her.

After a second of thought, she strolled over to Tia and removed the saddle. Why not take a proper break? Tia deserved the rest. Deryn could use it as well. Her bunk at the marshal's station was as comfortable as if the mattress had been stuffed with pebbles. Between that and Ross's snoring, she had not been sleeping well.

Deryn returned to the knoll and lay down on the grass, using the saddle as a pillow. The sky was brilliant blue, with just the faintest wisps of high cirrus. The soft breeze carried the scent of grass and sagebrush. The chirp of crickets made a background to the trill from a songbird and the occasional snort from Tia.

Suddenly, Deryn heard footsteps. Someone was walking through the grass, coming in her direction. Nobody had been in sight when she lay down, and the open hillside offered no nearby hiding place. How could anyone have reached her so quickly? It was not as if the person was racing toward her. The pace was the gentle, rhythmical swish of a slow stroll, with no suggestion of threat, yet something about the sound made Deryn's heart pound in her chest. She jerked up, twisting onto her knees, while at the same time reaching for the knife in her boot.

Less than a dozen steps away, her mother was sauntering across the hillside. In her hand was a small log, like the one used for target practice back in Neupor. Deryn felt her mouth go dry and sweat break out on the back of her neck. However, her mother seemed totally unconcerned. She stopped by Deryn's side, taking in the view, and then pushed the hair back from her forehead. The gesture was so familiar. Despite all the years that had passed, Deryn would have known it, would have recognized her mother, even if she had not seen her face.

"It's nice here."

The voice was the same as Deryn remembered. She tried to answer, but her mouth was too dry. The sound stuck in her throat and nothing but a dull croak came out. Still her mother seemed unconcerned. She settled on the grass beside Deryn and took her hand. The touch was warm and very solid. Deryn stared down. Her mother's hand was so much larger than her own. Deryn's fingers looked childlike by comparison—just as they had the last time she held her mother's hand.

"Mom. I've missed you." The words burst out, and with them came tears.

"We all have."

What she said made no sense. Nothing made sense. "Mom, you... you were...you..."

"Hush. It's all right." Her mother's smile faded. "I'm sorry. We didn't mean to leave you."

Deryn dashed the tears from her eyes. "Wasn't your fault."

"It wasn't what I meant. But what I wanted to say to you was..." Her mother's grasp tightened slightly. "Promise me that you won't forget..."

"Forget what?"

Her mother turned her head away. "Oh, will you just look."

"Mom, you were going to say something. What?"

"Look at them."

Deryn faced the same way as her mother. Farther down the hillside, Cray was running through the grass, playing with Roana's puppies. Her brother's legs were still round with baby fat, but the boy he would become was starting to show through—the boy he would have become, had he lived long enough.

On a fallen tree to one side, Aunt Ninka was sitting beside her father. The pair were binding the fletchings on arrows, as Deryn had seen them do a thousand times. Her mother was now standing behind them, talking to Grandpa Jojo.

Deryn scrambled to her feet. "Mom. What were you going to say?"

Nobody looked at her, but her voice was not as strong as it had been, no more than a raw whisper.

And then Deryn saw the dark figures in the woods behind. Stealthily they emerged from cover, swords in hand, creeping forward. The figures blurred, changing from human to windigo with each step. Blades became claws. Helmets became fangs. A base rumble came from their throats, wild and inhuman. Yet Deryn's relatives paid no attention. Her mother wrapped an arm around Ninka's shoulder, laughing at a shared joke.

They can't hear the windigos. They can't see them. Deryn's guts had turned to ice. She opened her mouth, but the air would not release from her lungs. The sound was no more than the mew of a newborn kitten. She tried to move, but her legs were at once leaden and rubbery—too heavy to lift, too weak to move. *No. I can't watch them die again.* Howls from the advancing monsters rose ever louder, a deep, drumlike booming.

Deryn opened her eyes and bolted upright as the peal of thunder died away. A sudden gust of cold wind carried the scent of rain and lightning to her. The sun was hidden behind thick cloud, but Deryn did not need to see it to know that she had slept for hours. Daylight was reduced to an ominous early dusk.

The first splat of rain hit her cheek, no more than an isolated drop, but more was on the way. Deryn estimated she had less than a half hour before the deluge started in earnest. She would not get back to Neupor in time. She would be lucky to reach any sort of shelter. Deryn slapped her leg, furious with herself. She knew how to read the weather, and regardless of her tiredness, she should not have slept so soundly, and all to have such a stupid, maudlin dream. What on earth had gotten into her? *You're going soft—soft in the head.*

Tia had not strayed far. Within minutes, Deryn had the saddle on and was making what speed she could down the hill. Once she left the fire-scarred region, the pines were tall and thick enough to touch above the trail. They would offer the most basic protection, but they also reduced the light further still. Deryn reined Tia back to a walk. They were going to get soaked. Nothing would be gained by galloping the whole way. All it would do was risk a broken leg for Tia or a broken neck for herself.

Thunder boomed again. This time closer. Tia skittered a dancing step to the side.

"Easy, girl." Deryn patted the mare's neck.

Even under the trees, the wind blew cold. Deryn let go of the reins to pull the cape from her pack.

The sky lit up. The blazing white was dazzling after the gloom. Immediately, the screech of thunder shattered the sky directly overhead. Tia took off, ears lying flat against her head. Deryn had to grab the saddle horn to stop herself falling. Her left foot slipped from the stirrup.

"Tia. Whoa. Easy, girl, easy."

After a brief moment of struggle, Deryn steadied her balance and took hold of the reins. The effect was immediate. Tia's headlong gallop slowed. Iron Wolves' horses were well trained. Deryn was surprised that Tia had been spooked in the first place. It was out of character, but maybe the horse was picking up on her rider's state of mind. Deryn was hardly her normal self either. She could not believe she had let the storm catch her out, or that she could have such a inane dream. The strain of putting up with Nevin was getting to her—it was the only explanation.

The end of the thunderclap rumbled away in the distance, softer than the thud of hooves. Tia's ears lifted and her pace slowed still further, breaking from the gallop into a canter.

"Good girl."

Deryn released the reins with one hand to stroke the horse's neck. Abruptly, Tia's shoulders dropped and vanished. Deryn saw a streak of sky between the trees, and then the saddle was no longer under her and the path was rushing closer. She hit the ground hard and kept rolling, finishing up in a ditch that ran beside the track. Everything inside her had been shaken up. Her knee and shoulder throbbed. Her cheek stung.

"Tia!"

To Deryn's relief, her horse lurched up to her feet, although tottering slightly as if drunk and shaking her head. Deryn scrambled back up the track.

"Stupid animal." She then threw her arm around Tia's neck and buried her face in the shaggy mane. When she had sworn never to care about anyone again, she had not been including her horse.

Deryn had received no injuries worse than a few scrapes and bruises, a stinging that eased as her heartbeat returned to normal. Tia was also standing steadier on her legs. All four hooves were flat on the ground and looked to be carrying her weight. She batted her head against Deryn's hip in a gesture of shamefaced apology.

Deryn crouched and ran her hands down Tia's legs, to doubly reassure herself there were no breaks. Everything seemed fine, but when she got Tia to walk a few steps, the horse was obviously favoring her left front leg.

"You've gone and sprained it, haven't you?"

The forest was not a good place to see out a storm, especially with an injured horse. What hope was there of finding shelter? In both directions, the path disappeared into the gloom, but through a gap in the tree cover, Deryn could see a sheer rock face overhanging the route, a quarter mile or so farther on. Was a cave really too much to ask for? Deryn grabbed Tia's reins and led her on.

To Deryn's disappointment, the next bend took them away from the cliff. She considered branching off from the path, but the way ahead was looking brighter. Another bend and they reached the edge of the trees. Cultivated farmland stretched out before them, with a field of cut stalks to the left and a pasture on the right. The stocky shapes of cows were clustered by a barn in the gathering dusk. Either a fold in the mountainside had hidden this farm from the pass or Tia's headlong flight had taken them farther down into the valley than Deryn had realized.

Rain was falling in a steady drizzle. Worse was on the way, but smoke rose from the chimney of the farmstead that nestled in a hollow nearby. Shelter and a warm fire. Now all Deryn had to hope was that the farmer would be better disposed than Finn. Slightly cleaner would be nice, but she did not want to be greedy in her wishes.

Dogs barked as Deryn entered the farmyard, announcing her arrival even before she had the chance to knock on the door.

"Who's there?" The voice was female and not unduly hostile.

"My name's Deryn. I'm working with the marshal's men. I was on my way back to Neupor when my horse got lamed. I—"

The door was flung open. "You want to get inside before it starts raining for real."

Deryn could not believe her luck. Not only hospitable and quick-thinking, but the farmer looked as if she had taken a bath some time during the previous month. "Thanks. But my horse—"

"Needs seeing to." The woman called over her shoulder. "I'll take them to the barn. Jed. Go get Alana. Make it sharp. The storm ain't gonna hold off much longer."

An assortment of animals were already occupying the barn, but the farmer—who introduced herself as Eldora—shunted them around to make space, while Deryn removed Tia's saddle and harness. A couple of sheepdogs looked on with keen interest, as if they were taking notes in case were one day called on to perform the tasks themselves. The building was well maintained and sturdy, and certainly no worse than any other she had seen in the district.

Deryn stroked Tia's nose. "You'll be fine here."

"Nice horse." Eldora nodded in approval, and rose still further in Deryn's opinion.

"Thanks."

The promised cloudburst arrived in a deafening drumming of rain on the roof. A scant three seconds later, another horse clopped into the barn, making it back just in time to save its riders a drenching. Deryn had caught a glimpse of the young man when he left. His overall resemblance to Eldora made it obvious they were related. Both had a compact build, dark skin, and a rectangular, square-jawed face.

The woman riding behind him was of a similar age. Deryn would have put her in the mid-twenties range. In the dim light, her hair appeared black. Her skin was a soft mid-brown—darker than Deryn's and lighter than Eldora's. When she slipped down from the horse, she was shown to be a little below average height.

"I take it you're the woman with the lame horse." She smiled up at Deryn. "My name's Alana. I'm a healer."

"A good one too," Eldora added.

Alana's face was oval, with high cheekbones and a delicate chin. She had a wide, smooth forehead and full lips. This last feature was what caught Deryn's gaze. They were lips that just begged to be kissed.

The image rushed into Deryn's head, of kissing those lips and holding the body that went with them. The force and immediacy of her reaction made Deryn grin. *Dammit, girl, you're so predictable.* Maybe getting caught by the storm might not turn out so badly, if it led to a more entertaining evening than listening to Ross snore and Nevin fart. Of course, the owner of the lips would have some say in the matter, but finding out her answer was half the fun. Deryn raised her gaze a couple of inches and met the healer's eyes.

Alana took a half step back. Her cheeks darkened a shade more and her eyes widened. She raised her hand to a round silver pendant hanging at her throat.

I guess I was gawking. There was nothing wrong with that. Someone as attractive as Alana ought to be used to it, and signaling your interest could cut out a lot of time wasting. Besides, the Iron Wolves had a reputation to maintain. Deryn's grin widened. *It's a hell of a job, but someone has to do it.*

For her part, Alana was clearly surprised and flustered, but not offended. Deryn did not get any sense of a rebuff. Things were looking promising, but it would have to wait. Tia came first, and there was the audience to consider. She could hardly ask Eldora and her son to step outside.

Deryn looked away while rolling back events in her mind. What state had the introductions reached before she had become distracted?

"Er, yeah. My name's Deryn. This is my horse, Tia. She got spooked by the lightning and tripped."

"Right. I'll see what I can do."

Deryn felt Eldora's hand on her arm. "We'll go sit by the fire and leave her to it."

"I want to stay with Tia."

"Alana doesn't like anyone around when she works."

"I'd rather—"

The tug on her arm was insistent. Deryn decided not to fight it. Although being left alone with Alana had possibilities, Tia's best interest would be better served if she did not have to compete for the healer's attention. A whole night lay ahead. Plenty of time to see how things would run.

At the door of the barn Deryn glanced back. Alana was kneeling, examining the injured leg. Tia was standing still for the healer, watching closely, ears angled forward. The mare's tail swished slowly from side to side and her lips were slightly open. Tia had taken an instant liking to Alana. Deryn knew her horse well enough to tell that.

Tia always did have an eye for good-looking women. Like rider, like horse.

❖

Eldora's family, all ten of them plus their visitor, were squeezed into the main room when Alana entered the farmhouse. The scene was warm and cozy in the firelight. Jed shifted along on the bench to make room for her and held out a tankard.

As befitting the matriarch of the family, Eldora had her own rocking chair beside the hearth. "You'll stay here tonight?" Just the faintest hint of an inflection made it a question rather than an instruction.

Alana hesitated. The room was a bubbling tower of emotions, straining the limits of her control. Without constant vigilance, she might get swept away at any second. Despite this, the rain sweeping the hillside would have made the offer tempting, except Alana knew space in the farmhouse was limited, and arranging who she ended up sharing a bed with might prove awkward. Even choosing where to sit was not straightforward. She did not want to give false encouragement to Jed by taking a place beside him, but it would look rude to ignore his offer and go elsewhere.

"Thanks, but there's a bit of a break in the rain." It was almost true. "I thought I'd take advantage of it and dash back. You've got an extra body to make room for here as it is."

"I was planning on sleeping in the stable." Deryn smiled as she spoke.

"Why don't you come back with me? I've got more space than

Eldora has." The offer was out of her mouth before Alana had time to think.

"Are you sure?"

"We'll have to go now."

"Okay." Deryn stood and edged her way through the gaps between knees and shoulders.

Alana wished she could be certain which of the conflicting emotions she felt was coming from herself, and which she was picking up from Deryn, Jed, and the others in the room. Anticipation and dismay were the two strongest strands, bound up with the hot flare of desire. She remembered the devastating surge of sexual attraction when she met Deryn in the barn. Had it come from her or the other woman? Not that it made any practical difference. Regardless of the source, she was going to be battling raw lust all evening, and on the basis of what had happened so far it was a battle she might well lose—as with sudden impulse when she had invited Deryn to spend the night in her cottage. Most worrying of all, some treacherous parts of her mind were already eagerly looking forward to a defeat.

Mind? That was one point where she could be quite sure of the source. *Be honest. It's not your mind that's getting excited.*

The daylight was almost gone from the farmyard. Heavy raindrops pounded the ground in salvos, driven by the rising wind. Alana waited for Deryn to join her, taking advantage of what shelter she could from the low overhanging eaves of the farmhouse, although she did wonder if she should stand in the rain and see if it cooled her down.

"I thought you said the rain had eased off." Deryn peered up at the black clouds.

"Must have picked up again. Do you want to go back inside?"

"Do you?"

"No."

"Then let's go."

Alana looked up at the woman standing beside her and again felt the rush of desire. *It could be coming from me.* Deryn was certainly enticing enough. She stood half a head taller than Alana. Even in the dim light, the blue-green of her eyes was unmistakable, beneath a fringe of sandy-colored hair. Her body was that of an acrobat or a warrior. Something about her face made Alana think of a fox, although that might have been solely due to the pure mischief in her grin. It matched the relaxed amusement overlying the quick-fire flicker of emotions inside her. All the signs pointed to her being sharp, audacious, a risk taker, and quite possibly a heartbreaker.

Alana tore her gaze away. "My cottage is up there." She pointed.

As if to make her previous claim true, at that moment the rain stopped abruptly, and did not start again until they were within sight of the cottage door. They raced the final hundred yards and arrived muddy but mostly dry.

Alana had damped the fire down before leaving. It was the work of a minute to bring it back to life. The two women deposited their caked boots to one side of the hearth. Cleaning them would be easier once the mud had dried.

Alana turned to her food safe on the wall. "Are you hungry? I've got today's bread, cheese, and beef jerky."

"If you got some to spare. Thanks."

"There's plenty. I've got a flagon of beer here as well."

"Sounds good." Deryn dropped into one of the chairs and stretched her bare feet toward the fire.

While sorting out their supper, Alana glanced occasionally at her guest. The sight of someone else relaxing in her home felt good. It changed the space. The crackle of the fire filled the room with different echoes. Shadows were warmer. The walls and roof were more secure, holding out the storm, rather than holding her in. *I am lonely.*

The realization was nothing new, even without considering the word lonely as a euphemism. However, loneliness and celibacy she could live with. A demon-spawn hunting mob armed with agricultural implements was a whole different matter. Alana knew she had to be very careful. *And maybe you're not even attracted to her. You might just be picking up on the way she feels about you.* Alana glanced at Deryn again. *Although, if you're not attracted, then you ought to start worrying about your eyesight or your sanity.*

But she was probably doing okay on both counts. The more Alana prodded the feelings around in her head, the more she was sure that not everything was a projection from the other woman. The emotions were too typical of how she had been in the past, at the start of an affair, back in the days when she had been able to keep the world out of her head.

So was it all her? Was the attraction purely one-sided? The way Deryn had looked at her in the barn was suggestive, but perhaps she had soot on her face. Deryn had leapt at the offer of accommodation for the night, but who wanted to sleep in a stable, given another option? What was the chance that none of the desire she was feeling came from Deryn? Alana tried to persuade herself this would be a good thing and that she was not unhappy with the idea.

Alana caught sight of her bed out of the corner of her eye, and all attempt at rationalization was knocked aside. Her stomach kicked so hard the waves rippled out though her limbs. For a moment her knees were in danger of buckling, but she steadied herself with a hand on the table. Why had she invited Deryn to stay? *You've dropped yourself in it, and it's too late now to get a puppy.*

After a few seconds to ensure that her legs had recovered sufficiently to carry her, Alana went to her seat by the fire. She passed over a plate and mug, hoping Deryn would not see how her hands were shaking. The next thing was to think of a safe topic of conversation, although safe was a very relative term. Between mouthfuls of bread and cheese, she said, "I don't think I've seen you around before. Have you been in Neupor long?"

"Only a few days."

"What brings you here?"

"Bad luck, mainly."

"Pardon?"

"I'm working with the marshal's men in town. It wouldn't have been my first choice for a way to spend winter, but I was out of options. I needed the money." Deryn gave a self-deprecating smile. "I was stupid enough to let myself get robbed."

The way Deryn phrased it was not merely an attempt to make light of her misfortune. Alana could sense more shame than anger underlying the words. Why should a victim blame herself? "What do you do normally?"

"I'm an Iron Wolf."

It explained why Deryn felt humiliated by the theft. If her job was protecting the property of others, it was doubly bad if she could not protect her own. However, Alana was now confused for another reason. Her mother frequently expressed views about the Iron Wolves, and very little of it was flattering. Alana was sure the king's chief marshal would not approve of her officers employing mercenary warriors to bolster their numbers.

The subject was not one Alana could pursue. She could hardly repeat the views, or explain her relationship to the person who held them. "You ride the Misery Trail?"

"Yes. I got back to Oakan a few days ago."

For a while they ate in companionable silence. Alana put her empty plate on the floor. "Where did you come from, initially?"

"On the borders, down to the south of here." A ripple of disquiet flowed from Deryn. It coincided with the question, but was it caused by it?

People were so much harder to read than animals. There were no layers of abstraction in a cow's head. If a cow was upset, the cause was simple, proportionate, and generally close at hand. All Alana had to do was use her eyes. If a human was upset it might be because a random word association had sparked a memory of something that happened decades ago. It might even be due to wandering daydreams, utterly independent of anything that was currently happening.

Was there something about her origins Deryn did not want to discuss? Or had the indirect reference to distance prompted Deryn to worry about her horse or relive the accident? Equally, a pattern in the fire might have recalled a totally unrelated incident. Was Deryn hiding a secret or was it a pure coincidence of timing?

Alana had no way to know. Those who had never experienced magical empathy would never believe quite how useless the ability was, but one thing was sure—whatever the cause of Deryn's unease, it was none of her business. Alana pushed the questions from her mind.

"I come from the south as well, but on the coast. Ellaye."

"What are you doing here?"

"Getting away from the city." Alana paused. It had been a while since she had needed to recount her story. "I was a herbalist, with my own small garden in the city. I used to make medicines and other stuff for people, but I wasn't happy. I like plants and there aren't enough of them in the city, while there's far too many people. The hubbub was swamping me. So I moved up here about two years ago, with my partner."

At the word *partner*, Deryn's eyes flicked sharply toward Alana, accompanied by a flare of surprise that twisted into disappointment.

That swirl of emotions definitely came from Deryn, and was, for once, all too easy to decode. Alana looked down at her own hand, gripping her half-empty mug of beer, while she composed herself. The attraction was mutual, and with the last trace of doubt gone, things had just become far more dangerous, because now Alana knew she did not need to fear rejection. The only thing she had to fear was revealing too much about who and what she was, and thereby losing her home, the measure of sanity she had found, and possibly her life.

Alana put the beer down. Alcohol was the last thing she should be drinking. Instead she wrapped her fingers around the silver talisman, trying to force all awareness of Deryn out of her head. Quite apart from the fact that ignorance would be safer, the mental eavesdropping felt underhanded and sordid.

Deryn had been scanning the room, no doubt looking for signs of the absent lover. "You have a partner?"

"I did. She left a year ago. She missed the city too much."

"You chose to stay here without her?"

"Yes."

Deryn paused, tilting her head to the side. "So, either you're not kidding when you say you like plants, or the relationship had run its course."

"A bit of both. Plus, I really can't stand the city."

"You don't miss your family?"

"You haven't met my family."

Deryn laughed. "It sounds as if I wouldn't want to."

"Not if you have any sense." Alana had to shift the conversation away from dangerous ground before Deryn asked any more questions. The risk of getting caught out in a lie was high if she invented a false family. Yet Lady Kyra Quintanilla was too well known not to be recognized, no matter how heavily Alana disguised the details. "Do you miss your family, while you're out on the Trail?"

"No."

Deryn delivered the word deadpan, voice and expression tightly controlled, but she could not disguise her emotions. An avalanche of grief smashed through Alana's fragile barriers. The pain clutched at her heart and spontaneous tears blurred her vision.

"What's happened to your family? Are they all right?" The questions were out before Alana could stop them.

Deryn's faint shake of the head was clearly intended to dismiss the subject. She did not want to talk, but she did not need to. There was only one interpretation of her pain.

"They're dead. All of them. How?"

"Why should you think…"

Added to the mix, Deryn was also now startled. Alana had slipped up. The savage grief she had absorbed had wiped out her better sense. *Be careful. If you can't block her out, then make sure you don't reveal what the empathy tells you.* But confronted by the enormity of Deryn's pain, it was easier said than done. The emotions filled the room—pain, anger, and terror. Overriding it all was the utter sense of abandonment and the world ripped open, without love or security. The blend screamed of a child's vulnerability and incomprehension.

"How old were you?"

"Eleven."

"How did they die? W—" Alana broke off and clutched at her talisman. This was exactly the sort of danger she had foreseen, the reason why she dared not take a lover. She had to block out the pain and act as if she knew no more than what had been said aloud. And if she could not stop herself blurting out too much, then she should clamp her mouth shut and say nothing.

Deryn had slipped down in her chair, her eyes fixed on the fire. She did not want to talk, and it was wrong to use magic to take what she did not want to share.

"I'm sorry. Forget I asked, please."

Perversely, Deryn decided to answer. "Outlaws." As she spoke the word, part of the child's pain softened and was replaced by an adult need to understand and control. "Outlaws. A gang of them." Suddenly, the words started to flow. "My family were fur trappers. We lived in a cabin in the mountains—my parents, grandparents, a couple of aunts, my brother and sister. Nine of us. Late one day we saw a group in the distance riding our way. I said I'd get rabbits to make stew for them—me, as a kid, showing off. I was proud of how I could hunt. My dad laughed as he said okay. I'd just shot the second rabbit when the group reached our cabin. I was in the woods out the back, but I stopped to watch. I peeked through the bushes. The man in the lead pulled up by Grandpa Jojo. They were talking and then the man drew his sword and he…" The muscles in Deryn's jaw clenched.

Alana sank back. The initial shock of the emotional onslaught had faded. The hurt was Deryn's, not hers. She did not need to deal with it. "You don't have to tell me about it, if you don't want to."

"There's not much more to tell. They cut my family down. Killed our dogs. Even my baby brother. He tried to run away, but he couldn't run as fast as a horse. Cray wasn't yet three and the bastards butchered him. And I hid in the trees, watching them do it."

"You were only a child yourself."

"I know. Doesn't make it any easier."

"It wouldn't."

Alana reached over and took Deryn's hand. She had to make physical contact. Deryn flinched at the touch, but then relaxed. She turned to Alana. The firelight caught on her cheekbone, making dark shadows of her eyes and tinging her hair with red.

"Aren't you going to say how sorry you are for my loss?" Deryn's tone was cynical, challenging, but the driving emotions went inward. Alana was certain the root lay in a contempt for self-pity.

"Do I need to?"

"No. In fact, I'd rather you didn't."

I know. Alana held back the remark. She wished she did not know in the way that she did. The emotional eavesdropping was beyond her power to stop, but surely it was the worst violation possible of Deryn's privacy.

"You managed to escape from them."

"It would have been easy enough, if I'd wanted to. They didn't know I was there."

"If?" Something new and fierce was pushing to the forefront of Deryn's mind.

"I didn't try to run. I wasn't going to let them get away with it—not the bastards who'd murdered my family."

"But you were only…eleven, you said? How many were there?"

Deryn brushed her free hand across her face although no tears had yet fallen. "Six. They were dumb shits. Given an even chance, Cray could have taken them on. They found my mom's home-brew and got themselves plastered. They dumped my family's bodies in the shed and threw a party in our cabin. Just one guy on lookout, and he was as drunk as the rest. By midnight it was quiet in the cabin and the lookout had passed out cold, flat on his back. I thought about taking his own sword and slitting his throat. I probably could have, but the full moon was out and I had my bow. I knelt by his feet and put an arrow through"—Deryn touched her index finger to a point under her chin—"there."

"The others?"

"Our woodpile was ready for winter. I stacked the logs up outside the cabin door and set fire to it. The bastards were so drunk they didn't wake up until the thatch was on fire. One of them opened the door, and the burning logs fell in. That was when they really started screaming. Only two managed to get out of the cabin. One was totally on fire, so I left her alone. She was done for. The other stood in our yard, beating out the flames on the leg of his pants. With the fire behind him, he was way too easy a target to miss."

"That's…" Amazing? Awful? Impressive? Alana was not sure what her main reaction was. "You were just eleven?"

Deryn shrugged. "Like I said. They were dumb shits. But the marshal's men who turned up the next day were pretty stunned. They'd been hunting the gang for months." She twisted her hand so that it was palm up and she could wrap her fingers around Alana's, return the grip. "If only they'd caught up with the scum the day before. They should have hired Brise earlier."

"Who's Brise?"

"An Iron Wolf scout. My foster mother. She adopted me afterward."

"The marshal's men hired an Iron Wolf to help them track down the gang?" Just how common was the practice of employing mercenaries? Alana's mother would be alarmed if she knew. However, the issue was of no concern to Alana, and she was certainly not going to bother writing to her mother about it.

"The gang had been raiding the borderlands for a couple of years, hitting somewhere and then hightailing it back to their base in the wilds. The marshal's men didn't stand a chance of finding them. The Iron Wolves are the only people who understand the wilderness. If they'd hired Brise earlier, she could have tracked the gang to their base months before and my parents would still be alive, plus who knows how many others. But the marshal's men are fucking arrogant jerks. They were just farting around until the gang was stupid enough to raid the marshal's own home. That's the only reason they hired Brise. It's a fucking joke, them protecting the common folk of Galvonia. The only people the marshals worry about are themselves."

Deryn's chin sank onto her chest. Her face tightened in an agonized grimace and a sob shook her shoulders. The anger and the pain were understandable, but indulging in them was not a common experience for Deryn, of that Alana was certain. The tears Deryn fought held no resonances. They were not invoking and feeding off memories of other occasions. Undoubtedly, Deryn had cried for her murdered family before, but not as often or as fiercely as she had held back and stamped on her grief. She had been bottling too much in for too long.

Holding hands was not enough. Alana left her chair so she could put her arm around Deryn's shoulders. She struggled to find the right words to say, when she realized the only thing Deryn wanted to hear was nothing. So while the fire burned down to glowing embers, Alana held her in silence. Maybe Deryn would talk when she was ready. If Alana was the person she wanted to talk to, she knew where to find her.

"We should go to sleep." Deryn had her voice back under control.

"Sure." After a last gentle squeeze, Alana released Deryn's shoulders.

Her bed was big enough to hold two comfortably, and one danger was removed. Just about the only good thing to come from the story of Deryn's family was that Alana knew she could sleep beside Deryn with no risk of anything untoward happening. She was no longer in the mood, and she was quite sure Deryn felt the same way.

Alana removed her outer clothes and slipped under the covers, telling herself it was all for the best and she had absolutely no grounds for feeling disappointed. Yet once again, she had difficulty persuading herself. Common sense could be so dull.

I wonder if any of Eldora's dogs are due to give birth soon?

❖

A warm body was curled against Deryn when she woke and an arm lay across her stomach. For the briefest moment, Deryn enjoyed the contact, before memories swamped her. She slid away from Alana and rolled quickly out of bed. The air was chill on her exposed skin.

Deryn grabbed her pants from the floor and pulled them on hurriedly. As she did so, she glared at the chair she had occupied the night before. Deryn could not believe the way she had sat there and let her heart pour out through her mouth.

A soft groan announced that Alana had also wakened. Deryn glanced at the bed. The blankets were moving in a way that indicated Alana was about to sit up. Deryn turned away, focusing on where her boots stood beside the cold hearth. She did not want to risk a moment of shared eye contact with the other woman.

"Good morning." Alana's voice came with a yawn.

"Morning."

Deryn dare not look around. She did not know what expression she would see on Alana's face, but could not think of a single one she could cope with. Pity would be as bad as derision. Even complete unconcern would be a rebuff. She had never spoken about her family to anyone except Brise the way she had last night. What had made her blurt stuff out like that? Had it been a reaction to the dream? Or had it been the way Alana deftly avoided saying anything stupid? She seemed to understand so much from just a few words. Was that what was meant by being a good listener? In which case, Alana ought to get some sort of medal for her skill at it.

Whatever the reason, Deryn wanted to get away, before Alana tried to reopen the topic, or worse still, before she herself broke down and started going over it all again. Mostly Deryn wanted time alone, to get her head back in one piece, so she could face the world on her own terms. The sound of the blankets being thrown back meant that Alana was also getting out of bed. Deryn had to make her escape quickly.

"Do you want breakfast? I've got the end of some bacon here, and the hens are laying."

"No. I need to get back to Neupor. The sergeant will want to know what's happened to me." Deryn grabbed her boots and tugged them on. Brushing the mud off could wait.

The chances were high that Nevin had gotten drunk last night and passed out without noticing her absence, and he would not have lost any sleep over it, even if he had, but Alana was not to know.

"Will a half hour make that much difference?" The slap of bare footsteps on stone were getting close.

The faintest bands of daylight outlined the shutters over the windows. Even allowing that dawn had not yet broken, the light was weak. The clouds must still be there, although rain was not pattering on the roof. Deryn wrenched open the door. A sheet of rolling gray stratus covered the sky, showing signs of brightening to the east. The air was heavy with moisture. The weight of it hit her like a slap to the face.

"I'd like to see if I can make it back without getting too wet. It's not raining at the moment, but I don't know when it will start again, so the sooner I go the better."

"What about your horse?"

Deryn froze in the doorway. What sort of state was she in to have forgotten Tia? Momentarily confused and distracted, she turned around.

Alana had gotten out of bed and stood in the middle of the room. Her face was still flushed from sleep. Even in the cold light, her skin looked soft and warm. Deryn could not help imagining how it would feel to kiss her all over. Alana's shoulder-length black hair was in uncombed disarray. She was wearing nothing except a long shapeless shirt that hung to her mid thigh. The garment was suitably modest, but Deryn was hit by the memory of waking up with Alana pressed against her, and only that shirt between them.

Alana must have rolled over in her sleep, a habit from the time she had spent with her now-departed lover. She probably did not even know she had done it, but that did not make its effect on Deryn any less. Alana had a soft sensuality. More than just her pleasing shape and well-formed face, her appeal blossomed from the relaxed way she moved and spoke, her competence at her craft, her smile. She was somebody Deryn would like to spend time with, which was all the more reason to get away, and quickly.

Despite Deryn's fears, Alana's expression was one of thoughtful concern—caring enough to show she had not forgotten or trivialized anything, but reserved enough to show she was not going to press, or make an unwarranted fuss. *Of course. The only one who's likely to make a asshole of herself is me.* Deryn could feel the shreds of her composure disintegrate still further at the thought. She stared down at her feet, trying to give the impression that she was thinking.

"Tia…yes. Will she be okay to walk into town?"

"It would be better if she got a few days' rest. I'm sure Eldora won't mind her staying in the barn."

"Right. I'll come by and pick her up in three days. Will you let Eldora know? Tell her I'll pay her back for any costs."

"I'll tell her, but I doubt she'll accept the money." Alana was getting close again. Her bare feet came into Deryn's field of view.

"Right. Thanks. I'll be going, then. And thanks, for everything."

Deryn turned and fled. Not until a mile had gone did her brain start working again. Deryn stopped and turned to look back, although Alana's cottage was now out of sight. She shook her head in bewilderment.

What was going on with her? She had just spent a night in bed with a very attractive woman and she had done nothing there but sleep. It was not the way she had planned on the evening going when she accepted the offer of accommodation. Admittedly, Alana's wishes would have come into play, but her previous partner had been female, so there had to be a chance she might be interested. Yet Deryn had made no attempt to try her luck, and that was very definitely not her style.

Instead she had gone to pieces. She had spoken of things she had never told anyone. She had sat sobbing, and acted like an infant in need of a cuddle and a kiss-better. It could not have been an appealing picture. *And that's surely blown any chance you ever stood with her. You can't sob your way into a woman's bed and expect anything much to come of it.*

Deryn was disgusted with herself. But, pride aside, perhaps it was not such a totally bad thing. Alana had stripped aside her emotional defenses as if they did not exist. She had gotten under Deryn's guard and into her head. Nobody had ever done that before, and the more Deryn thought about her, the more she realized Alana might just be able to get into her heart as well.

Deryn clenched her jaw. That was something she very definitely was not going to let happen. She turned and carried on walking down the hill to the main Neupor road.

Neupor Marshal's Station, northern Galvonia
Two days later, octubre 18, early evening

In the not so distant past, someone with a truly staggering amount of patience had taught Ross to play "scissors, paper, rock." It marked the high point of his intellectual accomplishments, even though he could only remember half the rules, and it was never the same half from one round to the next. Playing games would never give Ross a chance to shine. He was far better at his current activity of standing in the station doorway, watching the world go by. The world would always be bypassing Ross.

Sitting on the edge of her bunk, Deryn studied his rear view, then sighed and let her head slump. She could not believe that she was seriously thinking about asking him if he wanted to play. Her stint at Neupor had barely begun. How desperate for entertainment would she be by the end of winter?

A pack of cards were in her bag, but the thought of trying to teach Ross the basic rules of any game was nothing short of a joke. Nevin probably knew how to play poker, but he would refuse if she asked him. For all his contempt of the Iron Wolves in general and her in particular, he was not so stupid or arrogant as to think he could beat her—which was a pity. While Deryn had no wish to socialize with the slob, the thought of taking money off him had its attraction.

The inkling of a scheme drifted into Deryn's head. Nevin would undoubtedly take up the challenge to play against Ross, confident of victory. He would also be certain to bet heavily. Could she work out a way to fix the cards so that Ross was guaranteed to win? Watching Nevin lose to him would be doubly sweet. Not only would the sergeant be out of pocket, but he would end up looking like a fool. Sorting it out would not be easy, giving that her accomplice would be unwitting (in every sense of the word), but it was something to occupy her mind.

Possibly the biggest problem with this was that Ross would then think he was a champion card sharp, and get fleeced by the next person he met. Deryn frowned. She would not want that to happen. Ross was a well-meaning man, who tried his best. It was not his fault that his best did not amount to much. When the brains were dished out, somehow he had ended up in the line reserved for beetles.

"Your horse is coming," Ross said from the doorway.

"Tia?"

"Looks like her."

"Why isn't she in the barn?" Deryn jumped off her bunk, alarmed.

"Don't know."

Admittedly, someone with far more intelligence than Ross might have had difficulty answering the question. There could be little to show how Tia had escaped and made her own way back. "Is she all right?"

"I suppose so. That healer woman is leading her. She might know."

"Right, Ross." Deryn patted his back, grateful that he had finally gotten the important information out, giving her a moment to ready herself before meeting Alana. She squeezed passed him, her face set in an expression of pleased surprise. "Hi. I didn't expect you to bring Tia back. I was going to collect her myself tomorrow."

"I know. But I was coming into Neupor, and she'd been doing well. I thought I'd save you the journey."

"Thanks."

Tia's greeting whicker was a welcome distraction, an excuse to switch the focus of attention to her horse. Deryn stroked Tia's nose while mustering her self-composure. She needed to. Deceiving herself was pointless. She had been both dreading and looking forward to meeting Alana again.

In breaking down as she had, Deryn knew she had handed over ammunition that could rip her apart. Would Alana try to use it? The unfamiliar feeling of vulnerability made Deryn's stomach knot. And how did Alana view her? As a sad victim? A new topic to spread gossip about? A wounded soul needing treatment? All of these were unbearable. Deryn desperately wished she could run away, but she was tied to Neupor for the winter, with no escape.

All this was bad enough, but some inane part of her was excited to see Alana. It was a part that still fantasized about kissing those lips, and imagined the evening in Alana's cottage could be erased from their memories as if it had not happened. It still hoped she could work a way back into Alana's bed. Worst of all, if Deryn did not get it under control, that inane part of her was readying itself to start flirting.

Ain't gonna happen. Even as the words went through her head, Deryn felt her resolve weaken. Why did Alana have that sort of effect on her? And more to the point, how was Deryn to put an end to it?

"It's good to have Tia back."

"She's pleased to be back. She trusts you."

Really? I don't trust myself, with you around. "I'll take her to the stable."

"I'll come with you."

Deryn did not know what bothered her more—the offer, or the surge of pleasure it caused her.

The stable stood on the outskirts of Neupor, close by the dock. A corral was on one side, and a hay shed on the other. Its standard of maintenance was better than many of the nearby houses. This was no great feat in itself, but it said enough about the owner that Deryn was happy to entrust Tia to his care. The doors shut and the straw thatch kept the rain out. Both of these features made it an improvement on the marshal's station. The horses were well fed and the smell was no worse than Nevin's farts. Deryn was more than half tempted to move in with Tia.

There was certainly enough space. One small building serviced the entire village, and even then it was half empty. The marshal's men were the only ones to make regular use of it during the winter, the only ones with dedicated riding horses. In summer, when the docks were busy, no doubt the wagoners needed the spare capacity.

Deryn got Tia settled in her stall and stowed her tack, while being all too aware of Alana's eyes on her. She tried to concentrate on the task. Tia ought to be her first concern, Deryn reminded herself, although this was not much of a distraction since Tia was clearly doing fine. Her leg was not unusually warm and she was moving freely.

"How long before she'll be okay to ride?"

"I'd leave it another couple of days, if I were you. Then just a little gentle exercise to start, not too far. But you know your horse. I'm sure you can judge how she's doing."

"Good. She doesn't like being kept inside."

"I noticed."

"Has she been misbehaving?"

"Not really. She was missing you. But she can be a handful and gets bored easily. She became a touch overexcited whenever I turned up."

Like rider, like horse. Deryn hung Tia's harness on its hook. "What do I owe you?"

"Nothing."

"Are you sure?"

"I normally take payment in kind from the farmers. I don't know if you've got anything I want." Alana smiled as she spoke.

"Maybe I'll think of something I can do for you. Is there anything you'd like me to do?" Flustered, Deryn turned to rub Tia's nose. *Ain't gonna happen. Ain't gonna happen.*

"Did you have anything in mind?"

"I could chop logs."

"I can chop them for myself."

Alana's tone was light, teasing. The humor in her voice brought out its soft richness. Her underlying intelligence was clear in her ease with the game of words. And her lips were still so very kissable.

Despite everything in her head telling her to back off, Deryn stopped stroking Tia and turned to face Alana. *Why fight it?* "Doing things for yourself can be a bit unsatisfactory, don't you think? It's much more fun having someone lend a hand. I could take care of you."

"Are we still talking about chopping wood?"

"Do you want to?"

"Do you?" Alana took a step forward so that she stood directly in front of Deryn, with barely a hand's breadth between them. Her eyes met Deryn's, dancing with both amusement and desire. Her lips opened just enough for Deryn to see the tip of her tongue.

"What would you like to talk about?"

And then, between one heartbeat and the next, Alana's expression changed. Her eyes broke contact with Deryn's, dropping first to her feet and then flicking anxiously to the door. She turned and half stumbled away. "Um…well, what I need to talk about is a bag of grain to see the chickens through winter. That's why I came into Neupor. I ought to be moving on. I'm pleased Tia's okay, and that I could help. But I'll, er… be off. See you around, soon, maybe."

The words came in such a rush that Alana was out the door before Deryn had processed them all. "Ah, yeah. Bye. And will you—"

Deryn stopped. Alana was no longer there to hear.

What the hell? Deryn felt thoroughly aggrieved. She stood with her hands on her hips, staring at the open stable door. Who said Alana got first claim on running away? That was her role. It always had been in the past.

Deryn turned and stroked Tia's nose. "What got into her? She looked like she was about to kiss me, and then she ran away. I didn't say anything to scare her off, did I? That was just weird of her."

The snort from Tia was in total agreement.

"Do you think it's her idea of playing hard to get?"

Tia appeared to give this serious consideration.

"It isn't going to work. If she thinks I'm going to start chasing after her, she's got a surprise coming. Dammit. The last thing I want is to get stuck with someone."

Now Tia looked a little skeptical.

"Oh come on! Don't you think I've learned my lesson? If it hadn't been for those whores back in Oakan, I wouldn't be in this god-awful dump to start with. Alana's pretty. Got a good body. She's easy company. She seems bright enough. Nice smile. But that's it. She ain't going to get me wound round her finger. I'm not that much of a fool."

Tia's nostrils flared as she rolled her top lip back.

Deryn scowled at her horse. "And you can keep that thought to yourself."

She checked the hay, filled the water bucket, and then stomped back to the marshal's station. Ross had left the door and was lying on his bunk, which was another of his favorite occupations. The bad news was that Nevin had returned and was at the table with a half-empty bottle of wine before him. He would not offer to share it. He never did.

"I hear you've got your horse back."

"Yes."

"That healer woman from up the valley brought it down."

"Alana."

Nevin took a swig of wine and belched. "Yeah, Alana. That's her name. I've seen her around a few times. She's got a nice pair of tits on her."

Ross sniggered. Deryn ignored him. He only had half a brain, and could not be held fully accountable. Nevin did not have the same excuse.

"Really? I didn't notice."

"She's got a cute face too. Definitely screwable. Don't tell me you haven't thought about it."

"My horse was lame. Alana was looking after her. That was the only thing on my mind."

"That's not what I've heard about you Iron Wolves. Anything with a pulse and two legs and you'll hump it."

Ross sniggered again.

The thought of battering Nevin to a pulp with a large club had never been more attractive. Deryn turned her back on him and stood in the open doorway. If Tia had been fit she would have gone for a ride. Anything to get away from the obnoxious fool.

Nevin would not shut up. "Her girlfriend walked out on her a year ago, so I've heard. She ought to be up for it." He belched again. "I reckon she ought to be damn well desperate. I might call round myself. See if I can interest her in my old one-eyed snake."

"She's a good healer. But I haven't heard she can bring the dead back to life."

Without waiting for a reply, Deryn set off at a brisk walk. Maybe she could find someone who could sell her a fishing rod. There was the river in Neupor and she had often though about learning to fish. Failing that, maybe she could find someone who could sell her a club.

❖

Alana plodded up the hill. The bag of grain over her shoulder was weighing her down, but not as heavily as her thoughts. What was wrong with her?

During the previous two days, Alana had gone over her feelings about Deryn often enough until she had everything sorted out. She had to keep the Iron Wolf at arm's length. They could be friends, but that was it. It had been all perfectly rational and under control, right up until the second she had set eyes on Deryn again, and then the good intentions had gone straight out the window. Yes, she found the woman attractive, but how could she be so enamored as to leave all common sense behind? What had she been thinking of? For a moment in the stable, she had been on the point of stepping into Deryn's arms and kissing her. Alana shook her head, amazed at her own recklessness.

When she lived in Ellaye, she had thought she understood how common people viewed the demon-spawn aristocracy. Her time in Neupor had provided many surprises, but possibly the biggest was finding out how wrong she had been. Not that the commoners held any love for the demon-spawn. Quite the opposite. They did not hold any marked feelings at all.

The apathy had been unexpected. Most commoners did not spare a thought for the aristocracy from one month to the next. The king himself was dismissed with a shrug, the few times his name came up. The remaining demon-spawn nobles never got mentioned at all. Alana had been wryly amused by her own reaction to this. The demon-spawn were the most important people in Galvonia. They ran the country. They owned most of it. How dare the peasants ignore them?

Scratch me, and a little bit of my mother will show through.

Even so, this did not mean Alana could divulge her background in safety. Maybe the commoners, on a daily basis, wasted little time, breath, or thought on their demon-spawn masters, but it did not mean they held no opinion at all. What little attitude they expressed had been utterly and unreservedly scornful. More significantly, there were a few who were far more hostile. Maybe because of personal history. Maybe because of strongly held political views. Or maybe because they were aggressive thugs with chips on their shoulders who were on the lookout for any reason to cause trouble. If Alana's heritage became known, one or two instigators might be all it took to inflame the rest. Could they rouse a large group to attack her?

Scratch a group of commoners and find a demon-spawn hunting mob.

The thought was chilling, but were her fears overblown? Eldora and her family were decent people, as were most others she had met since leaving Ellaye. Alana could not imagine them joining with others to harm her, but equally, if they knew what she was, they would no longer treat her as part of their community. She would be an outcast, and Alana had learned enough in the past two years to know that without the support of neighbors, life in the mountains would be impossible.

Alana shifted the bag of grain on her shoulder. Would Gavin, owner of the small store, have sold chicken food to one of the demon-spawn? Would anyone tend her cow and hens if she fell ill? Would anyone help put out the fire if a thug with a grudge set her cottage alight? The answer to these questions might not be beyond doubt, but one "no" was all it took. The result was unavoidable. Alana dared not let anyone deep enough into her life that they might uncover the truth about her. So what was it about Deryn that made her ignore the risks?

Where are you keeping your brains these days?

Alana gave a wry grimace. Was that the answer—simply that she had been celibate for far too long? Maybe all she needed was to get laid. In which case, why not Deryn? The thought brought Alana up short, both literally and figuratively. She stopped and turned to stare back at Neupor, in the distance. *Why not Deryn?*

Keeping her demon-spawn ability hidden from a serious, long-term partner would be impossible, but a long-term relationship was not on offer. Deryn's work with the marshal's men was only for winter. Unlike everyone else in Neupor, Deryn was a temporary fixture. In the spring the Iron Wolf would be off on the Misery Trail again. Surely that made her safe.

A short-term fling. Why not? Alana felt an immediate recoil from the idea. Why? *Because it isn't a short-term fling you want with her.*

Alana frowned. That made no sense either. She had spent one night talking with Deryn and five minutes when she took the horse back. She did not know the woman well enough to make any sort of judgment about how serious a relationship with her might become. And if she went into the affair knowing they would part in a few short months, of course she would not, could not, lose her heart—not to a low-born Iron Wolf mercenary.

Oh yes. There's my mother again. Alana turned and carried on trudging up the hill.

Deryn was definitely doing strange things to her head—or possibly doing strange things inside her head. Alana was sure that she was genuinely attracted to Deryn, but she was equally sure that part of what she was feeling was picked up from the other woman. The sudden panic that had sent her running from the stable had seemed as though it was prompted by fear of exposing her demon-spawn ancestry, but it matched the way Deryn had run from her cottage the morning after they met.

Alana frowned, probing into her emotions, hunting for a response. Was that why the idea of a short fling felt wrong? The absurd, conflicting emotions were all Deryn, maybe due to her tragic background? Who could say what Deryn was looking for in a relationship? Unless Alana could push Deryn out of her head, how on earth could she work out what she truly wanted for herself? And without knowing the answer to that, how could she ever hope to be happy?

Instinctively Alana's hand clasped the talisman at her neck. She so desperately wanted to regain her barriers and shut the world out. Part of her reason for going into Neupor that day was to see how much progress she was making. The small hamlet was not much of a test, but she thought she was coping with the massed bombardment of emotions better than before. She might never be able to return to Ellaye, but this was no problem. She was far happier out of that game and had no wish to go back. She just desperately needed to be sure of who she was.

Her cottage came into view. Alana raised her eyes. Above the flank of Mount Pizgar, the distant peak of Voodoo Mountain broke the skyline. The mountain held a grim place in local legend. Alana had heard all the stories tying it with the Age of Chaos, the demons and those they possessed. Alana sighed. The evil villains of the stories were her ancestors. The past was not forgotten and could not be undone. It still cast its shadow over the living. If the commoners hated the demon-spawn, it might not be fair, but it was not without cause.

Beads of sweat were trickling down her back, due to the exertion of climbing the hill with the heavy sack. Despite this, Alana shivered.

Nyla's farm, 2 miles south of Neupor, northern Galvonia
Five days later, octubre 23, mid morning

Nyla's farm lay at the head of Sprig Valley, on the same road as Finn's, but several miles closer to Neupor. Tia had made the short journey without problem. Deryn tied the mare's reins to a post and stood, puzzling over the ramshackle farmstead. From what she could see, the farm's most noteworthy feature was that it lay in an even worse state of repair than any of the others along the way. Why was Nevin bothered about this one?

"What's so important about Nyla?"

Although many would have claimed it was impossible, Ross managed to look more confused than normal. "Nothing. She's just a farmer."

"I mean, why has Nevin dragged us out here?"

"Like he said. Because she's had some sheep stolen."

Deryn rested her forehead on Tia's flank, trying to summon strength from her horse. There had to be something special about Nyla, or her farm. Unlike the previous report of lost sheep, as soon as the news arrived, Nevin had chivvied her and Ross into saddling their horses as if he had a hot coal up his butt. They had ridden off to investigate, without a chance to talk outside his hearing.

Deryn stepped away from Tia's side and raised her head. Nevin had not reappeared from the farmhouse. Would she have long enough to wheedle any information out of Ross? Would it be worth the effort if she did?

"There has to be more to it. When Finn's sheep went missing, Nevin couldn't have cared less. But one word from this Nyla and it's like his ass is on fire."

Deep furrows appeared on Ross's brow as he struggled with the problem. At last he shrugged. "I dunno. I guess he likes his sister more than he likes Finn."

The door to the farmhouse opened. Deryn took one look and smiled. If only she had waited a little longer, she could have saved herself the effort of questioning Ross. As far as appearances went, the main difference between the two siblings was that Nevin's chins were covered in dark stubble. Most likely, his sister was clean faced only because she did not need to shave, but Deryn wanted to reserve judgment until she got a closer look at the farmer.

"Right, you two. Get over here." Nevin bellowed the order.

His sister had already plodded off, leading the way along a muddy track, past a horse trough covered with a layer of green slime, a hay barn that looked on the point of collapse, a vegetable plot that seemed to be used mainly for growing weeds, and the remains of a cart with a snapped axle. The conclusion Deryn drew was that Nyla was as good a farmer as Nevin was a soldier. Even the sheepdogs acted bored.

Nyla stopped by a pasture that was half stocked with dejected-looking sheep. Admittedly dejection was the natural demeanor for sheep, but these did seem less happy with their lot than normal. Deryn was not surprised.

The farmer pointed at the gate. "What are you going to do about it?"

Deryn was aware both Nyla and Nevin were glaring at her, obviously waiting for an answer. She frowned. It was not a very nice gate, but in no worse a state than anything else in the farm.

"What do you think needs doing?"

"My sister has had some of her sheep stolen. She doesn't need smart-ass comments from you," Nevin snarled.

"Sorry. I'm just confused what role this gate has in the theft."

"The fucking gate was open when I woke up this morning. Sheep were wandering all over the damned place. I was pissed enough about that. But when I rounded them up I found the fucking bastards had swiped two." Nyla clearly had a turn of phrase to match her brother.

"You think thieves left the gate open?"

"Who the fuck else would it be? The sheep can't open it themselves."

"You're sure you didn't leave the gate open last night?"

"Of course I'm fucking sure. Do you think I'm a fool or something?"

Definitely "or something." Deryn kept the thought to herself. "Where did you find the ones that had strayed?"

"What's that got to do with it?"

"Because if I'm looking for prints, I don't want to start tracking sheep you've already brought back."

Nevin always seemed to take malicious satisfaction from withholding information and refusing to answer questions. Judging by Nyla's frown, she would have liked to play the same game, but her desire to get her sheep back stood in the way. "Most hadn't gone far. They were hanging around outside the gate."

The sheep clearly lacked ambition. If Deryn had been one of them, she would have been off to find a better farm and would still be running. "And the rest?"

"They were up in the woods, weren't they?" Nyla's tone implied Deryn was stupid not to have guessed. "It's taken me hours to round the buggers up."

Nevin folded his arms so that they rested on top of his stomach. "So go on. You're supposed to be the shit-hot scout. Look for tracks. Show us how the Iron Wolves do things."

Ignoring her sneering audience, Deryn took a moment to examine the gate. Despite its poor condition, it would not have swung open on its own, although this was not proof that thieves were at work. Deryn's own personal bet still went on Nyla neglecting to latch it properly. If she shared her brother's drinking habits, she would rarely go to bed sober. Deryn's second guess was a prank by one of the neighbors' children, or even someone older who held a grudge. Anyone blessed with Nyla's personality had to have more than her fair share of enemies.

The ground around the gate was pockmarked by the passage of small hooves. Deryn shook her head. "Any tracks here have been trampled by the sheep."

"So what are you going to do?"

"I'll run a wide sweep and see if I can pick up any trace of the missing two."

Nevin pouted, mimicking deliberation. "Right. Report back to the farmhouse when you're done. And take Ross with you for backup."

While you and your sister put your feet up by the fire. Deryn cynically watched the siblings trudge back down the path. "Who'd have thought Nevin's sister would be even more lovable than him?"

"You think Nevin's lovable?"

"Don't you?"

"Not really." Ross frowned for a few seconds but then his confusion changed to excitement. "Do you think we'll catch the thieves?"

"No. But we might find the sheep."

"Won't the thieves have them?"

"I doubt it."

Deryn was sure the sheep were missing only because Nyla's search had not been thorough enough. But where to start? *Try to think like a sheep. Which direction looks like being the most fun for wandering off?* The trouble with this approach was that sheep were notorious for not thinking.

On the other side of the river, the long ridge leading up Mount Pizgar's peak formed the western flank of Sprig Valley. Alana's cottage was just over the tree-lined crest. *I could go visit her. This time it would be my turn to run away.* Even though the distance was about three miles, Deryn knew she could convince Ross that finding the lost sheep there was a genuine possibility. Unfortunately, he was the only one. Nyla and Nevin would not be so gullible. Deryn sighed and turned around.

Nyla's farm backed onto the slopes of Voodoo Mountain. The region was scored with steep-sided valleys. In places, bare rock broke through the tree cover. The forest ended only a few dozen yards away. Ranks of conifers were densely packed, with undergrowth covering the ground between, more matted than in the forest behind Finn's farm.

It did not look promising territory for sheep. Surely the lush water meadows would attract them more. However, Nyla claimed a few had ventured into the forest. Why would they do that, unless bleats from other members of their flock had drawn them in? This still left the question of what had prompted the first few sheep to explore the forest, but it made as good a rationale as any for where to start the search. It was not worthwhile trying to analyze sheep's motives in too much detail.

"Okay, Ross. We'll start by checking out the woods."

"It's not a good place."

"You're right. It's going to be very hard to find sheep in there."

"Not talking about the sheep. It's the mountain."

"What about it?"

"It's haunted."

"What?"

Ross was staring up at the peak of Voodoo Mountain. "The Witch-Lord lives there. He's evil. He'll kill us if he catches us."

What do you say to a frightened three-year-old? "Don't worry. He's probably out visiting someone today."

"He killed Delmar."

"Was Delmar a friend of yours?"

"In the story. The Witch-Lord tricked Delmar and killed him. Then the Witch-Lord got smashed to pieces, but his spirit is still on the mountain."

"It's just silly make-believe."

Somebody who ought to know better had obviously been telling ghost stories to the halfwit. Deryn sighed and marched toward the trees. Either Ross would follow, or he would stay put. She was not prepared to humor him any more.

The edge of the forest presented an unbroken barrier. No obvious paths led in, not even the short incursions of people collecting wood for the fire or picking berries. For all Deryn could see, nobody ever set foot in the forest. Was Ross not the only one who preferred to avoid the mountain? Was that why Nyla wanted someone else to find the sheep for her?

Deryn paced along the line of the trees, looking for signs of sheep. At last she found a faint trail, leading between the moss-coated trunks. The ground was damp and soft, and clearly held the small marks of sheep's hooves, leading in and out, as well as the broader paw prints of dogs, but the farthest any human tracks went was a scant two steps.

Deryn grinned. Nyla had sent the dogs in to bring back those sheep they could, but she was too frightened to go in herself. Who would have thought it? The surly farmer was scared of ghosts.

The track was clearly the work of deer, or some other animal. Deryn slipped along the trail, ducking under the low-hanging branches. She had gone a dozen paces when she heard heavy breathing and the sound of snapping branches behind her. Ross had summoned his courage and was following. His face was pale, but determined.

"Can't let you fight the thieves on your own."

"Good man."

Fifty yards into the forest, the trail reached a small opening on the hillside, caused by the fall of an ancient fir. Grass sprouted in the sunlight. From reading the tracks, Deryn could tell that this was where most of the sheep had stopped, and where the sheepdogs had found them. Several deer trails converged on the spot. Deryn examined each one in turn.

Not all the sheep had arrived by the path she and Ross had followed. A couple had made their way to the fallen tree via another faint trail, and clear in the mud beneath the hoof marks was a set of human footprints. Deryn frowned, examining the marks in more detail. Was it possible that Nyla was right? Had someone taken her sheep? The hoof marks overlay the human prints and both sets were less than a day old. That might mean the person had been dragging the sheep along behind, or the two sets might be completely unrelated. Deryn could not make an accurate enough estimate of timing to say.

She looked around, thoughtfully. Maybe one of her neighbors was not as superstitious or nervous as Nyla. If most folk avoided the forest, the glade would be a good rendezvous for anyone who was keen not to be caught out, perfect for a illicit lover's tryst. Deryn grimaced. She wished the idea had not occurred to her while she had the image of Nyla in her head.

Guessing was a waste of time. The answers could wait until after she found the sheep. Deryn carried on with her search. The ground on the uphill side of the opening was dry, stony, and devoid of prints, but a tuft of wool caught on a thorn showed where the two lost sheep had gone.

Deryn led the way farther into the forest, climbing higher. This new trail was wider than the first one they had taken, and caused by something bigger than deer. Deryn had no trouble slipping along it in total silence. However, Ross was a large man, and anyway, stealth was not his style. Luckily, it was not required. The bleating of sheep in Nyla's farm faded into the distance, drowned out by the sounds of Ross, wheezing as he crashed through the vegetation. The trail was going to be wider still by the time he finished with it. Then, faintly from up ahead, Deryn caught the bleat of a sheep.

"Ross. Stop."

"What is it?" He sounded frightened.

"Shush. Listen."

"To what?"

"I heard a sheep." Or Deryn thought she had. Ross had been making too much noise to be sure, and the sound did not repeat.

Deryn set off again. For a while, the track scrambled along the bottom of a narrow ravine, between sheer faces of broken rock. Even though there were no more branches to snap, Ross was still making enough noise for a small army. His boots set off cascades of pebbles and his labored breathing was reminiscent of his nightly snoring. He fell farther behind.

His wheezing and clattering were distant enough that, when the next bleat came, Deryn was able to be certain. She stopped and looked up. The sound had echoed around the ravine, but it appeared to come from directly overhead.

The walls of the ravine had been dropping as the trail climbed, but they were still a good thirty feet high. Trees and shrubs overhung the top. The upper branches swayed gently in the breeze. The lower bushes were also moving, but to a different tempo. Something was moving around up there, pushing through the undergrowth.

Deryn was about to press on when a louder cracking came from above. She looked up again. The rim of the ravine was shifting, disintegrating. Irregular black shapes were silhouetted against the gray sky, getting bigger quickly—very quickly. Deryn was already diving back, out of the way, even before her mind had recognized the shapes as falling stones.

Deryn rolled tight against the rock face, shielding her head with her arms. The ground shook as boulders landed, fortunately missing her completely, but fist-sized rocks punched her sides and another, more painful blow pounded her knee. Despite the protection of her arms, one stone clipped the top of her head, hard enough to daze. A hail of chippings stung the backs of her hands and exposed neck, and then everything went quiet.

"Deryn." The clatter of Ross's feet came close.

"I'm okay."

Deryn could hear that her voice was weak enough to cast doubt on her words. She rolled onto her back, readying herself to stand, but stopped, hissing with pain. Her knee joint felt as if it had been replaced with red-hot coals. Stars swam in her vision, either from the pain or the knock to the head. The liquid trickling through her hair had to be blood.

Ross's anxious face hovered over her. Far above him, at the top of the ravine, another head appeared over the edge, peering down—a sheep's head—and then it was gone.

"What happened?"

"Rocks fell on me."

"I saw." Ross paused, clearly trying to think of another question. "Can you stand up?"

"I don't think so. My knee isn't good."

Ross face cleared. "Do you want me to carry you?"

Not really. Except Deryn was short on options. "Do you think you're up to it?"

"Oh yes. I'm pretty strong. I'll try not to drop you."

"Try hard."

"I'll do my best." Ross smiled. He meant well.

❖

Deryn lay on her bunk. The fire in her knee was not getting any better. Every time she moved, the damaged joint sent daggers up her leg. She had hardly slept the night before, and now tiredness was adding to her general discomfort. Thankfully, the other two station residents were both gone for a while, so she did not have to be quite so stoical about it. Whimpering like a whipped child did nothing for the pain, but it made her feel better.

In truth, Ross had been surprisingly supportive, fetching food and helping her to the latrine and back whenever she asked. While Nevin had done nothing but gloat, while continuing to bitch about his sister's lost sheep. As far as Deryn was concerned, those sheep had better stay lost, because if she ever caught the one that had knocked the stones down, it was going to end up as stew.

The station door started to open. Deryn gritted her teeth and closed her eyes. Was it too much to get just five minutes alone? There was a limit to how much she could put up with. If Nevin made one more snide remark, she was going to demonstrate that her throwing arm was still working perfectly.

"I heard you were in an accident." The voice was Alana's.

Deryn's heart leapt. The accompanying surge of joy was infantile, and Deryn knew she would be annoyed with herself when she looked back at it, but for the moment she did not care. She opened her eyes and attempted to sit up. This was a mistake. Her squeak of pain was equally infantile and regrettable.

Alana dropped the bag she had been carrying and hurried to her side. "Stay still."

"Ah, yeah. Good idea." Deryn gasped the words. She sank back onto the bunk and took a deep breath. Why did Alana always have to see her when she was at her weakest? The truly worrying thing was it did not bother her as much as it should. She was simply happy to have Alana there. What was going on with her? *Cry on a woman's shoulder once and you're lost.*

"What happened to you?"

"A sheep kicked rocks at me, yesterday."

Alana laughed. "That's not the story going around."

"People are talking about it?"

"One of the marshal's men getting attacked by evil spirits on Voodoo Mountain? Come on. That's the most exciting thing that's happened in Neupor all year."

"It's also not true."

"I suspected as much." Alana paused. "You should have sent for me."

"It's not that serious."

Alana's expression showed she was not convinced. "Was it really a sheep that did it?"

"Yes. I was searching for some strays."

"Honestly? I thought that was what shepherds were for. I didn't think it would be part of your job with the marshal's men."

"It is when the sheep belong to the sergeant's sister."

"Right."

"We were getting close when one started a small avalanche. Unfortunately, I was standing under it."

"How badly are you hurt?"

"I'll live. But one fair-sized rock clipped my knee."

"How about your head?"

"A bit of a knock, but nothing serious."

"Look at me." Alana sat on the side of the bunk and held up her hand. "Now keep your head still and follow my finger."

Deryn felt her heart start to thud and her mouth go dry. She tried to concentrate on the moving finger, but it was not easy. Alana's expression was calm but intense, staring into her eyes. Alana's lips were slightly parted and just as kissable as the first time Deryn had seen them. Her own lips tingled in desire. If she groaned, could she pass it off as being due to pain in her leg?

"I think you're okay."

Deryn fixed her eyes on the ceiling, fighting to get herself back under control. "You're not so bad yourself."

"I was referring to your head injury." Alana sounded amused.

I wasn't. "As I said, the only real damage is to my knee."

"Let me see."

Deryn tugged the blanket back, bracing herself for the touch of Alana's hand on her skin. She was wearing a loose shirt that came down to mid thigh, but with the way she was feeling, she might as well have been naked under Alana's gaze. She felt her nipples harden. If Alana noticed, maybe she would put it down to the cold.

Alana sucked in her breath. "That's a quite wonderful bruise you have."

"Uh-huh."

"And some swelling."

"Yup."

"Can you bend your leg?"

"A little."

Alana pressed down gently on her kneecap. Despite all her preparation, Deryn gasped.

"I'm sorry. Did I hurt you?"

"Not really. Carry on." To be honest, Deryn did not have the first idea whether it hurt at all. She ground her teeth together.

Alana finished her examination. "The good news is that nothing's broken, including the skin, so I can give you this." She retrieved the bag from where she had dropped it.

"What?"

"A compress. Among other things, it's got wolfsbane in it, which is good for numbing pain. It will help get rid of fluid around the joint as well. It's potent. So much so it can be dangerous on an open wound."

Wolfsbane. The way winter is shaping up, you'll be the bane of this Wolf. "How dangerous?"

"As in fatal. Don't worry. As long as your skin is intact, it'll be quite safe. Just don't start chewing it." Alana smiled and pulled out a small bottle. "But this you can drink. It will help you sleep."

"Thank you."

"You're welcome. And maybe I will take you up on the offer to chop logs." Alana met her eyes, steadily and deliberately.

Deryn's stomach contracted in a throb that set fingers of ice wriggling in her nipples and groin—a sensation that ought to have been unpleasant, but most definitely was not. "You'll have to wait a while."

"I know."

"Any idea when I'll be up and about?"

Alana considered her knee again. "You'll be able to put your weight on it in a few days. By next week, you ought to be walking."

"Just in time for the Night of the Lost."

"Yes, but don't expect to dance too much."

"Not even a slow dance with someone to hold on to?"

"Only if it's very slow."

"Will you be there?"

Alana hesitated, looking uncertain. Her hand rose to the silver pendant at her throat. "I don't normally."

"Why not?"

"Maybe this year, I might."

"Then maybe I'll see you there."

Alana leaned forward, staring down at her. For a moment Deryn was certain they were about to kiss. *Not fair. I can't run.* But did she want to? A little voice of panic screamed that she was about to get sucked in, over her head, that she would lose her way and there would be no getting back. The little voice did not stand a chance. Deryn wanted Alana. The rush of desire was so strong it made her toenails ache. Deryn reached up, to wrap her arms around Alana's shoulder and draw her close.

The station door opened. "How's our shit-hot Iron Wolf tracker doing, then? Do you want to—" Nevin's voice cut off at sight of Alana.

"Oh, I, er…didn't know anyone else was here." He smarmed back his thinning hair with both hands and then stood up straighter—at least his shoulders did. His stomach continued to sag groundward as before. "I'm Sergeant Nevin. It's good of you to have called in on my subordinate."

Alana stood. "I think I've seen you around."

A leering smile plastered itself on Nevin's face. "Well, if you'd like to see more of me, I could sort something out. Maybe I could do you some good."

"That's a kind offer, and there certainly seems to be plenty of you to see."

Nevin clearly missed the sarcasm in Alana's voice. Possibly he mistook the direction of her gaze and thought she was looking a few inches below his waist. "Yeah well, I tell you, I've got something pretty big and explosive in my pants."

Alana turned back to Deryn. Judging by the wry tilt to her eyebrows, she was far more amused than anything else. "Why don't you take tips in sweet-talking from your sergeant?" She bent down and planted a quick kiss on Deryn's lips. "I'll meet you in the square for the Night of the Lost."

Deryn had been trying to think of a witty response, but at the kiss, all rational thought left her head. "Uh."

Alana smiled and picked up her bag to leave. She stopped at the door. "And, Sergeant, regarding that big explosion in your pants, black cherry tea is very good for diarrhea."

Deryn raised her hand to her mouth. Her lips were throbbing, her pulse was racing, and she was growing wet. *It was just a quick kiss, like she was my sister.* Yet still the reactions swept through her body. *This is stupid.*

She was barely aware of the thump as Nevin tried to slam the door, or his muttering afterward. "Fucking Iron Wolves…anything with a pulse…lost sheep…too busy chasing tail…"

Deryn blocked him out. She had more important issues to deal with. What was happening to her, and did it matter? She was never going to let herself get seriously involved with anyone. She had sworn that on Shea's grave. In the years since, there had been enough women. Was there anything so different about Alana?

She's the one who can get you to talk. If you're not careful she'll get you to fall in love as well.

Deryn shook her head, bemused at herself. The idea was ridiculous. She did not fall in love. She was not the type. So what was there to worry about? An affair with Alana stood no chance of getting serious. It might last a while longer than normal—anything over two days would meet that criterion—but long-term was not an option. In spring, the work with the marshal's men would finish and traders would be hiring Iron Wolves for the Misery Trail. Deryn would leave Neupor and never come back.

Why not have an affair with Alana? It would make the winter go quicker, and be much more fun than playing scissors, paper, rock with Ross. She might even be able to sleep in Alana's cottage each night, away from Ross's snores and Nevin's farts.

Alana was an attractive woman who was very definitely flirting with her, even if she did alternate between that and playing hard to get.

Deryn smiled. The injured knee should be mostly recovered in time for the Night of the Lost. The festival would present the ideal opportunity to see if she could persuade Alana to play some different games.

Approaching Neupor main square, northern Galvonia
Night of the Lost; octubre 31, dusk

From sunset to sunrise, in every town and village across Galvonia, bonfires would burn for the Night of the Lost. Even isolated homesteads and travelers camped beside the road would keep a lantern burning throughout the night. However, there was no general agreement as to whether the main purpose of the light was to keep malevolent ghosts away or to guide home the sprits of the beloved departed. Answers varied from region to region, and even from person to person within them.

Having never attended the Neupor celebration before, Alana was unsure which way the prevailing local view went. Tonight she would find out, although this was not the most important question on her mind. From the hillside above the village, she traced the column rising from the village square, following the trail of smoke to the point where it dispersed as a smudge on the pale blue sky. The festivities had started on cue. In the west, the last wisps of pink and orange hung over the mountains. The full orb of the moon was climbing.

From the amount of smoke, Alana tried to estimate the size of the bonfire, and from that extrapolate the number of people who might be there. She could not help laughing at herself when she realized what she was doing. The calculation was completely spurious. Easier to assume that everyone who lived in Neupor would be present, plus a fair proportion of those in easy walking distance. The gathering would be bigger than anything she had been exposed to since leaving Ellaye. Would she be able to cope? And what would be the consequences if she could not?

A renewed attack of doubts and fears beset her, and Alana toyed with the idea of giving up and returning to her cottage, but she wanted to see Deryn, and if she never put herself to the test, she would never know if her abilities were improving. She just had to be ready to make her excuses and slip away at the first sign that the strain of holding back the mental barrage was becoming too much for her.

The Night of the Lost marked the end of summer and the start of winter. For the nobles in Ellaye, the changing season meant little more than the move from summer residences by the ocean to the warmth of the desert springs, inland. According to rumor, Orrin had ideas for other purposes the festival might fulfill, as he sought to claim a divine ancestry for the king, but for now, the absurd display of ostentation in the king's winter palace was merely the chance to show off a different set of clothes, in new surroundings.

For the peasants, the festival had a different significance. The harvest was over. Animals that would not be kept through the winter were slaughtered and their meat preserved. The Night of the Lost was about eating as much as you could, and not worrying whether food would be on the table in the months ahead. Bringing in the harvest had required working from dawn to dusk in the fields. Now it was over, the farm laborers had one night to do as they wished, with the hope of catching up on sleep the next day.

Where the festival had gotten linked to the spirits of the dead, was anyone's guess. The association held for both nobles and commoners. Allegedly, it went back to the Ancients, before the Age of Chaos. Whatever the reason, the festival was an occasion for ghost stories. For nobles, troupes of professional actors and musicians would perform spine-chilling plays, with a little bit of magic to add effect. For peasants the stories would be recounted around the bonfires, by anyone who was sober enough to remember how they went.

Daylight was fading fast when Alana reached the edge of the village. The flickering of the bonfire shone through the gaps between buildings. Sparks drifted up above the rooftops, joining the bright specks of stars high overhead. The rumble of voices was swelling, blossoming into the night, and with it came excitement, expectation, and an overriding sense of fun. The emotions ran as thick as treacle. Alana had the sense of wading into them, and feeling them flow around and coat her. Unpleasant was not the word for it, yet it was unsettling. She was losing herself, but there were worse states to get lost in.

Alana rounded the corner of the marshal's station and stood at the edge of the square. Warm red light washed over the ring of faces.

Thirty or so people were gathered and others were still arriving. As she watched, a family of four took their place at the bonfire to a greeting of cheers and laughter. Alana hugged the shadow. She wanted to acclimatize herself to the environment before attempting to interact with anyone, although there was little likelihood the preparation would have achieved much, even without interruption.

"You made it."

"Ah...er..." The sudden rush of excitement threatened to topple Alana, but at least she was sure that it originated within herself.

Deryn was standing in the station doorway. She moved forward, smiling. "I'm sorry. You don't have to answer that. I was stating the obvious. I'm spending too much time with Ross."

"Pardon?"

"Have you met Ross?"

"I think so. He's one of your colleagues, isn't he? I treated him for a cough last winter. But how does he fit in?"

"He doesn't. That's the point."

"He...?"

Alana stopped and tried to assemble her thoughts. Was the conversation skipping steps, or was she succumbing to the intoxicating atmosphere in the village square? Whatever the case, she needed to keep her head clear and move to a subject that she did understand.

"How's your knee?"

"A lot better, thanks to you." Deryn's smile broadened. "But I don't think the music's going to work with my dance plans. From what I've heard, it won't amount to more than the blacksmith singing some bawdy drinking songs."

"The blacksmith?"

"Have you heard him sing?"

"Is he any good?"

"Unfortunately, no. But he's the loudest, and he seems to know more words than anyone else. A few join in with the chorus, but they aren't enough to drown him out."

Alana smiled and rested her shoulders against the wall behind her. She tried to relax, but it was not easy with Deryn standing so close. A scant inch separated them, and then the back of Deryn's hand brushed against hers. The effect of the touch shimmied up Alana's arm in a wave of goose bumps. She was so very aware of Deryn's eyes fixed on her. A ripple of panic swirled in her mind, telling her that she should make her excuses and go, but she calmed it, and then very carefully returned the pressure against Deryn's hand.

"The prospects for dancing don't look so good, then?"

"We'll have to think of something else." Deryn slid her fingers around Alana's. "I'm pleased you're here."

A rush of sexual desire sliced through the torrent of other emotions, and for a moment, everything dissolved into chaos. Alana gasped and closed her eyes, fighting to keep a grip on her own mind. The pathetic barriers holding the world out threatened to dissolve, but by an effort of will, she forced herself to focus on the single thread of experience that was bound within the confines of her own body.

"Are you all right?" Deryn had seen her reaction.

"I'm sorry. I'm a bit overwhelmed."

"By what?"

Alana tightened the grip of her fingers and Deryn laughed, clearly taking it as an answer. "Okay."

Deryn's hand felt firm and warm. The skin was hardened by exercise, but the texture was smooth rather than rough. Deryn ran her thumb over Alana's knuckles and gave a gentle squeeze. The gesture was both a question and a promise, eliciting an undeniable response. Alana felt her nipples harden. Maybe she should make her excuses and leave after all, but drag Deryn away with her.

"Why have you avoided the festival before?" Deryn asked, before Alana could act on the impulse.

"I fear I've become a bit of a recluse. Maybe it's an overreaction to escaping the crowds in Ellaye."

"Did you go to the festivals when you lived there?"

"I had to."

"Why?"

"My mother insisted the whole family turned up to make a good showing for the k—"

In trying to juggle too much at once, she had slipped up. Alana stopped herself just in time but the realization left her off-balance, and her concentration wavered. In that instant, the whole village flooded into her head, an avalanche of excitement. Alana struggled to pull herself together enough to make some saving remark, but the more she scrambled for a way out, the weaker became her ability to ignore the emotional maelstrom around her. She grabbed the talisman at her throat, snatching at it as a lifeline. The onslaught softened, but not enough to allow much in the way of rational thought.

A high voice broke in. "What did the demon look like?"

Alana opened her eyes. They were surrounded by a gaggle of small children, the oldest no more than eight.

"What?" Deryn asked. She was clearly the focus of interest.

"The demon you fought on Voodoo Mountain. The one that knocked you out, what did it look like?"

The other children joined in, excitedly. "Did it have hornth?" a small boy lisped.

"Did it walk like this?" A girl hunched her shoulders and stomped along, elbows and knees bowed out to the side. "Hurr. Hurr. Hurr." She added growled sound effects for greater impact.

Alana felt a succession of quick responses flip through Deryn, ending in amusement.

"Oh, much worse than that."

The children all failed to pick up on Deryn's mock-serious tone. Their eyes opened wide. "How?"

"It had teeth. Load and loads of little peg teeth. And it had cloven hooves. Its nose came out like this"—Deryn cupped both hands in front of her mouth—"It had orange eyes, like slits. And when it spoke, it went, baaaaa."

The children had been enraptured, hanging on every word. Their faces had held identical expressions of delighted fear, but at Deryn's bleat, the reaction diversified. Some giggled, some looked disgusted, some were clearly confused.

"It made a sound like a sheep?"

"More than that. It had disguised itself as a sheep."

"Don't be silly. Demons don't disguise themselves as sheep."

"Now that's the clever bit. Nobody expects a demon to look like a sheep. That was how it got the jump on me." Deryn nodded seriously. "Next time I see a demon disguised as a sheep, I'm going to be ready for it."

The children stood, mulling it over, until one at the rear cheered and rushed off. "When I find a demon, I want one disguised as a pig."

The others followed. "No. A cow."

"A huge rabbit, with furry ears. No one expects that."

"Yeah."

Alana laughed, watching them go. The interruption had been what she needed to take charge of her head, and with any luck, Deryn would have forgotten what they had been talking about before. For the moment she was okay, but common sense said she should not push her luck any further. The crowd was too volatile. Any unexpected disturbance could smash aside her feeble attempts at control.

Then Deryn turned, smiled at her, and all common sense vanished. "What's the big deal about Voodoo Mountain?"

"You don't know?"

"I wouldn't have asked if I did."

Without stopping to consider the wisdom, Alana tightened her hold on Deryn's hand and towed her across the square. "Let's see if we can find someone to tell you the story. This is the night for it."

Regan was sitting on a bench in the warmth of the bonfire, accompanied by two other elderly inhabitants and a small beer barrel. According to Eldora, the town mayor was the best storyteller in Neupor.

Alana hailed her. "Excuse me, Regan."

"Yes?"

"Deryn wants to hear about the Witch-Lord and Voodoo Mountain."

The mayor smiled. "Ah now, she should have gotten the story before she went running up there."

"Could you tell it to her now?"

"I'm sure people don't want me yammering on, telling silly stories."

The disavowal was not in earnest. Others had heard the request and already an audience was gathering. In seconds, word spread across the square. Groups broke off what they were doing and drifted in Regan's direction. Children squirmed between the taller adults, and then sat cross-legged on the ground in front of her.

Regan laughed, accepting the role as storyteller. She cast her eyes over the listeners and nodded. "The Witch-Lord. Yes, now there's a good tale for the Night of the Lost." Her voice dropped and she hunched forward, adopting a singsong lilt. "Long, long ago, in the Age of Chaos, there lived a weak, cowardly, petty-minded man. Some say his name was Grigor, although nobody much cared what it was then, and it matters even less now. He fell in love with a beautiful woman from Oakan, called Caylee, but she'd have nothing to do with him. Her heart was given to a brave, handsome hunter called Delmar. When Grigor realized this, he was consumed with anger. But what could he do?" Regan paused, dramatically. "I'll tell you what he did. He prayed to the demons that were ravaging the earth."

A soft gasp came from those gathered, even though they all must have heard the story many times before. The ripple of anticipation jolted Alana, forcing her to concentrate on holding herself steady.

Regan continued. "He offered himself to them, and asked them to possess him. Because that was the only way the weak man could avenge himself on those he thought had wronged him. One of the demons heard his plea. The demon entered him, and ate his soul. The man became one of the possessed, and the name Grigor was lost forever. He became, and will always be known as, the Witch-Lord. He excavated a mighty citadel for himself in the roots of Voodoo Mountain, and he set about inflicting as much pain, misery, and evil upon the world as he could."

Was Grigor one of my ancestors? The question popped into Alana's head. In the minds of the people gathered, there was no doubt about the guilt of the evil villain. But had any of her demon-possessed ancestors really been willing collaborators? Or had they been mindless puppets, the demons' most cruelly abused victims? Yet regardless of the truth, and whatever her ancestors had done, it was unfair to hold her, or any of the demon-spawn, responsible. She scanned the faces around her. How many people in the village square would see things that way? Alana suddenly felt very isolated.

Regan's story had moved on. The beautiful, but unfortunate, Caylee had been captured by her rejected suitor and held prisoner in the mountain stronghold.

"Delmar swore to rescue his love. He took up his shield, sword, and bow. He put on his helmet, and he bravely set out for Voodoo Mountain. Yet no mortal man could compete with the demon's magic. The Witch-Lord made his own four weapons: A sword so sharp it could cut through steel. A shield that bestowed invulnerability, so that nothing could harm the bearer. His helmet cast a spell that made everyone fall to their knees in terror when they saw it. His bow shot magic arrows, powerful enough to go through stone."

How much of the story was true? If Delmar went up against

someone armed with weapons like that, he was not only brave, he was also a complete fool. Alana hung on to the cynical thought. The story was binding the audience together. The single beat of shared emotions was overpowering her mind. She had to remove herself, physically as well as mentally.

Alana loosened her hand from Deryn's grip. At the querying expression she pointed to the side of the square, where Gavin the trader was selling rough cider. Drinking alcohol was not a wise move, but food should also be around somewhere. It gave her something safe to focus on, and a valid reason to leave the storytelling. Deryn nodded and let her go.

The few yards across the square barely took the edge off the massed emotional onslaught. Alana knew she should put a mile or more between herself and the festival, but she could not go. Her hand still tingled with the memory of Deryn's touch. She needed that touch, and not just on her hand. If she could withstand the emotions for a little while longer, surely it would be very easy to talk Deryn into leaving with her. She could do it, and at least now that she could not hear Regan's words, it was possible to resist the sway and assert her own consciousness.

Alana waited until she judged the story was nearly complete before returning.

"When Caylee saw how she'd been betrayed, she threw herself from the crag where she'd bid good-bye to Delmar, and her body was broken on the rocks below. The lovers were thus united in death, but the Witch-Lord was still bound by his oath. His body and his four great weapons lie in state beneath the mountain but he can have no release from this world. The demons have gone, but the evil they wrought remains. The shade of the Witch-Lord haunts Voodoo Mountain, a spirit of cruelty and malice, forever seeking Caylee, until the day he will rise again from the dead and fulfill his oath."

The story finished and the crowd drifted away. Beer and cider had been flowing freely, and the mood across the square was getting ever more riotous. The blacksmith and his friends embarked on another vulgar song. The activity described in it was physically impossible, or so Alana suspected, but it would be fun putting it to the test. All she needed was a willing helper, and she was not the only one to feel that way. Certain spikes in the emotions around her were getting harder to ignore. Alana could not withstand the bombardment of sexual tension for much longer—not when it so closely coincided with her own desires. She had to leave but she would not go alone.

Alana slipped her arm through Deryn's "Let's walk a bit."

"Do you have anywhere in mind?"

"How about somewhere where there aren't so many people watching?"

"That's an interesting idea."

Together, they strolled toward the river along the path between two buildings. With each step, Alana could feel the impact of the people in the square fading. Everything was going to be okay. She had survived the festival, and now it was just her and Deryn. Alana was sure she could cope with that. Deryn walked with only the faintest limp. Her knee was clearly much better. Alana was pleased, and not just in her role as healer. She did not want any impediments to physical activity.

"Didn't you like the story?" Deryn asked.

"What makes you think that?"

"You missed part of it."

"I've heard it before, and I was hungry. It's a good tale, and it explains why everyone keeps away from the mountain."

"Not everyone. I saw footprints up there."

"Really?"

"Yup. Of course, it could have been the Witch-Lord's ghost, but I don't think ghosts leave footprints." Deryn was obviously not overly superstitious.

They reached the river and wandered a short way along the bank, eventually stopping in the shelter of a clump of trees. Sounds from the village square were a distant hubbub, punctuated by the occasional whoop. The full moon reflected in the water. Its beams picked out the surrounding envelope of mountains, dotted with the lights of distant farmsteads. A breeze pulled strands of Alana's hair across her forehead. The day had been warm for the time of year, but the temperature was dropping fast—not that Alana needed an excuse to snuggle into the circle of Deryn's arms.

She stood in the embrace, getting used to the feel of Deryn's body pressed against hers. Her head fitted into the curve of Deryn's neck. The warm scent of leather, horses, and smoke was so right for the mercenary warrior. Alana ran her hands over Deryn's back. The muscles were hard and defined.

The implied strength was intriguing. All Alana's previous lovers had been aristocrats, for whom an hour-long stroll was unusual exercise. The nearest any had gotten to being athletic was one devoted horsewoman, and even she had preferred petting her horse to riding it. Reyna had been soft and round, even after a year in the mountains. Deryn's body was so very different.

"I want to kiss you." Deryn breathed the words in Alana's ear.

Alana pulled back her head and stared up into Deryn's eyes. The blue of them was lost in the moonlight, but the rakish glint was still there.

"That sounds like another interesting idea."

Their lips met. Deryn's hand cupped the back of her hand, gently guiding Alana's movements as the kiss became more ardent. Alana opened her mouth, inviting Deryn's tongue inside, a prelude to what would follow. Alana had no doubts about how that evening would finish. She felt herself grow wet at the thought and moaned into Deryn's mouth.

A sliver of fear crawled into Alana's mind, at first no more than an easily dismissed discord against the desire that was consuming her, but then the fear grew, no longer ignorable. Alana had recognized the emotion and was trying to control it, even as it abruptly surged forward, a blinding white panic, pushing out all rational thought. She broke from Deryn's grip and staggered away.

"What's up? Are you all right?"

The fear was so strong Alana could barely form words. "Fire. Get me away from it."

"Fire? The bonfire?"

"Get me away. I'm tied. Can't run. Want to run. Smoke. I smell smoke."

"You can smell the bonfire? What about it?"

"Smoke. Stable. Fire. Let me out."

"The stable?"

"Smoke. Fire. Let me out. Let me—"

Alana was vaguely aware of Deryn trying to hold her shoulders, but there was no room in her head for anything other than fear and smoke. Tears of terror ran down her face, Deryn's hands became ropes, and then nothing existed except the fear. She could not see, could not think. She knew nothing except that she had to run as far as she could. Twigs whipped her hands and face. A tree leapt out of the dark before her and she barely fended it off. Still she ran, until a bush snared her foot and brought her crashing to the ground, where she lay, dead to everything except terror.

Time passed in a haze of fear, and then slowly the world cleared and the panic slid from her head, allowing thoughts to return. Alana was alone, lying curled in a ball beside the river. She grasped the talisman at her throat with both hands and, by an effort of will, pushed the last tendrils of panic from her mind. She was herself again. Alana staggered to her feet and looked around.

How long had the panic blanketed her mind? Minutes certainly, maybe longer. Yet her crazed flight had taken her only a few dozen yards from the clump of trees where she had been standing with Deryn. She might even have been running in circles. Deryn was nowhere in sight. Had she fled from the madwoman?

Alana took a deep breath, steadying herself, but the blinding panic had gone. She no longer needed to resist it. The fear had not been hers. It had not been human. Alana recalled the wordless desperation. Now she could identify it.

"Horses. The stable."

What had upset the animals? Had it been no more than the wind carrying smoke from the bonfire, or had they been in real danger? Whatever had given rise to the terror was now over, one way or another. Had the horses been rescued, or died? Or was it merely that the wind had shifted? Alana had to find out. She jogged back along the riverbank, toward the village.

As she approached the jetty of the dock, Alana felt a new bubbling up of emotion, but this was a very human blend of excitement and concern. The sound of voices followed, shouting instructions. She rounded the corner of the dock warehouse and arrived at a scene of hectic activity surrounding the stable. The festival had been abandoned while the revelers worked to put out the fire, but it was clear that the drama was nearly over. The air was acrid with smoke and bundles of smoldering straw littered the ground, but the blaze in the hay shed adjoining the stable was out.

In the corral, over a score of horses were milling nervously back and forth. They were not happy, but they were unharmed. The wave of relief left Alana weak. Having shared their fear, she felt a bond with the horses, although this was a source of concern in itself. In the past, she had always been able to keep a mental distance from animals. Never had she been taken over like that. Why now? Was it a reaction to the strain she had put herself under that night? Was it the number of animals, in the grip of the same utter terror? Or was it that she had been so totally off guard and open? All barriers had been set aside when Deryn's lips met hers.

Deryn. At the thought of her, Alana closed her eyes. That was something else to worry about, and even more serious. What must Deryn have made of it all? Alana buried her face in her hand, trying to remember exactly what she had said in the grip of the panic. How much had she given away? Would Deryn know that magic was involved? Or would she think—

Alana bit her lip. What? That she had suffered a mental breakdown, linked to a smoke phobia, that by a wild coincidence had occurred at the same time as a fire broke out nearby. Deryn might not realize she had mentally bonded to the horses, but the exact form the magic had taken was irrelevant. At the very least, Deryn must suspect that she had a trace of demon-spawn in her ancestry.

With the fire in the hay shed out, people started to drift away from the stable. The party was due to continue, with a whole new edge of excitement. The force of it battered Alana's mind. She had to get away, gather her strength, and maybe after a night's sleep she could work out a plausible explanation for Deryn.

"Good job you spotted the fire when you did." Regan's voice was close, but not loud enough to be addressing her.

Alana raised her head. A few feet away, the mayor stood with Deryn.

"Pure luck. Me and Alana were—"

They were both looking at the stable, standing with their backs to Alana. Presumably they had not seen her in the deep shadow. Alana tried to slip away, but the sound of movement caught Deryn's attention. She glanced over her shoulder and their eyes met. Surprise and confusion were easy to read. Was there also hostility and fear? Before she knew what she was doing, Alana reached out to feel the emotion, but in the overexcited atmosphere of the interrupted festival, picking out Deryn's thread was impossible.

"You and her were doing what, eh? As if I need ask." Sergeant Nevin waddled over. His voice held an undertone of crude innuendo. "I saw you creeping off, hand in hand for a quick fuck. It's what they say about Iron Wolves—anything with a pulse."

"We were just walking by the river." Deryn glared at the sergeant in unconcealed dislike and then turned back to Regan. "And we heard the horses neighing."

"Didn't hear them in the square."

"It was quieter by the river, and I've got good hearing. I need it for my job."

Regan patted her arm. "Anyway, it's a damn good job. Wouldn't have wanted to lose them." The mayor smiled and left.

Deryn's eyes returned to Alana. The doubts were hardening into anger. Even without sensing her emotions, her scowl said it clearly enough. Without another word, Deryn also turned and walked away, back to the town square.

Deryn dismounted and stared at Alana's cottage. Her doubts multiplied. For a moment she thought about getting back on Tia and riding away again, but she had to understand exactly what had happened the night before. She needed answers, and the only person who could give them was Alana.

The cottage was in silence as she approached, but then she heard the rattle of pans inside. Deryn raised her fist and knocked. The rattle stopped at once, but almost a minute passed before the door opened.

Alana's expression provided half the answers on the spot, not from what was there, but from what was missing, no surprise, no reproach, no confidence.

After an awkward moment of staring at each other, Alana stepped back. "Do you want to come in?"

Did she? Would turning around and leaving be the wiser course? Yet wisdom never had been Deryn's guiding light. She ducked under the doorway.

The room was unchanged from the last time she had been there. Alana went to the same chair and sat, waiting. Her face was impassive, but Deryn read other signs; the rapid pulse beating in her throat, the raised tendons from tightly clasped hands, the paleness of her lips.

Deryn had intended to remain standing, but intimidation was for thugs, and whatever else Alana might be, she was also a beautiful woman who was frightened. Deryn shoved the chair around so that she sat facing Alana rather than the fire.

On the ride up, Deryn had rehearsed her questions a dozen times, and variations on them. Now they all seemed naive, duplicitous, boorish, or out-and-out inane. From Alana's face, she could tell there was no need to browbeat or trick her way to the answers. They would come. Deryn crossed her arms. She would give Alana the first go at picking the route.

"Have they found out how the fire started?"

Was that really the most important issue on Alana's mind?

"No. It might have been a spark carried from the bonfire. More likely it was somebody who doesn't want to own up being careless."

"There'd be a lot of angry people to own up to."

"True. Normally only a half dozen horses are in the stable, but a lot of folk had ridden in for the festival."

Alana nodded, but her eyes were fixed on the wall. She was not interested in details of the fire, any more than Deryn was. Why waste time, skirting around the real issue? Deryn's mood hardened. She had given Alana a chance. Now it was her turn to call the shots. "How did you know the stable was on fire?"

Alana flinched, but answered steadily. "I sensed the horses' fear."

Deryn had guessed as much, leaving only one possible explanation. "Do you know which of your ancestors was demon-spawn?"

"All of them."

The answer went beyond anything Deryn had expected, or feared. She paused, making sure she had her voice under control. "All? Who are you?"

"Alana"—she paused, catching her lower lip in her teeth— "Quintanilla."

"You're related to Lady Kyra?"

"She's my mother."

Deryn felt sweat break out on the back of her neck and her pulse speed. *I'm a fool to have come alone.* Not just demon-spawn, but a member of the second most powerful family in Galvonia. "What are you doing here?"

"Like I told you, getting away from Ellaye."

"Why?"

"I'm an empath. I can feel the emotions of others. The city was overwhelming me. I had to get as far away from as many people as I could."

"People? It's not just frightened animals?"

"No."

"Can you feel my emotions now?"

"Yes."

The simple answer hit Deryn like a fist of ice in her gut. She looked down trying to calm her breathing, fighting the urge to flee. *Don't let her see you're frightened.* But was there any way to hide it?

"You're reading my mind?"

"No. It's not like that." Alana's sigh was somewhere between weariness and defiance. "I know that you're scared and angry, and think I've cheated you. You feel betrayed and invaded. But I could work that out from looking at your face and using a bit of common sense. It's how anyone would feel in your place."

"But you could tell if I was trying to hide something."

"Depends. Maybe I'd pick up on your anxiety. But even if I did I couldn't be sure of the cause, and I certainly wouldn't know whatever the something was. Maybe you have an important secret. Maybe you want to fart and are worried about making a noise."

The attempt at humor failed. Deryn stared at her hands, resisting the urge to ball them into fists. This was not something she could fight, but nor was there any point in acting calm. Alana would know exactly what she was feeling. That had been the case since the first time they met. No wonder Alana had been able to draw so much out of her. *She got inside your head.* Deryn had thought the same words before, but she had not realized the literal truth of them. *The demon-spawn bitch toyed with you, like a cat with a mouse.* The thought was intolerable. How could she stand this? How could anyone?

Deryn raised her head. "Was that why your partner left you?"

"Reyna? No. She was demon-spawn too. We were lovers in Ellaye. She moved up here with me, but didn't love me enough to stay, once it became clear I could never go back."

Alana's story had holes. How much was she still hiding? "Why did you come here?"

"I told you. I can't cope with loads of people, they drown me out."

"But you used to live in Ellaye, so what changed?"

"The king's high counselor, Orrin, supposedly tried to help me."

"Supposedly?"

"I think it was more a case of getting rid of a potential rival. I used to be able to block everyone out of my head. I had barriers, but he destroyed them. I would have gone mad if I'd stayed in Ellaye."

"It wasn't because your family didn't want you snooping around inside their heads either?"

"No. I sense your cynicism, and your anger and fear. And I don't blame you for feeling any of them. But believe me, if I could shut you out of my head, I would. Can't you imagine what's it like, being swamped by other people? Half the time, I don't know what I'm feeling on my own account and what I'm picking up from others. I lose myself. At the moment I'm feeling really angry, but I suspect it isn't me. I'm absorbing it from you. What have I got to be angry about, except that you're blaming me for things I didn't want and didn't choose and are hurting me far more than they hurt you?" Alana's shoulders slumped. "I just want to be me and nobody else."

"Easy for you to say that."

"It's the truth. With all my family's money, do you think I'd be living alone in a decrepit shack like this if I didn't have to? Do you think I enjoy living like a louse-ridden peasant?"

"I only have your word on who you are and why you're here."

"How dare you accuse me of lying." Alana reached up and clasped the silver pendant at her throat. Her eyes closed while the fury slowly left her face. At last she opened them again and met Deryn's gaze. "So what are you going to do?" Her voice was calm and resigned, a half shade from despair.

"Do?"

"Are you going to tell people in Neupor about me?"

"What if I do?"

"Then I couldn't stay here. I wouldn't be safe. So, if you are going to tell people, I'd rather you did it while the weather is still good enough for me to travel."

Some folk, with less justification than Deryn, might try to hurt Alana if they knew the truth. That was undeniable, and at the thought, Deryn felt her anger ebb. But did she care what happened to any of the demon-spawn? She stood and went to the doorway. Outside, Tia was grazing on a patch of grass.

"Last night, when you started acting odd, at first I was confused. I thought you were having a fit. Then you neighed and ran off. If it had just been the running off, I'd have gone after you. But the neighing? There's a limit to how weird I'll put up with. I let you go. But I was"— Deryn bit her lip, searching for a word she could admit to—"upset. And you'd put me in mind of Tia. I thought I'd check her before I went back to the festival. Which is how I found the fire."

Deryn recalled walking back along the path, battling with hurt and rejection, thinking that if she could not hold Alana, she wanted to hold someone or something she could care about. Then there had been the horror when she saw the flames lapping the side of the stable. It was a barrage of remembered emotion. How much of it was Alana now reading? Did she know how much Deryn had wanted her? The desolation after she had run off? The pathetic joke where an Iron Wolf needed to hug her horse for comfort?

Deryn stamped down on the memories and turned back to face Alana. "If it hadn't been for you, Tia would have burned to death. I owe you. I'll keep my mouth shut, and we can call it quits."

"Thank you." Alana's eyes again met hers.

Deryn caught her breath. *I almost became her lover.*

Alana was still sitting in her chair, hands clasped in her lap. She was demon-spawn, and she was alone and vulnerable. The last of Deryn's anger slipped away. Alana's lips were just as kissable as before. *I can't still want her, can I? Dammit. Is Nevin right? Anything with a pulse?* Before she could give in to the urge to wrap Alana in her arms, Deryn turned on her heel and left.

Neupor Marshal's Station, northern Galvonia
Early winter, diciembre 2, afternoon

Was there any sadder state for an Iron Wolf to be reduced to than playing solitaire? Apart from anything else, it brought to mind all the tired old jokes about playing with yourself, and giving yourself a good hand. None of which Deryn found in the slightest bit funny. She muttered a string of obscenities, prompted by frustration, irritation, and plain out-and-out boredom. As ever, the universe was indifferent to her swearing. Nothing changed. Deryn scowled as she dealt the top row of cards out on the table.

The light in the room dimmed. Deryn looked up to see an adolescent boy standing in the doorway.

"Do you want something?"

"Is Sergeant Nevin here?"

Before replying, Deryn made a show of leaning to the side and peering under the table—the only possible hiding place in the room. "No."

"Sorry. That was a bit of a stupid question." At least the lad realized it.

Deryn relented and smiled at him. "Finding the sergeant under the table isn't as rare as you might think."

"Do you know where he is?"

"He went to get something. He'll be back soon. Why don't you sit down and wait for him?"

"Thanks." The boy slid onto the bench facing Deryn. His face was vaguely familiar.

"I've met you before, haven't I?"

"I'm one of Eldora's sons, Shaw."

"Right."

"Mom's sent me with a message."

"What is it? Or does it have to wait for the sergeant?"

"Not really. One of our neighbors has gone missing."

Alana. Deryn looked down and rubbed her forehead, trying to act indifferent. *I don't care if anything has happened to her. I never want to see her again so it doesn't matter.* Yet Deryn was lying to herself, and she knew it. "Who?"

"One of the dairy farmers who lives below us at the bottom of the valley."

Her surge of relief annoyed Deryn just as much as her initial reaction had. "How long has the farmer been—"

The light dimmed again. Nevin had returned with his purchase, a bottle of wine. He snarled at the boy. "What do you want?"

Shaw scrambled off the bench. "One of the dairymen in the valley has gone missing."

"Who?"

"Alejo."

"Probably passed out somewhere, drunk."

There's nothing like judging the world by your own standards, or is he a beer buddy of yours?

Shaw shook his head. "Nobody has seen him for three days."

Even you don't get that drunk.

Nevin's forehead wrinkled in a deep frown. "Did Alejo tell anyone where he was going?"

Deryn could see that Nevin was trying very hard to think of a way to get out of doing anything, but he was clutching at straws. If the missing farmer had said where he was going, he would not count as missing when he went there.

Shaw's answer confirmed this. "No. Mom says you need to organize a search party to find him."

"Yeah? Well, I make the decisions here. Not your damned mom."

Nevin slumped onto the vacated bench and put the bottle on the table, scuffing Deryn's cards aside as he did so. This last part was an act of petty spite. The table was quite big enough for the bottle and the card game. Its only rationale was that Nevin wanted to show he could claim the whole table as his own whenever he liked.

"What decision are you going to make...sir?" Deryn made no attempt to downplay her contempt, turning the last word into an insult.

"What?"

"The lost dairyman. What are you going to do about him?"

Nevin spat on the ground. "We'll give it a couple of days. See if he shows up."

"On top of the three days he's already been missing?"

"I don't need your fucking advice." Nevin gave a sarcastic sneer. "I wouldn't have thought you'd been so keen to start searching for lost people. You made a real fucking mess the last time. My sister never got her sheep back."

Deryn gathered her cards and stood. "Good point."

"What is?"

"The marshal's men don't have the resources for this manhunt. We couldn't even find the sheep."

"You couldn't." The emphasis Nevin put onto the first word turned it into an accusation.

"You looked for them as well, didn't you, sir?"

"No. I mean yes. I mean…"

Make your mind up. Do you want to confess to failure or laziness?

Nevin settled for a scowl. "Do what the fuck you like."

I was going to. Deryn smiled at Shaw. "Come on." At the doorway she added, "We'll find Regan and tell her about Alejo."

The mayor liked organizing things—this had been obvious from the way she shouted orders to the firefighters—which made it rather a shame there was so little in Neupor for her to organize. Regan would surely make the most of this chance. She would call on every available person for the manhunt, and some of the people it was her right to call on were the marshal's men. As a break from playing solitaire, Deryn had spent a couple of dull afternoons reading the marshal's rule book. In coordinating a citizens' posse, the mayor outranked the sergeant.

"Hey. What the…"

Deryn made no attempt to hide her grin as she strolled away, ignoring Nevin's shout. She had seen that the mayor did not have a high opinion of the sergeant (who would?), but had not yet had the chance to gauge how Regan's sense of humor ran. What chance she would order Nevin to personally check that Alejo had not accidentally buried himself in the farm's dung heap?

❖

Nevin muttered to himself for the entire ride from Neupor to Alejo's farm. However, since he was muttering to himself, and not her, Deryn was unconcerned. It was a beautiful, crisp morning for a ride and she was not going to let him spoil it.

Winter was on the way. The white-capped peaks of distant mountains were pristine perfection against the crystal blue sky. Although dawn was an hour past, the temperature was still freezing. The night had brought a heavy frost, coating leaves and branches in glittering rime. Snow might not fall that day, but it could not be far off. Steam formed in the horses' breath and punctuated Nevin's muttering.

"...Iron fucking Wolves...poxy mayor...stupid, fucking waste of fucking time..."

Deryn grinned. Despite Nevin's rank of sergeant, he had no real power over her. The worst he could do was write to Marshal Palemon in Oakan and recommend that she be dismissed or that her pay be docked. The risk was low, since her pay was mostly in the form of board and lodging. She could hardly be put on half rations all winter, and if Nevin had her kicked out then he would have to do all the work that Ross was incapable of. Furthermore, in Deryn's brief meeting with the marshal, while they might not have got on well together, he had not struck her as enough of a fool to pay the slightest attention to anything Nevin said.

The road emerged from a small stand of trees. A quarter mile ahead was a rickety hovel, held up by lean-tos. The humble structure did not merit the name of homestead, but from the group of people clustered in the enclosed yard, Deryn guessed it was Alejo's farm.

"You're late," Regan called once they were in hailing distance.

Deryn tipped her head in Nevin's direction. Not that she thought the mayor needed the hint to explain their poor punctuality. She reined Tia to a halt beside the gate to the yard. Several of the gathered faces she recognized, Eldora and her family among them. Deryn scanned the rest for anyone else she knew.

Who am I trying to kid? She was looking for Alana. Deryn told herself she was only doing it in the hope that the demon-spawn healer was not there, but this was another failed attempt at self-deception. Her stomach did a flip and her pulse raced when she spotted Alana standing at the far side of the yard, some way detached from the rest of the assembled group.

Deryn swung down from Tia's back. Maybe she was still attracted, but there was no way she was going to give in to the temptation. If learning about Alana's true nature had not put her off, it only showed how serious things might get. *And I'm never going to get serious over anyone. Certainly not her.* Deryn knew she should view it as a lucky escape. What did it matter if she was losing sleep?

"Okay. Now we're all here. Listen up." Regan was in her element. "I'm going to divide you into pairs, and give you each an area to search. Eldora. Pick one of your kids and take East Sprig Woods. Sal. You and Connie check the fields to the south. Yanna…"

Regan carried on, working her way through the assembled locals, until she reached Nevin.

"Sergeant. I'm worried Alejo might have drowned in the marsh at the bottom of his field. I want you to take one of your officers and check it out."

Deryn ducked her head, while pinching her mouth, to hide her smile. She was sure the assignment was not random. Who better to spend the day up to his knees in cold mud? Annoying the mayor by turning up late had not been a clever move on Nevin's part.

Even though Deryn liked the mayor's decision, she did not want to be the person roped in to help Nevin. "Is anyone going to check Voodoo Mountain?"

Deryn's question clearly caught Regan off balance. She paused, frowning. "That might be an idea. Um…Would anyone like to volunteer?"

Most of the crowd found a sudden interest in the state of their shoes. The rest started looking for clouds. The reaction was exactly what Deryn had hoped.

"I'll do it. That's why I mentioned it. I've got a score to settle up there."

"Great. Would someone be willing to go with Deryn?"

"I will."

Deryn felt her stomach clench. The voice had belonged to Alana.

"Right. So. Sergeant Nevin. You and Ross take the marsh. Deryn and Alana have Voodoo Mountain." Regan smiled and continued telling people what to do. She was clearly having a wonderful time of it. She finished by waving a bugle in the air. "That's it. When Alejo is found, I'll signal with three blasts on this, to let everyone else know the search is over."

"Supposing we don't find him?" someone on the other side of the crowd asked.

"Let's be positive. I'm sure we will. But if not, we'll meet back here at dusk. Right. Off you go."

The crowd drifted away in their assigned pairs. While waiting for Alana to weave a path through and join her, Deryn leaned against the gatepost and tried to act nonchalant. *She's demon-spawn. Remember that. Incredibly attractive, fun-to-be-with demon-spawn.* As a thought to firm up her resolve, Deryn had to admit it left a bit to be desired. *She can get inside your head. She probably can read that you've been going crazy thinking about her and if she gave you one more kiss you'd dissolve quicker than a snowball in a furnace. She could snap her fingers and you'd be on your knees, and she knows it.* Deryn tried to convince herself that this was a frightening thought.

"Hi. Ready to go?" Alana appeared through the crowd.

"Yeah. Sure."

Alana did not speak again until everyone was out of earshot. "Sorry about dumping myself on you like that, but I knew nobody else would put their hand up."

"It's all right. It's not like I feel any need to avoid you." *Like hell it isn't.*

"Really? I've been avoiding you." Alana carried on without a sideways glance.

Deryn stopped as if she had walked into a wall. *And if she doesn't snap her fingers... Does that mean she's no longer interested?* Deryn pinched her forehead. Why was that thought so much more upsetting than all the rest? *Shit. Shit. Shit.* Deryn hurried to catch up.

The Sprig River might warrant its name in spring, when it was swollen with meltwater, but in early autumn it could not count as anything more than a stream. Deryn and Alana crossed, hopping from stone to stone, without getting their feet wet. The forest covering Voodoo Mountain grew close on the other side. Deryn crouched to examine the prints between wood and water.

"Can you tell anything?"

Deryn pointed. "That's a cow. And so is that. These are sheep." She cast around. "Sheepdogs. At least three people. Otter. Chipmunk. Lots of chipmunk. Deer. And a few more chipmunks. All of it in the last day. Alejo's footprints are gone, if they were ever here." She stood. "Maybe in the forest we can find a spot that's seen less traffic."

"How do we get into the forest? I can't see any paths."

"There aren't any proper ones. We'll have to find one the deer have made."

"Supposing we can't find any way into the forest?"

"Then we rule out the idea that Alejo might be here. If we can't get in, he couldn't either."

However, it did not take long before Deryn found a clear trail. The ground around the entrance had been well trodden, with a mass of deer prints, and the occasional coyote thrown in. Unfortunately, the profusion of prints left no chance of spotting any sign of Alejo.

Before following the path into the forest, Deryn took a last look back. On the other side of the stream, Nevin and Ross were ankle deep in sludge, probing with long poles. Ross looked like a little boy playing in mud puddles. Nevin looked totally pissed off. Deryn grinned at the sight and then slipped between the trees.

It soon became clear they had found a deer highway that widened rapidly as more spiderweb-draped trails merged with their own. The path was still not quite wide enough to walk side by side, but they no longer needed to duck under branches and shove through thickets.

The awareness of Alana walking behind her made Deryn's shoulder blades tingle. But she could handle it, she told herself. They were going to concentrate on the task at hand and keep conversations to the mundane. So why did she feel like a roasted snowball? It was not as if there was any risk of them kissing—was there?

After a half mile, the deer trail reached a wide glade around a woodland pool.

"Why would Alejo have come this far?" Alana asked.

"Maybe one of his cows strayed and he was going after it."

"Okay. So why did his cow come this far?"

"I don't know. But the path here is the only one big enough for a cow. So if it was straying, it's here or nowhere."

The pool in the middle of the clearing was clearly the goal for the deer. The water's edge was pockmarked by their hooves. A patch of mud, close by the trees, was less heavily trampled, and this was where Deryn spotted the first clue that they were on the right track.

"Here we go." The broad print underlay the smaller deer marks.

"A cow?"

"A cow."

"Yea." Alana gave a soft cheer.

Another patch of mud, farther on, caught Deryn's eyes. "More cow prints and…there"—she pointed—"see that? A heel. Someone was here."

"Alejo."

"I guess s—" Deryn pushed back a tuft of grass for a better look at a second partial footprint.

"What is it?"

Deryn chewed her lip, comparing the two prints. "That's someone's toe, but I don't think it's a match to the heel."

"What?"

"We've got two different people."

"Are you sure?"

"Not totally. Maybe Alejo was wearing odd boots, but it's where I'd put my money."

"Alejo can't have had anyone with him. Nobody else is missing."

"The other possibility is…"

"Is what?"

"You mean you can't read my mind?" Deryn mainly intended it as a joke, but the seeds of apprehension added an edge to her tone.

Alana clearly did not find it funny, and an expression of irritation crossed her face. "No. I've told you that. But I can tell something is bothering you."

Deryn sighed and stood, looking around. "Nevin's sister reckoned someone had stolen her sheep. I put it down to carelessness on her part. But I found footprints in the forest. Now this." She pointed at the ground. "Maybe a farmer has started stealing livestock from the neighbors. It would explain why the cow wandered so far."

"Do you want to get your comrades?"

"Who?"

"Ross and Sergeant Nevin."

"Oh, them. Sorry. I didn't recognize the description." This time Deryn's words did get a smile. Her stomach flipped at the sight and she looked away quickly. Making Alana smile was not safe or wise. Deryn ran a hand through her hair, trying to pretend she was thinking. "Um, no. Even if it is a thief at work, neither of those two will be any help at all. I've got my bow, and a dozen arrows. That should do."

Deryn rarely went anywhere without her bow, usually in hope of rabbit stew rather than battling thieves. Unfortunately, she had left her sword behind at the station. It had not occurred to her that it might be needed. She could return to collect it, but that would mean the long round trek to Neupor and back. The sword was never her best weapon, anyway.

"We go on?" Alana asked.

"I do. You can go back if you want."

"I'm going with you."

"Okay. It's probably nothing to worry about. If his farm's anything to go by, I wouldn't be surprised if Alejo can't afford a proper pair of boots and has a couple of his neighbors' mismatched cast-offs."

Even so, Deryn strung her bow before moving on into the forest.

Why did I say I'd come? Alana repeatedly asked herself the question. A sudden impulse had struck her in the farmyard and she had volunteered without giving herself time to think. What had she been hoping for? That Deryn would have softened her attitude? That if they had time to talk they might reach some accord? Or was it just to spend a day with Deryn, watching her? In which case, why had she wanted this torture? Her hands still held the tactile memory of how Deryn's body felt. Her lips still burned with their kiss. She wanted Deryn, and all she could do was look.

Why she wanted Deryn so desperately was another hard question. *Is it just that I've been alone too long?* Or was there something special about the Iron Wolf? Maybe that was it. Deryn's background was part of the picture. Alana's previous lovers had all fitted into one of two molds: either smart and ambitious and therefore motivated as least as much by politics as love, or sweet and not too bright, like Reyna. Deryn was sharp, without having one eye on the Quintanilla family connection.

The other part of the package lay in the way Deryn had latched a hold on Alana that first night with the heart-rending combination of the tough warrior exterior and the emotional vulnerability from her childhood tragedy. There were layers to Deryn. Alana wanted to peel them off, one by one, and heal the woman at the core. *Oh yes, that's me. A healer through and through.*

On Deryn's part, the reaction was complex. Alana was sure that not all the sexual desire she felt was her own, but mostly what she sensed in Deryn was unease and irritation that increased whenever they spoke. Deryn would undoubtedly be happier with some other companion in the forest. *You're demon-spawn. What do you expect?*

While they walked, Alana studied Deryn's back. *Suppose I came straight out and said something like, "Give me one more kiss and I promise you won't set eyes on me again."* Alana pouted. Of course, she would never have the nerve to say it, and Deryn was unlikely to agree, but it made a starting point for a nice fantasy to play with. Alana sighed. Maybe she should simply enjoy the view and stop tormenting herself.

Midday was just past. For the last quarter mile, their route had run along the top of a cliff, with a sheer drop of fifty feet or more on their right and the forest on their left. The cliff top was fully exposed to the winter sunshine. Added to the exertion and her heavy clothes, Alana was feeling a little too warm. She toyed with the idea of stripping off her coat, but if she did, the trail would be sure to dive back into the shadow of the trees and she would be too cold again. A short rest would be nice, though.

Deryn stopped to examine the ground, as she had been doing all morning, flicking a pinecone aside with her forefinger.

"Anything?" Alana asked.

Deryn's face was more pensive than normal. "The ground is too stony to be sure, but I'd say there's been a lot of people through here for somewhere that everyone is so keen to avoid."

"It's not just Alejo?"

"Nope."

"So there is a thief?"

"Can't tell their occupation from their footprints, but there's more than one of them, I'd say." Deryn's tone was calmly professional, but her underlying emotion was sharp, not with fear, but wariness, honed to a razor edge.

"Any idea how many?"

"No. The prints aren't good enough to be sure. Could be two or three. Could be a whole gang."

"A gang? We can't handle them on our own."

"Not if they're outlaws." Deryn stood, brushing the dirt off her hands. "It still might be a bunch of prospectors, but we can't take the chance. We need to go back for support."

Alana faced out over the cliff face, preparing herself for the long walk back. The rocks below formed a flat-bottomed gorge—suspiciously flat, now that she stopped to look at it properly. The angle between floor and walls was geometrically precise. Then she spotted knots of rusted metal pipes and glittering spots that might be broken glass.

"This isn't a natural valley. Someone excavated it."

"Yes. I'd noticed."

"You didn't mention it."

Deryn shrugged. "I didn't think you'd be interested. You see lots of places like this on the Misery Trail."

"The demons made this valley?"

"Maybe, or it might have been the Ancients in the Age of Wonders. They built roads like this. If you look, you'll see patches of the black resin stuff they covered them with."

"People dug this out, just for a road?"

"Yup. When a mountain got in the way they'd cut straight through it."

Alana was speechless. She had seen ruins of the Ancients before. Ellaye itself was built on the site of one such city, but nothing remained on the same scale as this. Suddenly, all the stories about the Age of Wonders, before the demons came, seemed less like fairy stories.

Once humans had ruled the world, the Ancients. They had machines that could fly. They raised buildings so tall they scraped the sky. They sent messages around the world in an instant. No one was hungry. No one was cold.

Then the demons came. Who knew from where or why? Nothing about them made sense. They destroyed human civilization, but was it war or a game to them?

Alana's ancestors had been the mortal face of the demons, avatars for their spirits, but had they been possessed humans, or were they like the windigos, the demons' creations let loose? Not that it mattered now. The demons had gone, as suddenly and inexplicably as they had arrived, leaving a world in ruins. The demon-spawn descendants of their avatars were all that was left for the survivors to vent their anger on.

Of course Deryn would not want anything to do with you. Can you blame her? Alana bit her lip. *Maybe not, but neither is it fair for her to blame me.*

Alana turned away from the ancient roadway and started back down the trail, but after a couple of steps, she realized that Deryn was not following. She looked back. "What is it?"

Deryn was standing close to the edge and staring up the valley, shading her eyes from the sun. "There's something fluttering between two boulders up there. It looks like cloth. It's certainly not part of the ruins."

"Do you want to check it out before we go?"

"Why not? It's only few dozen yards. Won't take long."

They reached the cliff top point directly above the object that Deryn had spotted and peered over the rim. Lying at the foot of the cliff was an elderly man. The only sign of movement was his cloak, scuffing in the breeze.

"Does that look like Alejo to you?" Deryn asked.

"Yes. Do you think he's dead?"

"Doesn't look good, but we have to check, just in case. I'll climb down." Already Deryn was slipping off her backpack, then she turned and lowered herself over the edge.

The cliff face was sheer but not smooth, offering plenty of handholds. After a moment of indecisiveness, Alana dropped her pack beside Deryn's and followed. She agreed that Alejo's chances were slim; even if he had survived the fall, three days lying out in the cold would surely be fatal, but as a healer, she was the one who should examine him.

When she got to the bottom, Deryn was already crouched beside the motionless figure.

"Is he dead?"

"Yeah."

"He must have tripped and fallen." Alana looked up at the top of the cliff. The path along the edge had been wide enough, but if Alejo had been distracted, or trying to make his way at night, one false step would have been all it required.

"I don't think so."

"Pardon?"

"Dead people don't usually trip. He was dumped over the edge."

"Why do you—"

Deryn shifted back, giving Alana her first clear view of the body. Alejo's throat gaped open in an obscene parody of a smile. The straight line could only be the work of a blade, rather than an injury from his fall.

"Not just thieves. Murderers."

Deryn's tone was calmly matter-of-fact. Her revulsion and disgust were tightly controlled. But of course, the Iron Wolf would have seen violent death many times before. Alana could not muster the same composure. She clamped a hand over her mouth, trying to hold back the nausea.

Deryn stood. "We need to get back."

"Yup."

Alana turned away, trying to force her eyes to focus on the rocks before her, but her hands were shaking. She needed to get a grip on herself before she started to climb, else she might be joining Alejo.

"Be still."

In her tense state, the sharp tone was more than Alana could take. She barely restrained a scream. "Wha—"

Deryn clamped a hand over her mouth. "Hush."

At first Alana could hear nothing over the blood roaring in her ears, but then the faint sound of voices drifted down, and the crunch of footsteps.

"Shit." Deryn's whisper was more breath than sound.

A shout echoed like a whip crack between the rock faces.

Deryn pulled her hand from Alana's mouth. "They've seen our stuff up there."

"What do we do?"

"Run like fuck."

Deryn grabbed Alana's hand, hauling her away. They sped along the valley's flat bottom in a frantic slalom between the fallen boulders and ripped-up slabs that littered the ancient highway. A riot of shouts broke out above them on the cliff-top path, and then a sharp hiss. Alana flinched as an arrow struck the ground in front of her.

"They're shooting."

"Yeah. Save your breath for running."

Still Deryn led the headlong flight. A second arrow hummed by, close enough that Alana felt the draft on her neck. Deryn made a sharp break to the right, veering toward a narrow gap in the valley wall on the opposite side to the one they had climbed down. The entrance was no more than fifteen feet across. Even more than the main valley, this showed the signs of mechanical excavation. The sides were steeper and smoother.

Alana spared one backward glance. Five figures were climbing down into the valley behind them.

"They're following us."

"Then run faster."

But Alana did not think she could. The morning's hike over rough ground had tired her out. Now her lungs were burning and her legs were turning to rubber. The surge of adrenaline could not carry her much farther. If it had not been for Deryn towing her along, she would have been overtaken by the gang already.

The man-made ravine took a sharp bend to the left and then the right. The way split. Without hesitation Deryn took the smaller side branch. The sounds of pursuit echoed through the narrow chasm, bouncing off the perpendicular stone walls.

"We have…get to trees…hide. Too exposed…" Deryn gasped the words.

Alana glanced up. The rock faces on either side showed no sign of getting lower or less sheer. If anything, they were smoother than before, devoid of handholds, impossible to climb.

They sped around another right-angled bend and came up short. The ravine widened out into a square, fifty feet across, like a room with an open roof, carved into the mountain. The walls were sheer and unbroken on all sides except for the one facing the entrance, where twin stone doors were carved into the rock face. There was no other way out.

Shouts and the pounding footsteps were getting louder. The gang was very close, but Alana did not need sound to tell her this. A rising furor of savage excitement was bearing down on her, wild bloodlust and aggression, and through it all ran a yet more terrifying thread, a cold hunger, utterly without mercy. She had felt this bestial emotion once before, Alana realized, walking home from Eldora's farm. How long had the gang been watching the citizens and farmers of Neupor?

Deryn was still not giving up. She grabbed a brass handle on the door and threw her whole weight into pulling it. "Help me."

The stone door started to move, but they were out of time.

"Freeze."

Alana tried to stand still, but her legs gave out and she sank to her knees, gasping. She twisted her head toward the entrance. Five outlaws had entered the rock chamber, four men and a woman. Two held drawn bows. The others had swords. They also were breathing heavily from the exertion. Their clothes were one step up from rags. Clearly they had been living rough for a while, yet the man in the center carried himself with an arrogant confidence that marked him as leader.

He was tall and broad shouldered. His graying hair would once have been jet black. His face had crooked nose and an even more crooked smile. He was the center of the inhuman malice that Alana could sense. His followers were fired up with the excitement of the chase. Without doubt, they were dangerous criminals, but the leader was the one who would kill without guilt, motive, or hesitation, and enjoy doing it.

His aura added to the sight of the bows pointing at them, turning Alana's guts to water. The arrowheads drew her gaze, mesmerizing her with fear. For all the tales of battles and adventure she had heard, she had never realized quite how menacing it would feel. At her side, Deryn had released the brass handle and stood motionless, both palms pressed flat against the stone door. Alana could feel her mood, bitter, defiant, but also despairing. She realized the Iron Wolf did not have much hope for their chances. Deryn took another deep breath, then raised her hands in surrender and turned around.

Shock ripped through Deryn, as sharp as it was unexpected. Alana was still dealing with the surprise when, without warning, Deryn dropped, lunging left. Alana saw Deryn's hand brush her calf as she rolled. Bowstrings twanged, but the archers were too slow and the arrows ricocheted off the stone door, missing their target. Deryn's momentum took her over in a roll and then up onto one knee. Her hand shot out and Alana caught the flash of metal. She turned her head, following the trajectory.

The gang leader was also moving, diving sideways. A metal object hit the wall behind where he had been standing and clattered to the ground. A dagger. Meanwhile, one of the gang was fumbling for another arrow, and the other three were charging forward, toward Deryn. They arrived in a storm of blows, knocking her down.

The gang leader had landed on the ground. His malice and self-assurance had been blown away by the wave of alarm, but now they slithered back into place as, grinning, he hoisted himself to his feet. The fighting was over, while Alana was still trying to catch up with what had happened and how it started.

No. Not quite over. Deryn was the focus of a frenzied attack. Three outlaws were laying into her with their feet, stamping and kicking. Deryn was curled on the ground, arms wrapped around her head. Alana was still on her knees, a yard or more away. Without bothering to rise, she threw herself forward, desperate to help. The ankle of one outlaw was just beyond her grasp, but if she could trip him—

"Hold on, there." The gang leader's voice was not loud, but it held the surety of someone who does not need to shout to be confident of obedience.

All movement stopped, apart from the woman with the bow, who completed the action of nocking a new arrow on the string. In the sudden calm, the leader strolled forward, dusting grit from the seat of his pants. At his nod, his followers reached down and dragged Deryn to her feet. She looked dazed. Blood tricked down the side of her face and a raw graze marked her chin.

"You know, I don't like people throwing knives at me." The leader's voice was quietly conversational. Then he drew back his fist and slammed it into Deryn's stomach, twice. His next blow backhanded her across the face.

Alana started to scramble to her feet, but a movement from the archer stopped her. The arrow was aimed straight at her heart and Alana did not have the speed to avoid it. All she could do was watch.

The feral excitement from the gang was monstrous, sickening. Each grunt and gasp from Deryn added a fresh surge of satisfaction. Never had Alana wanted so much to block out the emotions of others.

At last the leader stepped back. The outlaws holding Deryn released her, and she collapsed senseless to the ground, still and silent.

"Say, boss, isn't she the one who tracked us onto the mountain before? The one we got with the rockfall?"

"Could be. We'll have to make sure she doesn't interrupt our lamb barbecue again." The leader turned to the stone door while nonchalantly rubbing his knuckles. "Right, now. What have we here?"

"We gonna open it, boss?"

"Don't see why not." He gestured impatiently to his followers. "Well go on, then. Don't just look at it."

The doors opened to the sound of grinding, while a shower of dust rained down from the top. The air that flowed out was stale and smelt of mildew. Matted spiderwebs coated the inside of the doors. How long had passed since they were last opened? Beyond them, a tunnel vanished into the darkness.

One of the outlaws took a step forward.

"Hang on."

He looked back. "Yes, boss?"

"Supposing there's a trap in there?"

"Oh." The outlaw retreated.

The leader's smile broadened. "That's why we're going to send her in first."

Alana's guts clenched. He was staring at her.

"And she won't get any clever ideas, because we've got her friend here to play football with." The leader planted a swinging kick on Deryn's ass.

"I promise. I won't try anything. I promise." Alana heard herself babbling. The most worrying thing had been Deryn's lack of response to the kick. She was clearly unconscious. Alana could only pray that she was not more seriously hurt. Asking for permission to examine Deryn's injuries first would be a waste of breath.

After a last anxious look at Deryn's motionless body, Alana entered the tunnel. She ran her left hand along the wall, while holding the other out in front. Despite the outlaw's talk of traps, Alana was so concerned for Deryn that she had walked a dozen paces before the idea struck her that maybe she should also be concerned for herself.

Alana stopped, straining her senses. The echoes suggested that a large void lay ahead, but she could see nothing. The wind gusted down the corridor, stirring up centuries-old dust, clogging her nose. The stone wall was as smooth against her fingers as polished marble. Alana took another few cautious steps forward. Abruptly the wall vanished on her left. Alana stopped and then realized the darkness was no longer so complete. Her eyes were adjusting after the bright sunlight outside.

The passageway had led her to a large chamber, cut from the

rock. Alana stepped forward, into the open, and looked up. A barrel ceiling arched, high overhead, hazy in diffuse daylight. The chamber was fifty or so feet across. The walls were smooth as glass, devoid of ornamentation, glinting with a faint blue sheen. The floor was empty apart from a carved rectangular block in the middle.

"Well. What have you found?" The voice boomed from the entrance.

"Nothing. There's a room in here."

"What's in it?"

"Like I said. Nothing, apart from a block of stone." Alana turned in a circle, looking around. "It's—"

"What?"

The blue sheen on the walls had come from three deep recesses at the far end of the room. "There's some weird blue lights in here. But they're not moving or anything."

Blue eternal lights. Demon magic. *And that's one thing that really shouldn't worry me. They wouldn't even count as a party trick for Mom.*

Footsteps echoed around the walls. The outlaws were coming.

"What do the lights look like?"

"Statues or something. They're in niches on the wall. There's a helmet, a shield, and a s..."

The word froze in Alana's throat. Three of the four magical weapons from the story. The stone block was a sarcophagus. How could she not have recognized it immediately? She stood in the Witch-Lord's tomb beneath Voodoo Mountain.

"What the..."

The outlaws had reached the chamber. Two were half carrying Deryn, with her arms hooked over their shoulders, but she was now awake. When they dropped her, she rolled onto her back and raised her hand to her face.

"Boss, I know this. We...we n-n-need to get away." One of the outlaws spoke in panic, backing toward the exit.

"What?"

"The Witch-Lord. His ghost will—"

The leader grabbed a fistful of the man's hair to stop his retreat. "Ghost stories are for kids."

"But…"

While the outlaws' attention was elsewhere, Alana sidled around the edge of the chamber. Deryn levered herself into a sitting position as Alana dropped down at her side. Even in the dim light, Alana could see her wince.

"You should lie still."

"Why?"

"You're injured."

"I know that. But it's not going to be a problem much longer, is it?"

They slit Alejo's throat. Alana was struck by the understanding of what Deryn meant. *They won't let us go alive.*

Deryn's eyes met hers. "Sorry."

"It's not your fault."

"I should have—"

"Yes." The outlaw leader's voice was a shout of triumph. "A sword that will cut through steel, a shield that won't let me be hurt, and a helmet that will bring everyone to their knees before me. Now, which one will I try out first?"

His voice was getting louder, closer. Alana looked up. The shield was apparently out of the running. The leader was marching toward them, the sword in one hand and the helmet in the other. He stopped, looming over them, and then raised the helmet and placed it over his head.

Primordial terror cascaded through Alana's soul. Death, and undeath. Pain and ruin. Horror to stop a heart beating. She heard screams, but the sound was only a fitting backdrop to the fear. And yet, not all reason was scattered. Alana recognized the familiar taint of imposed emotion. This was not her fear. She could renounce it. Instinctively, she went to grasp the talisman at her throat, only to have her hand knocked aside.

"That's a nice-looking bauble. But you won't be needing it anymore. So if you don't mind…"

A hand wrapped itself around the talisman. Alana felt it as a blade in her mind, dissecting her thoughts. A sword passed in front of her eyes, and the talisman—her shield against the world—was gone.

Six sets of emotions snapped into sharp focus. Blind terror

consuming Deryn, and four others, the outlaws, nearly as savagely affected, but farther away. Closest of all was crazed joy from the gang leader. Alana had thought she could feel the emotions of others before, but she had only seen the blurred reflection. This was the full force of it, in fine detail. Greed, bloodlust, doubt, alarm, and hatred. And yet—Alana pressed her clenched fists to her head—and yet, with the detail came comprehension. The emotions were precise and clear, and she could finally see which ones where hers.

Alana reached out with her mind and closed the doors.

The sudden shock of calm made her keel forward, flat on the ground, almost at the point of passing out.

"Well, what do you know? It works." The gang leader's laughter echoed around the tomb, becoming less muffled as he removed the helmet.

"Boss, boss, that was, oh…" The outlaw was crying.

"What? Did you feel it too?"

"Yeah, it was—" Another one spoke, a quaver in her voice. "But I don't think I got it quite so bad, 'cause I was standing right behind you."

"Boss, you can't use it again… you can't—"

"Stop whining. I'll try to make sure you're behind me. But just think what this means." The leader laughed again. "We're going to go and have ourselves a good time."

"What are we gonna do with them?"

Alana guessed that she and Deryn were the subject of the outlaw's question, but was too happy to care about the answer.

"Ah. We'll leave them here. They can keep the Witch-Lord company."

Footsteps clipped past her head. They echoed along the passage and faded. Only the boom of the doors shutting roused Alana from her daze. She sat up, shaking her head, still dumbfounded by her own stupidity. The talisman. Why had she ever trusted Orrin that it was for her benefit?

Deryn groaned beside her.

"How are you?" Alana asked.

"Fuck. What the…" Deryn gave a few deep breaths. "That helmet… it…I…"

"Don't think about it."

"I'm trying not to. Believe me."

With the doors closed, it was even darker in the tomb, but slits near the ceiling allowed enough light in to still make out the surroundings. Alana helped Deryn slide across the floor until she was sitting with her back against the wall, and then settled down beside her.

"Okay. How about this as something to distract you—why didn't he kill us?" Alana asked.

"Because he's an evil bastard."

"But—"

"Listen."

The sound echoed down the tunnel, of something large landing against the door. Another thud followed, and a third. "They're sealing us in?"

"Afraid so."

Alana rested her forehead in her hand. "Damn. He's been crueler than he knows." She felt Deryn's fingers slip around her other hand and squeeze.

"How so?"

"He took my talisman."

"He'd take anything of value. But it…" Deryn trailed off, clearly confused.

"The talisman was given to me by Orrin, the king's high counselor, after he'd blown away my defensive barriers. It helped me cope. It's hard to explain, but it was like an emotional cushion. The world couldn't hit me so hard while I was touching it."

"Oh. Right. You…"

"What?"

"I'd noticed how you used to hold it. Does it mean that now you're being bombarded by my…um…"

"No. The opposite. Maybe once, some time back, I needed the protection of the talisman, but what it had been doing, for"—Alana shrugged—"I don't know how long, was blunting my senses. I couldn't learn how to block the world out because the talisman wouldn't let me see clearly enough what I needed to do. And I guess that doesn't make any sort of sense to you."

"Yes, it does. When you break your leg, you need a splint. But once you've healed you have to throw the splint away, even though it hurts, otherwise the muscles will wither and you'll never be able to run."

"That's not quite right."

"It's the same principle."

"Maybe. But anyway, now I know this, I could learn how to cope with people. I don't need to hide in my cabin. In taking the talisman he's given me the prospect of a whole new future, only to leave me with no future at all." Alana squeezed Deryn's hand. "I'm sorry you missed him with the dagger."

"I am too."

"You were surprised when you saw him, just before you threw it."

"I recognized him. He attacked a party I was guarding, years back."

"He didn't seem to know you."

"Probably not. I was just an apprentice at the time. But I've always hoped I'd bang into him again. His name's Martez. He's a renegade Iron Wolf, and he's responsible for the death of somebody I cared about."

"Not your family?"

"No. My first lover."

"A long time ago."

Deryn gave a soft laugh. "Yup, a long time. There have been quite a few since then, but I'd still like to avenge her."

The dull booms of rocks being piled against the door stopped. A voice sounded, too muffled to make out any words, and then there was nothing but silence.

"Sounds like they've gone."

"Uh-huh."

"I guess there's not much chance of anyone finding us here." Alana sighed. "I doubt Regan will get many volunteers to come looking."

"You and me going missing on Voodoo Mountain? She won't get any. They'll just write it off as the evil spirits being evil." Deryn started to stand.

"You don't need to move."

"I'll be okay. I'm bruised, nothing else. I can probably walk most of it off."

Alana was not convinced. "That's no reason why you can't sit still."

The light was just strong enough to show Deryn's smile. "If you want a reason, how about this—Martez didn't think to check if there was another way out."

"I can't see one."

"True, but either we can give up, or we can look for a secret passage. I know which way my vote goes." Deryn tapped her knuckles on the wall and then limped on a step.

Alana shook her head, smiling, then levered herself to her feet and joined in.

Despite three hours of poking and prying, the search turned out to be fruitless. As the daylight faded, they again settled down by the wall. Thirst and hunger were starting to niggle. The tomb was well insulated by the rock, but the temperature was bitterly cold, and only likely to get colder through the night.

Alana shivered. "I wish we had a blanket."

"I wish we had food and a water flask. In fact, I rather wish we weren't here at all. But wishing isn't going to help us." Deryn sighed. "The best I can think of is we huddle together for warmth. As long as you don't mind huddling close to me."

Alana opened her mouth, and then closed it again, but why not say it? "I'd happily snuggle up with you, even if it was a blazing hot summer's day. I'm demon-spawn and you want nothing to do with me. But so many times since the Night of the Lost, I've wished that the fire at the stable hadn't happened. That you and I had spent the night together. I know it's wrong of me to wish it, because it isn't what you'd have wanted if you'd known the truth, but—"

Deryn's finger on her lips halted the flow of words. "I don't mind you wishing it. It's what I wanted too. What I still want."

"But…"

The light was so weak that Alana heard more than saw Deryn lean toward her. Their lips touched in the softest of kisses, but even so, Alana knew immediately that it was not going to work. Her mouth was already so dry that their lips stuck together and Deryn winced as they parted.

"Ah, sorry. I've got a cut lip."

Alana laughed softly. "And a load of bruises. An empty stomach. And all we've got to lie on is a very cold stone floor."

"It's not looking good for a night of passion."

"No. Just sit by me. Hold me. That would be nice."

"Okay." Deryn adjusted her position. "There. Comfy?"

"Yes. Very." Alana paused. "Well, as comfy as can be expected, all things considered."

Alana twisted around slightly, placing her hand on Deryn's thigh and feeling the warmth of firm muscle. Deryn's shoulder was equally hard, but still so very good to rest her head on. "That first morning, after you'd stayed at my cabin. Why did you run away?"

"Habit."

"What sort of habit?"

"Maybe habit isn't quite right." Deryn paused, as if weighing up her next words. "I told you my first lover was killed by Martez. On her grave, I swore I'd never let anyone else get close to me. After what had happened to my family, it seemed the safest thing."

"I'd have thought it was a hard promise to keep."

"Running away a lot helped."

"So it became a habit?"

"Except it was different with you. I told you about my family, how they died, and I'd never spoken to anyone else about them before. That next morning, I was confused, but I also think, deep inside, I knew if I got to see much of you, I was going to break my promise." Deryn's arm around Alana tightened. "You've got to me, like no one else. I don't know if we could have a serious relationship. I've never had one before, so I don't know what they feel like. But you've got your hooks in me, and I don't want to run away anymore."

"Just as well, because you'd have a bit of trouble doing it right now."

"True. I've got a feeling I'm going to be with you for the rest of my life." Deryn gave a rueful sigh. "Damn."

"What?"

"Even though we're talking about days rather than years, it sounds good."

"Yup. I was thinking that too." Alana curled closer into Deryn's body. Given the circumstances, it was ridiculous to feel happy, but she did.

The light faded completely. Alana's eyes were closing. She was half asleep when a shudder ran through Deryn, waking her.

"Alana."

"What?"

"Can you see anything?"

"It's too dark. I…"

The prickle of goose bumps ran over Alana's skin, with ice flowing after. A thin faint line of blue danced before her. She rubbed her eyes, but it would not go.

"It's coming from the stone coffin, isn't it?"

"I think so."

"The legend said the Witch-Lord would rise again." Deryn sounded nearly as alarmed as Alana felt.

"It's just a story."

"Part of the story was true."

"The dead stay dead. My family may not know everything about magic, but I'm sure…" Alana clenched her teeth. Just how sure was she? Her heart was pounding.

"Maybe he wants his weapons back."

"Then he needs to go after Martez."

"The light's getting brighter."

"Or is it our eyes playing tricks?"

"I don't know."

Time trickled by as Alana sat, staring at the light. Even with it, the room was now so dark that she could see nothing else. Sometimes the light seemed to swell, sometimes it faded to almost nothing. The line wobbled and swam through her vision. Logically Alana knew it was tiredness. The light was unchanging, and if the Witch-Lord had not risen in the first hour, he probably was not going to rise at all. Exhaustion washed over her, threatening to sweep her away. Yet if she gave in, what nightmares would she endure?

In the end, Alana did not get the choice. The blue line finally dissolved in the blackness of sleep.

❖

The wayside fountain delivered a steady stream into its stone basin. Deryn dipped her tin mug in, raised it to her lips, and swallowed, but her mouth stayed dry. A closer check on the mug revealed the wide crack in the bottom. Deryn sighed and put the mug down. She bent to scoop up water in her cupped hands, but now the basin also was empty and the fountain had dried up. It was getting beyond a joke. She was really quite thirsty.

Deryn jerked awake and opened her eyes. The taunting dream faded, but things were not going to get any better. Before long, hallucinations would plague their waking hours as well.

During the night, she had slid down the wall and now lay on her back on the cold floor. Above her, a faint hint of daylight misted the ceiling of the tomb. As far as she could guess, she had slept most of the morning away, a consequence of staying awake half the night, staring at the blue light from the stone coffin. The multitude of cuts and bruises had made getting to sleep all the more difficult, as did the guilt at her failure.

I'm sorry, Shea. I'd have killed the bastard for you if I could. Should have spent more time practicing my aim.

Alana lay curled beside her, a soft weight on her shoulder. Deryn brushed her dry lips across Alana's forehead. Another source of guilt. What had she been thinking of? When she had seen the first clues that thieves were at work, she should have gone back at once. Nevin and Ross might not be any help, but not everyone in the region was so useless. Regan would have loved organizing another, bigger, better-armed citizens' posse.

Was it just that I wanted to spend a day alone with you and managed to convince myself it would be okay? Deryn grimaced at the thought. But maybe, just maybe, she could make amends.

Deryn eased herself from beneath the head on her shoulder, but the cold had stiffened her bruises, making her clumsy, and despite her attempt to be careful, the movement was enough to wake the woman beside her.

Alana groaned and rubbed her face. "So yesterday wasn't just a bad dream."

"Nope. None of it. I'm afraid."

"How about the light from the sarcophagus? It's not there now. Did I see it or did I fall asleep and dream it?"

"The stone coffin? That was real. I saw it too."

"What do you think it was?"

"I've got an idea, but rather than guess, I'm going to find out." Deryn stood, wincing at the complaints from her injuries. "I'm going to open the coffin."

Alana sat up, looking startled. "You're going to do what?"

"I want to find the source of the light. Whatever was shining through the crack beneath the lid."

"But it's gone now, hasn't it?"

"I don't think so. It's just too faint to see unless there's total darkness."

"But—"

"Do you remember the story about the Witch-Lord? I know you didn't stay for all of it on the Night of the Lost, but you said you'd heard it before."

"Which part?"

"His mistake when he fell from the tower. The story said he should have held on to his shield, because that would have saved him from being hurt, but his bow was his favorite, so he held on to that instead and broke his neck when he hit the ground."

"I remember, although I've heard variations on it."

"But they all mention the bow as his favorite?"

"Yes."

"Yet the bow wasn't here. I'm right about that, aren't I? I know I wasn't in a state to pay much attention, but I don't remember anyone mentioning it."

"No. There wasn't a bow. I assumed it was one point where the story got things wrong." Alana frowned. "You think the bow's in the sarcophagus?"

"Maybe, if the bow really was his pride and joy, he wanted to be entombed with it."

Deryn hobbled over and placed her hands on the stone coffin. The lid was going to be heavy. Would they be able to move it? She looked back. "Could you lend me a hand here?"

Alana got to her feet. "Okay. Supposing the bow is in there, how will it help us?"

"In the story, it shot magical bolts that could go through stone."

"And?"

"The door is stone."

Judging by her expression, Alana was not convinced, but she

added her strength to the effort. The pain of her injuries made Deryn grit her teeth, and at first, all for nothing. The lid did not budge.

Deryn changed the angle of pressure. "Maybe there's a lip on it. If we both push up under here…"

Alana placed her hands beside Deryn's. This time, the sound of hollow grinding came as the lid slid a half a finger's width—not much, but a start.

"It's moving."

"I saw."

Inch by inch, they slid the stone slab back. The blue light shone out from within, getting stronger as the gap between lid and base widened. At last, the opening was wide enough for them to peer in.

A tall skeleton lay in state. Its clothing had rotted long ago, but the items that remained showed its wealth. The gem-encrusted scabbard alone was worth more than Deryn would earn in her lifetime. A gold circlet still adorned the skull. Precious stones glinted on the rings around its finger bones. The leather belt was shriveled and decayed, but the engraved ivory buckle was unspoiled by time.

Despite these riches, the only thing that caught Deryn's interest was the shining blue bow. "You're sure the dead stay dead?"

"Yes."

The demon-spawn healer ought to know better than anyone. Deryn still felt a twinge of anxiety, but they were out of options. She squeezed her hand through the gap and was just able to snare the top with her fingertip. The shaft slid free from the skeletal grasp.

The bow was a little bigger than her own, but not the size of a full longbow. It had been left in a strung state. In fact, as far as Deryn could tell, the string was an integral part of the weapon. It also glowed with the blue light and could not be removed. She could only hope that the magical material did not stretch or weaken with age.

"No quiver." Alana peered into the coffin. "And no arrows."

"According to Regan's version of the story, it didn't need them."

"Oh well." Alana reached in and pulled out a thick gold chain. "If nothing else, we'll die rich."

"And can amuse ourselves thinking how sick Martez would be if he knew what he'd left behind."

Deryn placed her fingers on the string and tugged gently, testing the tension. It seemed good. She pulled a little farther and saw a new shimmering start to appear. At first it was hazy, but then it solidified into the shape of an arrow, on the string and ready to shoot.

"Let's see what it does to the door."

Deryn was hoping for an explosion and for the stone to crack. Instead, the arrow hit silently and vanished.

"Shit." Deryn let her hands drop to her side, and stared forlornly at the still intact door.

"That wasn't very impressive."

"I know. Maybe the magic has worn out over the years."

"The helmet still worked."

"Yes." Deryn shuddered at the memory and turned away. "I'm sor—"

"Hang on." Alana had gone to inspect the door up close.

"What?"

"The arrow did exactly what was claimed."

"It did?"

"Come here. You need to see it from the right angle."

Deryn peered at the spot where the arrow had hit. A small circle of daylight shone through. "Oh yes."

The hole was no more than a quarter inch across, looking as if it had been drilled through the stone by a master mason.

Alana grinned. "It's a bit small to climb through. But I guess, with enough of them, the whole door will cave in. Or maybe we can cut a line, and knock out a corner."

"It'll take a long time."

"Then it's just as well that we haven't got anything else we need to do. If you get tired, I'll take over."

❖

Several hundred arrows later, the top section of one door finally gave way and crashed to the ground, creating a gap big enough for them to squeeze though. By then, it was late afternoon, and Deryn's thirst was becoming a major source of discomfort, but just standing in the open air was good. Deryn's smile was so broad it made her face ache.

Alana looked equally happy. She wrapped her arms around Deryn's waist and rested her forehead in the hollow of Deryn's neck. "I never thought we'd get out."

"Uh." Deryn's stomach melted and sank down to flop around on other, lower, parts of her body.

Alana seemed unaware of the effect she had caused. "It looks like the rest of your life might be a little bit longer than you'd expected last night. Are you having second thoughts?"

Alana's tone was light, teasing, but her words set off a wave of doubt in Deryn. *I did say that, didn't I? Does it still sound so good?* Maybe, but the doubt was trying to turn itself into panic. Alana's body pressed against hers made Deryn feel as if the other half of her soul was coming home, and she did not want that. She was complete in herself. She always had been in the past. Could she go back to that state? Did she want to? *Which thought is more frightening, losing Alana or losing myself?*

Mainly what Deryn wanted was the time to answer that question, and be sure her answer was the right one. She needed space, to think things through. She peeled Alana off her, and immediately felt the emptiness flow back into her life, but she tried to ignore it. "We've got to be careful. We don't know where Martez is."

Alana sighed. "You're probably right. Especially since you're in a worse state to outrun the outlaws than before. What do you think he'll be doing now?"

"Making plans to go on the rampage and steal as much as he can. We need to get back to Neupor and raise the alarm, but we don't want to bump into him on the way." Deryn raised the bow. "This will give us the advantage in a ranged fight. We need to pick our battleground."

Alana scooped up Deryn's free hand, kissed each knuckle in turn, and then let it drop. "You'd better lead the way. I haven't got a clue how to find our way home."

"Right."

Deryn took a moment to steady herself and then crept back to the main valley where they had found Alejo's body. She forced herself to concentrate on her surroundings, alert for the first hint of danger, but it was not easy. Her head and heart were in turmoil. She wanted to hold Alana's hand again so much it frightened her. She was lost and unable to fight. So why risk making a fool of herself by trying? *Because it's a whole new world for you, and on occasion you can be a bit of a coward. Alana deserves better than that.*

Sometimes, the voice of Deryn's conscience sounded exactly like Brise.

❖

When the hovels of Neupor came into sight, Deryn felt some of the knots leave her shoulders. Her relief was not only due to the prospect of getting reinforcements. Her bruises were sending jolts of pain through her limbs with each step. Deryn was aware that Alana kept giving her sideways looks, but was thankfully silent. She desperately wanted to lie down, rest, and work out what she was going to do. Before she took any irrevocable steps, Deryn wanted to reassure herself that it was a good idea, and that she could live in a serious relationship with Alana. Although if she was honest with herself, the real issue was whether she could live without it.

The farmlands looked as peaceful as ever in the soft twilight. Deryn tried to draw strength from the view, while gritting her teeth against the raw aches in her legs and sides. How could any great danger or drama play out here? The run-down farmsteads were not the right backdrop, the smell of wood smoke and cow dung too prosaic. The miserable backwater was so tediously boring it could not be anything other than safe.

Two miles outside the village, a side track led away from the main road, climbing the hillside. Alana stopped and pointed. "My cottage is up there."

"Yes. I know."

"So why are you going straight past the turning?"

"It's not the…" Deryn drew a breath. *Please, just a bit more time.*

Alana caught hold of her hand. "You're coming home with me."

"Don't I get a say in it?"

"No."

The certainty in Alana's voice only emphasized the doubts overwhelming Deryn. She pulled her hand free and stepped back. "I'm sorry. I have to go to Neupor."

"Why?"

"In case you've forgotten, there's a gang of dangerous outlaws on the loose. Sergeant Nevin needs to be told." The absurdity of what she was saying only added to Deryn's discomfort.

Alana sighed. "Okay. I'll come with you."

"No. You should go home."

Deryn's clipped tone must have registered. Alana looked first surprised and then annoyed. "You mean you want to run away again."

"No. I've just got to…" *Run. Now. Because otherwise I'll never be able to run again.*

Alana rubbed her forehead as if she had a headache. "Look, I know you have issues because of your past."

"I know that you know. And the bits I haven't told you, you've found out by trawling through my head." Deryn told herself she meant it as a joke, but even she had to admit the delivery was off, and it would not have been very funny regardless of how she had said it.

"If I could have stopped doing it I would. I've got quite enough problems of my own, without taking on yours." Alana was starting to sound angry. Deryn could not really blame her.

"I didn't mean it as an attack."

"It sounded like it. I don't understand why you're suddenly so… so…" Alana waved her hand, clearly hunting for the word she wanted.

"So what?"

"You really do want to make an argument of this, don't you?"

"You're the one who's arguing."

"Me! Don't be stupid. It's you."

"That sounds to me like you're arguing."

"Right. Fine. I'll see you around sometime."

Deryn watched Alana storm away. She opened her mouth, about to call out. But what? That she was sorry? That she knew she was being stupid?

"I'm sorry, Alana. I'm stupid." Deryn spoke the words too softly for the departing woman to have any hope of hearing. "But I'm scared. I've got used to being me, and how I act, and what I do and don't do. It's all going to change. I don't know who I'm going to become, and it will take a bit of getting used to. Give me time, please."

Alana was now fifty yards away, fading into the dull light of an overcast dusk. Deryn was seized by the urge to run after her, but her legs would not move.

Tomorrow. I'll go visit her tomorrow. Give her a bit of time to calm down, and I can have a night to sleep on it. I'll feel better when I don't ache so much. I'm going to be spending a lot of time with her. One more night to get my head in order won't matter. She's angry, but maybe if I take her some flowers...

Deryn felt her face freeze in an expression of utter amazement. Her shoulders sagged. She had never given anyone flowers before in her life. Never even thought about doing it. What had gotten into her, and more importantly, would the flowers work the way she had been told, and make Alana happy? What flowers were available in winter? Would an artistic posy of cones and berries work instead?

This is bad. Why even try to fight it?

For a moment, Deryn teetered on the point of giving in to her heart and hobbling after Alana, but then she turned away and started her slow, lonely walk for the last few miles to Neupor.

When Alana got over being angry she was going to be very upset. She felt she owed it to herself. What was going on with Deryn? Never had Alana felt such a strong urge to throttle anyone—well, anyone apart from her parents. She marched up the hill, trying to vent the anger in long firm strides. This had the added advantage that she would reach the security of her cottage quicker, so she could shut out the world and give way to the upset. *Damn her.*

The day was almost over. The sun would have set behind the mountains, were it not that clouds had rolled over from the west and covered two-thirds of the sky. Rain or even snow was likely. Fortunately, Alana was almost home. When she rounded the next clump of trees she would be a stone's throw from her own vegetable patch. Lights from Eldora's farmhouse glimmered in the dusk, a short way off her route.

Alana's stride faltered. Should she call in on the way past? Although she had no desire to talk to anyone, it would count as basic politeness. Surely Eldora had been concerned when she and Deryn did not return the previous day. She ought to let them know that she was all right, and maybe give a warning about the danger at hand. It was also the case that if anyone saw light coming from her cottage, then Eldora would be certain to send someone to check on her. Alana sighed and changed course for the farmstead. Much better to get the conversation over now, and on her own terms.

A lone sheepdog whined and barked from the barn as Alana stomped into the farmyard. Even in her preoccupied state, the sound was enough to distract her from brooding about Deryn. She glanced at the closed door. The wooden pole had been slid in place, barring it shut. Had the dog been locked in by mistake? In which case, why had nobody gone to let it out? Maybe it was ill and had been put there in quarantine.

However, now Alana's attention had been caught, other discrepancies jumped out. No voices came from the farmhouse, and Eldora's large family was normally anything but quiet. The cows were clustered by the barn, their udders swollen and pendulous. A hoe was lying discarded in the mud by her foot.

Alana came to an uncertain stop and stared down at it. The cows had not been milked, and tools were not something the farmers would neglect and let rust. Something was very wrong. Alana's stomach contracted in a knot. There had to be other possible explanations for what that something might be, but a sickening dread gripped her.

Alana took a step back and bumped into someone who had crept up behind her. She yelped in shock.

"You don't really want to go, do you?" A hand landed heavily on her shoulder and a cold edge touched her neck, pressed hard enough to let her feel the blade's sharpness, although not quite enough to draw blood.

Alana was rooted to the spot, until a shove propelled her toward the farmhouse door.

Martez and the rest of his gang were in the main room, relaxing by the fire and helping themselves to Eldora's beer and food. They looked up as the door opened.

"Look who I've found sneaking around." A hard thump in the small of her back sent Alana stumbling into the middle of the room.

Martez was the only one who managed to mask his surprise, but Alana felt a degree of satisfaction when she sensed his bout of confusion and alarm. This was one case where she felt no guilt at all in probing inside someone else's head, and now the talisman was not blurring her perception, the boundaries and nuances were so much clearer, so much easier to read.

Martez was sprawled in his chair, feigning a casual lack of concern, his legs stretched out straight. He snapped his fingers. "Bring her here."

An outlaw grabbed Alana's elbow and yanked her forward so she stood scant inches from the tip of Martez's boots, with her back to the fire. She saw that she was not the only prisoner in the room. Eldora and Jed were bundled in the corner behind the door, their wrists and ankles tied. There was no sign of the rest of the family. Alana prayed they were unharmed. The memory of what had happened to Deryn's family flashed through her mind. The floor did not show any bloodstains, but it was no guarantee. A better guide was that although Eldora was scared and angry, she was not grief-stricken.

The four other members of Martez's gang had taken positions around the walls, watching eagerly. Their mood of savage anticipation did not auger well.

"There was another way out of the Witch-Lord's tomb." Martez reclaimed her attention. He took a deep swig from his tankard, looking thoughtful. "Silly of me. I should have checked. I guess I let myself get a touch overexcited by my new toys."

"What are you doing here?"

Martez shook his head, mimicking disbelief. "My first thought is that you don't seem to have grasped the situation. I'm the one who gets to ask questions. And my second thought is you must be very stupid. Isn't it obvious? I'm taking over. Whatever I want is mine."

"The marshals might have something to say about that."

"I don't think so. Any marshals with sense will be taking my orders pretty soon. With the Witch-Lord's weapons, I think I can take care of any that don't. I'm going to be the new ruler around here. But I won't be greedy. I'll become king of Neupor. Oakan as well…Sattle if I feel like it. That'll do me."

You don't know what you're up against. Any half-competent fire-mage will turn you to smoldering ash before you can grab your weapons. Alana did not say it. This far from Ellaye, the demon-spawn nobility were little more than a distant fable. Most commoners did not understand the power they wielded, and nothing would be achieved by

Alana trying to explain, other than putting herself at risk. Martez was insane with self-love. He would not believe her because he did not want to. Alana could tell that much from the swirl of his emotions.

Martez could defeat the marshal's men. Sergeant Nevin would present no obstacle at all. Maybe a weak demon-spawn marshal might not be up to the challenge that the magical weapons posed. This did not mean that King Alvarro II would sit back and let an upstart fool carve a chunk off Galvonia. Whatever weaknesses he might have, Alvarro was a very good fire-mage. The outlaws would stand no chance. Alana's guess was Martez and all his gang would be dead inside a month. The only issue was to limit the damage they did before then.

Martez's smile broadened. "Now we have the rules sorted. My first question. Where's your friend?"

"I don't know."

"I don't believe you."

"We parted when we got out of the forest. She said she was going to get help. She didn't tell me any more of her plans."

"How about if I see if I can do something to improve your memory?" Martez stood and stretched lazily. His wide yawn added to the theatrical display of nonchalance. "You remember these, don't you?"

The Witch-Lord's sword and shield were propped against the side of his chair. Martez, patted them, as if they were pets, then scooped the helmet up from where it hung over the armrest.

A wave of fear swept around the room, so sharp that Alana flinched. In the corner, Jed whimpered, which tied in with the strongest epicenter of the emotion, but even the gang members were terrified. Clearly Martez had been using the helmet to intimidate Eldora's family, and any attempt to protect his own followers had failed.

But had he really tried, Alana wondered. She could feel his love of power, the joy he took in dominating others, the pleasure he felt in causing suffering. Had he also enjoyed scaring his own followers? Did he feel more secure, thinking he had intimidated them into obeying him without question?

Martez took a half-step toward her and smiled, waving the helmet tauntingly. "What do you think? If I put this helmet on, will your memory improve? Will you be able to remember where your friend with the twitchy knife hand is?"

The farmhouse door crashed open with the force of a kick.

"You don't need to ask Alana where I am. I can tell you myself." Deryn stood in the doorway.

Martez spun to face her. A bolt of disbelief shot through him, surely due in part to Deryn's dramatic arrival, and in part to the unmistakable shimmering blue light that played over the bow, half drawn in her hands. His surprise was followed by a quiver of doubt, which was in turn washed away by anger and then malice. Alana could trace them all, as clearly as it they were laid out on a page. She could not be fooled by his manner, which did not waver in its disdainful self-assurance.

"Oh good. That'll save us having to leave the fire to find you. I've spent too much of the last few years being cold."

"You'll be warm enough in hell."

"So I've been told. But you'll get to find out before me."

"This is the Witch-Lord's bow."

"I guessed, but there are five of us. You won't be able to kill us all."

"I'll shoot the first one that moves. I'll probably get the second one as well. Who wants to try their luck?"

Alana held her breath. Would the desperate bluff work? And it was a bluff, because if the outlaws thought about it, they had little to lose by charging at Deryn as a group. True, she would kill one or two, but not all. Whereas, if they threw down their weapons and allowed themselves to be taken prisoner, then they would all assuredly hang. Yet none seemed willing to take the lead, and when there was no reply, Deryn continued.

"Okay. You can put that helmet down on the floor, but make sure you do it very slowly. Any sudden movement and I might just let go of this bowstring."

Deryn's eyes were darting back and forth, covering all the outlaws in the room, but she kept the bow trained steadily on Martez. The outlaw leader was frozen, looking at the Witch-Lord's helmet in his hands, as if he was evaluating his chances, but then he started to lower it.

A loud clank from the corner made Alana jump. One of the bandits had knocked a pewter tankard onto the floor, either by accident or as a diversion. Deryn's head snapped toward the sound and the bow started to follow. Alana could tell that it was only a split-second lapse in the

Iron Wolf's concentration, but that was all Martez needed. He ducked to the side, out of the line the blue arrow that flashed harmlessly across the room, while at the same time slipping the helmet over his head.

Screams of terror erupted all around. Deryn sank to her knees, her face twisted in horror. Despite the fact that his own followers were affected as much as anyone else, Martez was unconcerned. He rested his fists on his hips and threw back his head, laughing in delight at the power he wielded. The helmet was not a weapon for anyone who wanted to keep their friends around. Yet the fear it projected was merely a rootless overlay, feeding off nothing. Alana could read it as easily as Martez's emotions, and she could see its foundation and its limits. Without effort, she blocked it from her mind.

Martez had his back to her, confident that she presented no greater threat than anyone else in the room. Despite the advantage of surprise this gave her, Alana needed a weapon of some sort. Martez was tall and well built. Living rough in the wilderness showed no sign of weakening him and he would be able to overpower her easily in a straight fight, even without the Witch-Lord's sword, which he now picked up. He sauntered across the room, idly swinging the sword, like a cow herder waving a switch, but his intentions toward Deryn had nothing idle about them.

Alana had mere seconds to act, and the only thing at hand was a pile of cut wood, laid ready beside the hearth. She grabbed a heavy log, a foot and a half long and thick enough that the fingers of both hands could barely touch around it. At least she did not need to worry about moving stealthily. Martez stood no chance of hearing her over the uproar of screaming and crying.

As well as its magical ability, the helmet would surely fulfill the normal function of protecting Martez's head. Alana swung her makeshift club down with all the strength she could muster, striking him square across his shoulders at the base of the neck. Martez stumbled to his knees, dropping the sword. Alana tossed aside the log, clasped the helmet in both hands, and ripped it from his head.

The Witch-Lord had not gone merely for show when creating his magic devices. The helmet was made of half-inch-thick steel, heavy in Alana's hands. She raised it up and then swung it down, cracking the kneeling outlaw over the back of his head. Martez keeled over like a felled tree.

Still, the danger was far from over. Across the room, Deryn was still on her knees, shaking her head as if to clear it. When she looked up, her eyes were dazed. The full force of the helmet had been directed at her and she was recovering slower than the others in the room.

The female outlaw was the first to seize the advantage. She yelled a challenge and charged while ripping a dagger from its sheath on her belt. The distance between her and Deryn was a matter of three paces, giving no time to stand or fully draw the bow. Deryn loosed an arrow from half set, with the bow held horizontal at her waist. Even so, her aim was good enough to hit its target. The blue arrow vanished as it struck and the woman screamed and spun away, her left hand clasping her right shoulder. Blood streamed between her fingers.

A second outlaw also rushed the door, only to trip and fall. Alana was still looking for the cause and to see if he would rise again, when the helmet was batted from her grasp. Martez was back on his knees.

The helmet rolled across the floor. Martez scrambled after it, but he had left the sword where it had fallen. Alana bent and scooped it up. She struck out, intending to do no more than use the extended reach to flick the helmet out of Martez's grasp, but she did not allow for the sword's heaviness or keenness. The weight pulled on her wrist and the tip of the blade sagged groundward, failing to reach the helmet. It did not matter. The sword sliced through the flagstones as if they were paper. Martez's flesh offered no more resistance. He yelled in pain and snatched his bleeding left hand back from his prize, leaving three fingers behind on the floor.

Footsteps sounded to Alana's right. She whirled around. The outlaw planted his feet firmly, his sword held out before him. The point flicked left then right, drawing Alana's eyes with it, and then he leapt forward, thrusting the blade directly at her. Alana's guts contracted in a spasm. She did not have any sort of martial training. She could not parry to save her life, and that was exactly what she had to do—or would have, had she been holding a normal sword.

The outlaw's attack was coming straight for her heart. Alana brought the Witch-Lord's sword across in a clumsy reflex counter, and the outlaw's blade was cut in two. The momentum of Alana's wild swing carried the sword on, slicing through the man's chest with the same lack of effort as it had cut through everything else. In the space of a half second, the outlaw's emotions went from surprise at the pain, then shock, then confusion, then disbelief, and then nothing. He dropped, lifeless, to the floor.

Alana stared at his body in horror. She had not meant to kill him. She had not meant to take his life. In unthinking revulsion, she tossed the sword down beside him.

"I'm sorry." Alana's words sounded so weak, stupid, and utterly inadequate.

"Behind you!" Eldora shouted.

Alana lifted her head, confused. The outlaw was dead, on the floor. She had killed him. Then she heard someone else. The fighting was not over. Alana twisted to look back over her shoulder. The last outlaw brandished twin daggers in his hands. Already he was within striking distance. His face was locked in a snarl of rage. He swung one dagger across in a lightning-fast blur of motion, slashing out at her throat, and Alana was frozen on the spot. Too much had happened too quickly. She could not move.

A flicker of blue light appeared in the middle of the outlaw's forehead. It immediately changed to a red dot and the dagger dropped from his hand. He jolted to a stop, then stumbled a step back before his knees gave out and he started to crumple. His eyes glazed over and closed as he fell. Alana stared at his motionless form on the ground in incomprehension. A sound at the door made her look over. Deryn was standing there, still with the Witch-Lord's bow held out in an archer's pose.

Deryn lowered the bow. "Are you all right?"

Alana nodded and lifted her hand to her head, as if it could steady her thoughts. Now the battle was really over. The room was quiet, apart from the crackle of flames in the hearth, her pounding heartbeat, and whimpers from Martez and the female outlaw. In the corner, Jed was sitting astride the back of the outlaw who had fallen—tripped by him and Eldora at a guess—and using the rope binding his wrists to choke the man.

Eldora tapped his arm. "That's good enough, son. He's out cold. You can stop now."

Alana turned back to the man she had killed. Her initial shock was fading, but the awful guilt was not. She listened with half an ear to the conversation as Deryn removed Eldora's bonds.

Deryn appeared at her side. She put her hand on Alana's arm. "Are you sure you're okay?"

"I'm not hurt."

"We need to get Martez and what's left of his gang tied up and under guard as soon as possible."

"Right." Still Alana could not tear her eyes from the dead outlaw.

"You don't look okay."

"I'm just…I'll be fine. Do what you have to."

"If you're sure."

"Yes."

"I'll talk to you later." Deryn's tone was quiet and meaningful.

Alana nodded, but did she want to talk? Deryn's phrase "what's left of the gang" was rolling around in her head. One part of the gang was no longer there because she had killed him. Suddenly, all Alana wanted was to get away and forget it all. Forget that she had taken someone's life. She could not bear to be in the room an instant longer, staring at the evidence of what her own hands had done.

Alana retreated a step, then turned and fled from the farmhouse.

Red firelight shone beneath the door of Alana's cottage. Deryn raised her hand and knocked. When she received no answer, she knocked again and tried the handle, but the door was barred on the inside. The urge to flee tried to establish a foothold in her mind, telling her that she had made the effort to talk, and that was all she was obliged to do, but the cowardly thought stood no chance. Deryn needed to see Alana.

She took a step back and called out, "Alana, if you don't open the door, I'm going to kick it in." The threat was empty. Even were she fit, Deryn would not have carried it out, and in her current state she would have trouble managing the feat.

Alana did not call her bluff, although she did no more than lift the latch, leaving the door to swing open on its own. Deryn followed her in, uninvited. The only light in the room came from the fire burning in the hearth. Judging by the state of the bedclothes, Alana had not been asleep. She slumped down into a chair and sat, staring blankly into the flames, paying no attention to her visitor.

Deryn took the other chair and studied her with concern. "Alana, what's wrong? It's not just that you're pissed off at me."

"I killed a man."

"Ah." This one Deryn knew. She had seen it before in her comrades, enough times that she should have guessed. A moment's thought would have told her the aristocratic healer was unlikely to have ever been in a fight to the death before. But what could she say? Her own experience was of little help. "It was a man who was trying to kill you."

"I know it's stupid." Alana wiped her eyes. "And I know you have to deal with it all the time."

"Not really. It doesn't happen very often. Mostly I'm fighting windigos."

"But when it does happen, how do you cope?"

"I think it gets easier with time." Deryn pursed her lips. "Some Wolves never get used to it. I wish I could say I know what you're going through, but the first time I killed, I was too young to understand what I'd done. All I cared about was that they'd taken my mom and dad away from me."

"You'd think, as an adult, I'd be able to cope better."

"Doesn't work like that. Children can be so self-absorbed. I was too upset to care about anyone else."

Alana slipped down in her chair. Her eyes were still locked on the hearth, but then she gave a sad half-smile. "Thank you."

"For what?"

"For putting things in perspective. I've been wallowing."

"You're allowed."

"No. You were just a child, and you'd suffered much more. I should—" Alana broke off, chewing her lip. "How is Eldora? Her family? Had they been hurt?"

"They're fine. The gang had the rest of the family shut up in the barn. They wanted to keep a couple in the house as hostages so the others wouldn't try running away. Eldora and her son got picked out as the two most likely to cause trouble if unwatched."

"Good call. Those are who I'd pick too." Although Alana still sounded withdrawn, she had a touch of humor in her voice.

"The gang wanted to keep an eye on them. But it worked out well for us. They were pretty sharp. Even though they were tied up, they took care of one outlaw. They tripped him over and half throttled him."

Alana glanced across quickly, not long enough to count as eye contact, but it marked a further improvement in her state of mind. "I'm sorry. I shouldn't have run off and left you to deal with everything."

"It's okay. There wasn't much to do. We freed the others in the barn. Eldora sent one of her kids to Neupor with a message for Regan and Nevin. She's organized the rest to keep a watch on Martez and his friends."

"Martez—how is he? I didn't mean to cut his hand."

"Really? If I were you, I'd be regretting I'd only taken off three fingers."

"He kept going for the helmet. If he'd grabbed the sword he'd have done much better."

"He should have listened to the legend. The Witch-Lord valued his bow too much, and forgot the shield. Martez likes scaring people. He's a bully at heart. The helmet was his idea of the perfect weapon." Deryn tilted her head to the side. "It was pretty amazing you got it off him. I don't know how you did it. I couldn't bear to look at him."

"It's mind magic. I could see what the helmet was doing and I knew how to block it. It was a fake emotion."

The words delivered an uncomfortable dig to Deryn's conscience. She licked her lips. "Um…on that subject, I'm sorry about what I said before, about you reading my emotions. I was being an asshole."

"I overreacted."

"No, you didn't. It was me, or part of me, a really stupid part. I was frightened, and I let it take over."

"Frightened?"

"Yes. I was scared about having a relationship with you, and how much it's going to change me."

"I don't want you to change."

"You've already done it. The frightened part of me wanted my life to stay the way it's always been. But that can't happen, because I'm not the same person anymore."

"I don't think people change that easily."

"It feels like it." Deryn stopped, trying on different emotions to see how they fitted. "Maybe I've been changing for a while, and meeting you has made me notice it. But after we parted I went about twenty steps down the road before I realized that walking away from you was the most stupid thing I've ever done in my life, and if you knew what the competition for that title is like…" Deryn gave a wry grimace. "You were going too fast for me to catch up. I was still some way back when you reached Eldora's farm, but I was just close enough to see the outlaw take you prisoner."

"Thanks for coming to my rescue."

"I had to. Though it wasn't the smartest move on my part."

"I'm pleased you did."

"It worked out okay, but I should have gone for help. Bursting in like I did, I hadn't really thought it through. It wasn't very clever of me. I was outnumbered and I wasn't in a good shape for a fight anyway. But I couldn't leave you."

Alana bounded up from her chair. "Of course. You're injured. I'm sorry. I forgot. I shouldn't have let you just sit there talking." She grabbed an open basket from her dresser. "Here. I've got stuff for your bruises."

"It's all right. I'll be—"

"No. Sit still." Alana dropped the basket beside Deryn's chair and knelt. "I've got what I need here. Take off your shirt."

Only the matter-of-fact delivery stopped Deryn sliding to the ground in a molten pool, but her hands could not move. Alana did not wait. Seemingly utterly unaware of the effect she was having, she slipped open the row of buttons on Deryn's heavy woolen shirt and tugged up the lighter cotton undershirt.

"Ooh. That's nasty. But I've got some salve here, with more wolfsbane. It should be fine." Alana opened a bottle and poured liquid onto a sheep's-wool pad.

Deryn gasped at the contact.

"It probably tingles." Intent on her work, Alana did not look up.

"It's not that."

"The bruises won't—"

"It's that you're touching me."

Alana froze mid-action and looked up to meet Deryn's eyes. "I'm trying to concentrate on treating your injuries."

"Don't."

"You don't want me to do this?"

"Don't concentrate on being a healer. Concentrate on me." Deryn shifted off her chair and sat on the floor.

Alana's eyes were dark hollows in the firelight, with only the flickering red flames reflected in their depths. Her lips were parted slightly, maybe in surprise, maybe in desire, maybe in preparation to speak. They were every bit as kissable as the first time Deryn had seen them. This time, there was no reason to hold back. Deryn leaned forward and claimed them.

Deryn liked to think she was good at kissing. She certainly had practiced enough, with more women than she could count. But in the past, kissing had only been a way to arouse passion, one of the required steps along the way, something expected from her as a precursor to sex, and never an end in itself. This was different. The faint sting from her cut lip was lost in the softness and the sweetness. Deryn's need and desire overrode all other awareness. Alana's mouth was the only thing that existed. Kissing her was the only thing Deryn wanted to do.

Eventually, Alana broke away. Her breath was ragged. "We should stop."

"Why?"

"I'm worried I'm going to lose all self-control."

Deryn smiled. "Really? I'm counting on it."

"You might have a cracked rib, or a concussion."

"I think I'd know by now if I had."

"Even so, you're injured, and I don't want to hurt you."

"Then you'll have to be very gentle with me."

Alana rested her forehead on Deryn's shoulder. "I guess we could take it slow and careful. See how things go."

"I think you could talk me into that."

Once they were in bed, Alana's naked body was soft and welcoming, pressed against hers. They lay facing each other, while their mouths and tongues played a teasing game of tag. The warmth of Alana's skin soaked into Deryn like sunlight on a summer's day. She burrowed her hand between them, her thumb seeking the hardness of a nipple. Alana moaned into her mouth when she succeeded.

Deryn's hand moved on, in slow exploration, stroking the side of Alana's breast, running over the furrows of her ribs, and cupping the soft mound of her ass. She slid her hand down farther behind Alana's leg and pulled it up, over her hip. Her fingers traced the line of hard tendons at the back of Alana's knee. The weight lying on her drew a sting from a bruise, but it did not matter and the position allowed Deryn to slip her own knee up between Alana's legs, so that her thigh pressed against the wetness there.

Alana's back arched, forcing her stomach yet harder against Deryn and she gasped, but then she pulled away slightly and stared into Deryn's face.

"What are you worried about?"

Deryn had not been aware that she was. "You're reading my emotions again?"

"No. I can see it in your expression."

"I'm not wor—"

Deryn stopped. Was she? And if so, what about? But there was a niggle—and maybe a tad more than just a niggle. Why? It was not as if she was inexperienced. Far from it. Deryn had no doubts about her ability to satisfy a lover. She knew the spots on a woman's body, inside and out. She could try each one in turn and discover which worked best for Alana. Deryn's mobility was impaired. Her bruises might not let her perform as acrobatically as she would have liked, but her hands and tongue were fine, and they were all she needed. She knew she could make Alana come, and more than once, but that was not the issue.

Deryn's goal was something far more ambitious, far more complex, and far more important. Could she do it?

"I want to make you happy."

Alana smiled. "You already are."

Neupor Marshal's Station, northern Galvonia
Five days later, diciembre 9, morning

The stubs on Martez's hand had scabbed over and were showing no sign of infection. Shock and the effect of blood loss had passed days before and he was now well enough to put on a display of sneering bravado.

"You know you ain't seen the last of me. You've taken these three fingers. Do you want to guess what I'm going to take from you in exchange?"

Alana ignored him as she replaced the bandage on his left hand. She could sense Deryn standing behind her, and knew her lover was watching the outlaw closely, ready for the first sign that action was needed. Not that it was likely. Martez's words were nothing but empty bluster. The rope around his wrists and the Witch-Lord's bow in Deryn's hands ensured that.

Alana turned her attention to the female outlaw. The woman was in a frailer state than her leader. Her skin was pale, yellowish rather than white. A fever had set in, slow to shift. She was now over the worst of it, but still very weak, and she would never regain the use of her right arm. Although for her, never was not going to be a long time. Once the outlaws were delivered to the marshal in Oakan, they would certainly be tried and hanged within days. The woman glared at Alana from under hooded eyes, but said nothing.

The last outlaw was in the best physical condition, having no injury apart from the raw rope burn around his throat. Yet, of the three, he was the one acting the most sorry for himself. He flinched when Alana put her hand on his wrist to judge his pulse rate and temperature, and cowered even farther into the corner.

"Why you bothering with checking him?" Nevin spat the question.

"I like to do a thorough job." The sergeant really was one of the most unpleasant people Alana had met. She did not envy Deryn, working with him every day. "If you want, I'll try to find someone to explain the concept to you."

A faint release of breath came from Deryn, choking her laughter. The mayor did not bother with restraint, and gave a loud chuckle. "Nice one."

Alana stood and backed out of the tiny cell in the marshal's station. "They're all okay to move. They'll be fine on the journey."

"About time. Get them on the wagon now. Move it." Nevin snapped the order almost before the words were out of Alana's mouth. Most likely to ensure that he was the one to give the command, rather than let Regan get a word in first.

Deryn and Ross transferred the outlaws, one at a time, from the tiny holding cell to the back of the wagon waiting outside. Alana followed Regan into the street and watched the checking of bonds on the outlaws' wrists and retying of their ankles.

An hour had passed since dawn, and although a faint covering of cloud blocked the sun, the light was bright. Alana looked along the road toward Oakan. The fields around Neupor were white. Snow had come later than normal that year. The first to settle that winter had arrived only two days before, and no more than six inches deep. The route to Oakan was still passable, and with luck, no more snow would fall that day, or tomorrow. The prisoners and escort would reach their destination without trouble from the weather and return safely.

Alana shivered, but not from the cold. A nagging sense of fear was scratching at the edges of her mind. Undoubtedly, it was only her picking up on Martez's vicious fury. However, Alana would not be happy until Deryn was back, safe, sound, and in her bed, and the sooner the better.

Once the work of loading the prisoners on the wagon was finished, Nevin also came out. He dropped the Witch-Lord's helmet and shield on the driver's footboard, but kept the sword in his hand as he clambered onto the seat.

"You can put that bow up here too." From Nevin's tone anyone might have thought Deryn had helped herself to the weapon as part of a juvenile prank.

What was wrong with the man, Alana wondered. Was he totally incapable of saying anything in a civil manner?

"Are you sure that's wise, sir?" The scornful way Deryn delivered the line made it clear she was not intimidated.

"Of course I'm fucking sure. You don't need it. I'll keep watch. I've got the sword if the prisoners try acting up. Ross can drive this thing. You can ride behind."

"Supposing they have some friends, lying in wait for us up ahead."

Nevin's face fell. "I thought you got them all."

"We got all that we know about. No saying if there are any more out there." Deryn nodded at Martez. "We can't trust any answer we get from him."

"They won't...it isn't...er..."

"What I was thinking, sir, was that I should ride ahead, with the bow, and make sure we don't head into an ambush."

"Sounds like a good idea to me," Regan said.

Nevin's face shifted through a few emotions before settling in its normal angry contempt. "Right. Well. You keep a fucking sharp watch. I'm sick of hauling your ass out of the fire. I don't want no fucking trouble on the way."

Nevin was clearly unnerved at the thought of any personal danger, and was covering with a more vitriolic display of stupidity than normal. The act was unlikely to fool anyone, even Ross. Alana certainly did not need her empathy to see through it—which she was very pleased about. This was one case where she was making full use of her newly gained ability to block people out. She had no wish to get drawn into the cesspit of Nevin's mind.

Deryn grinned as she turned away. Alana joined her by Tia's side. Deryn pulled the horse around to form a partial screen while she bent her head and kissed Alana. "I'll be back soon."

"Take good care."

"I always do."

"Nevin's an idiot."

"Is that supposed to be news to me?"

Alana rested her head on Deryn's shoulder. "You'd be safer without him along."

"But then he wouldn't get the chance to hand Martez and the weapons over to Marshal Palemon and claim all the glory and the reward."

"You're not going to let him get away with that?"

"No. But it won't stop him trying."

"Will the marshal believe him?"

"I doubt it. Even without me there to say my bit, I'm sure Palemon knows Nevin would never put himself in the way of anything resembling work or danger." Deryn's grin broadened still more. "I did enjoy scaring him about the ambush."

"Is one likely?"

"I'd say nonexistent. Martez would have wanted his whole gang along to feed his ego. But even if a couple were off somewhere else, they'd need to find out what happened, and then be willing to sit for days on the trail to Oakan, waiting for us to move him. On top of that, they'd be risking their lives against demon weapons." Deryn shook her head. "Outlaws don't stick together that well when things don't go their way."

Alana held Deryn tightly, hit by renewed fears. "Be very careful. Promise me that. I'm frightened, and I want you back safe."

"I promise. It'll be fine, even with Nevin."

As if hearing his name, the sergeant shouted. "Hey you, Deryn. Get your fucking ass on your horse. Don't think we don't know what you're doing round there. You can make out with your tart when you get back, not when there's work to do."

Alana grimaced. "Do you think you'll be able to make it all the way to Oakan without killing him?"

"I've survived so far. But why do you think I wanted to ride Tia far enough in front so I can't hear what he says?"

"Smart move." Alana smiled. "It's Ross I feel sorry for."

"He's good at ignoring things. Most of it goes over his head. Anyway, Nevin will probably get drunk and fall asleep before we've gone a few miles."

Deryn gave Alana one final kiss and hopped into her saddle. With a wave, she urged Tia forward, on the road to Oakan.

Alana stood outside the marshal's station, watching until rider and wagon vanished into the distance.

❖

The road wound its way along the bottom of the narrow valley, climbing ever higher. As it neared the top of the Pendorial Pass the walls closed in. This was the highest point on the road to Oakan, and the first stretch to be blocked each winter. The snow cover was a clear foot deeper than in Neupor. Not enough yet to close the route, but it could not be long before a heavier snowfall made the journey too risky to attempt in anything other than the gravest emergency. The river would be passable for a while longer, until that also froze.

On either side, the valley walls were covered with tall pines dressed in their new cloaks of white, but in places, bare rock lined the side of the route. These stone faces were all just a little too flat and a little too perpendicular to be natural.

Deryn considered one such cutting as she passed, and then the surrounding terrain. What sort of power must the Ancients have commanded that they would routinely knock holes in mountains, to save themselves the effort of going over minor obstructions? The section of hillside that the Ancients had removed would take a score of men months to hack away, using pickaxes. The easing of the route amounted to no more than a rise and drop of fifty feet, surely a negligible savings in the context of crossing the pass.

Deryn glanced over her shoulder, musing on the subject. The wagon with Ross in the driving seat was a short way behind, and showing no sign of trouble keeping up with her pace. Yet this would not have been the case over the original land contours, and the larger the wagon, the more trouble it would have. Maybe the question was, what sort of wagons did the Ancients use, that made steady inclines so advantageous? Did they never go anywhere by foot or horse?

Whatever justification the Ancients had for their monumental landscaping, Deryn was grateful, in that it shortened the journey time to Oakan for the wagon, if only by an hour, and increased the chances that she would be back in Alana's arms before the threatened heavy snowfall arrived.

The route to Oakan was a little over forty miles. If Nevin had gotten his ass out of bed early, they could have made the journey in a day, although at this time of year it would have meant starting and finishing in darkness. At the thought, Deryn shook her head despairingly. The chances of Nevin ever exerting himself were slightly lower than that of them all sprouting wings and flying to Oakan.

The upshot was that noon had passed and they were less than halfway. They would have to make an overnight stop at Buckie or Chatree, just north of Oakan, and finish the journey the next morning. If they could hand the prisoners over quickly, and turn straight around, maybe they could get back to Neupor before nightfall the day after—or maybe they could fly back.

Deryn rubbed her forehead to ease the frown. To be honest, the wasted time was an irritation, but not critical. The weather looked to be holding up well, and one more day away from Alana was not going to kill her, although Deryn was amazed at how much the thought chafed her heart. This whole relationship thing was affecting her more than she would ever have imagined.

The greatest problem was that, as far as Deryn knew, neither Buckie nor Chatree had a marshal station, or any secure lock-up for prisoners. Someone would have to stand watch over them all night. Nevin would certainly refuse to do it, and Ross could not be relied on. Deryn sighed. The outlook was not panning out well for her. Sleeping in the saddle was not one of her better skills, but if she wanted to stay awake that night, she ought to try a catch a little rest.

"Argh—" The scream from behind was cut short.

Deryn was reaching for her bow even as she wheeled Tia around.

The wagon was stopped thirty yards back, skewed across the road. One of the outlaws stood in the rear, holding the Witch-Lord's sword above his head in a two-handed grip. Ross had thrown himself from the driver's seat in a frantic bid to avoid the impending slash, but his feet appeared to be trapped in something and his shoulders were balanced ungainly across the carthorse's rump. The shouting and activity were unsettling the animal, and Ross was no longer holding the reins. If the horse decided to bolt, it would not be easy to stop. Other figures were moving in the wagon behind the swordsman, but they were not the immediate threat. Ross's arm had become tangled in the reins and his chances of escape were nonexistent.

Deryn drew the bowstring to her chin and released. The glowing blue arrow struck the standing man in the center of his chest and vanished. For the space of two seconds, the outlaw froze and then his knees gave way. He crumpled and keeled to the side, pitching over the side of the wagon onto the road. The sword fell from his grasp and clattered down beside him. Ross gave a yelp of surprise, but was unharmed.

Martez had been at the rear of the wagon, helping the injured female outlaw down. Her arm was draped over his shoulder. Ross's shout made Martez look up at the same moment that his dying follower landed like a sack of potatoes on the ground. Martez hesitated for only the barest instant. As Deryn again drew the bow, he shoved the woman away and ducked from under her arm. He dived, snatching up the dropped sword, and then carried on rolling.

Deryn loosed the arrow, but even as her fingers released, she knew her aim was off. The arrow did no more than nick Martez's shoulder. Before she could draw again, he was on his feet and leaping for the cover of the trees, and then he was gone.

Cautiously, Deryn urged Tia back down the road. The sword would give Martez the advantage if he charged her at close quarters, but as she neared the wagon, the fading sounds of him crashing away though the undergrowth were reassuring, if only in the short term.

Ross was still tangled in the cart harness, half upside down, with his feet on the driver's seat, but luckily, now the shouting had stopped, the horse looked to have given up any thought of bolting in favor of investigating what remained of the roadside vegetation. The outlaw on the road was unmoving, either dead or dying. The female outlaw was sprawled gasping on the bed of the wagon, and scarcely a greater threat than her comrade. Nevin lay beside her—or most of him did. A trail of red led Deryn to where his head had rolled, a few yards back down the road.

She grimaced, wishing she could find it in herself to be more sorry. A halfhearted prod of guilt tried to stir her conscience. Why had she not seen this coming, and stopped it? After all the time she had spent with Nevin, how could she have underestimated his incompetence? Yet even if she had predicted this, Deryn knew she would never have been able to make Nevin relinquish the Witch-Lord's sword, or make him take better care of it.

"Nevin…he…the sword…"

"It's okay, Ross. It's going to be okay." Deryn untangled his arm and helped him back onto the seat.

"But…but…the sword—"

"It's okay. I've got the bow and I'm going after Martez. I'll get the sword back, and make him pay for Nevin."

Ross took a deep breath, visibly composing himself. He was surprised, but not terrified. "Do you want me to come with you?"

Deryn shook her head. An ounce more brain matter and adequate training and Ross would be a decent soldier. It was not his fault that he had neither, but as things stood, he would be more hindrance than help. The sounds of Martez's flight had faded, but was he still running away, or was he silently returning, with an attack in mind?

"No. You stay here and guard the wagon. We don't want Martez to sneak back and make off with it."

"Martez has got the sword." Ross's eyes flicked toward Nevin's body as he spoke.

"Yes. But we've got the rest of the Witch-Lord's weapons."

"Are you going to take them all?"

"No. We'll share."

Deryn caught her lip in her teeth. How best to allocate them? The dense forest would work against the bow. Getting a clear shot at Martez was unlikely. Equally, the matted undergrowth presented ideal opportunities for an ambush, and in close combat, the sword had the advantage. Yet there was no point leaving the bow with Ross. His marksmanship was worse than useless. The carthorse would be in as much danger as Martez. Ross's own feet would not be safe.

The helmet would put any fight beyond doubt once Deryn caught up with Martez. But could she leave Ross with just the shield? Although he could not be hurt while he held it, presumably he could still be overpowered and have it taken off him. The helmet would make Ross safe, requiring nothing other than sitting with it on his head, a task that would not strain his abilities. He would not need the shield as well, but was it any use to her? Deryn shook her head, answering her own question. The shield was large, heavy, and a handicap to moving quickly and silently though the forest. Nor could she hold it and shoot the bow at the same time.

Deryn straightened her shoulders. The bow was her weapon of choice. The forest was her home ground. She could take on anyone there, regardless of demon magic.

"Ross, keep hold of the shield. Then Martez won't be able to hurt you, even with the sword, and if you put the helmet on, he won't be able to fight you anyway. Wait until I'm out of sight and then don't take it off until I come back. I'll stand down there"—Deryn pushed the shield into his hands and then pointed—"and wave when it's all safe. Tie up the prisoner again, not that I think she's going anywhere. Okay?"

Ross nodded. "Okay."

Deryn jumped from the wagon and stared into the forest. Was Martez still running? Or was he lying in wait for when she would pass within sword's reach? Until she knew exactly where Martez was, the important thing was never to take the route he expected. Deryn jogged up the road, toward higher ground, and then stepped under the cover of the towering pines.

The heavy not-quite silence of the forest enveloped her. Deryn let her ears take over, but there was nothing except the normal sounds of a forest in winter. The rustle of the wind through the treetops overhead; the crack of shifting snow on the branches; the flutter of a bird's wing; the beat of her own heart. Eyes came next. Despite the dense cover of pines, a dusting of snow had reached the ground. Prints of deer, fox, and other animals were clear, but no human feet had passed that way.

In all directions, the undergrowth was matted tangle of brown and yellow, the dead remains of summer. With a few thorny exceptions it would be easy to push through, but not without creating a lot of noise, as Martez had already demonstrated. Deryn had entered the forest on a faint animal track that would allow her to advance quickly yet silently, but she could not expect the deer to have made a path that went exactly where she wanted.

However, time was not an issue. She could go as slowly as she liked. Eventually, Martez would have to stop and rest. All Deryn had to do was to keep going just a little while longer than he did. She was younger, in better shape, and last night she had slept on a bed, not crammed into a five-foot-square pen with two others. Admittedly it had been Alana's bed, and she had not gone to sleep immediately, but when she did, she had slept very soundly.

Smiling at the memory, Deryn crept forward under the trees, on a course set to intersect with the line Martez had taken. After ten minutes of stealthy progress, she spotted an avenue of broken plant stems and twigs. The track was clearly made by something in full flight, and Martez was far and away the most likely prospect, but she needed to be sure. She did not want to end up on the trail of a panicked moose.

Before approaching, she double-checked her surroundings for any patch of vegetation big and dense enough to conceal the large man. A clump of vine maple was the only possible candidate. Deryn shifted to one side, until she could get a view straight through it. Only once she was sure did she creep close enough to see the imprint of boots. An accompanying splatter of blood confirmed that her arrow had clipped Martez, but the quantity did not suggest the wound was serious, or that it would hamper him. Deryn retreated a few yards, so she was close enough to see Martez's trail, yet distant enough to give her a chance to get a shot off if needed, and then carried on.

For another half mile she followed the trail of trampled undergrowth. The route crossed over a low ridge and then led down into a dip, where rocks broke through the covering soil. The tree cover here was thinner and the vine maple grew dense, supplemented by spikes of evergreen scotch broom. Deryn stopped and crouched down under cover. If Martez was going to try to ambush her, this was the sort of spot he would pick.

The hollow was silent, with no movement except for a woodpecker, hopping up a trunk. Then Deryn spotted a quiver run through a patch of thicket. Maybe it was another bird, but the motion had seemed a little too dispersed, suggesting it was caused by something large. Martez's trail ran straight past the spot without stopping, but of course, the outlaw would have the sense to go on a little way and then double back.

Was he there, waiting for her to go past? Deryn smiled. If so, he would have to wait a very long time. She raised her bow.

Normally, shooting blind into bushes was a good way to waste arrows, but the Witch-Lord's bow had an infinite number of arrows to waste. Deryn released the string. The leaves did not move as the arrow passed through, but Deryn heard a muffled gasp. On the third shot, Martez broke from cover, bounding away from her in wild flight.

Deryn smiled. Now that she knew exactly where he was, she could risk a closer pursuit. She could also follow in his footsteps, letting him do all the hard work of breaking the trail. Not having to plow through the undergrowth meant she could stick to a comfortable jog, while he would be getting more and more tired. Occasionally, she caught a glimpse of his back between the tree trunks, but mostly, she followed by ear. She had no need to try catching him. Much easier to wait until he collapsed from exhaustion.

Are you watching this, Shea? I hope you enjoy it.

When the sound of crashing stopped abruptly, Deryn froze. What was Martez planning now? His trail was heading down a steep incline. The lower branches of the trees merged with the undergrowth, blocking Deryn's view, but she could see that the light was markedly stronger, denoting a break in the tree cover. Were they reaching an area stripped by forest fire? In which case, she might get a clear shot at the outlaw and hasten the end of the chase. Was that why Martez had stopped running? Had he decided to turn and fight? Deryn took a tight grip on the bow and advanced with caution until she reached the edge of the trees.

The break was caused by a narrow ravine, thirty feet deep, slicing through the hillside. The walls were dirt and loose shale, too steep for trees to cling to. Twisted roots broke through the sides. A small river cascaded over the boulder-strewn bottom, cutting a black line through the white snow.

Martez had slithered down and was trying to clamber up the far side—something he was finding very difficult to do, largely because one of his hands was bandaged and missing fingers, while the other was holding the sword. He was a sitting target. Deryn stood on the lip of the gully and raised the bow.

The attempts to climb the gully wall were getting more and more frantic. His toe found purchase and he levered himself up a foot or so, but he still had a long way to climb. Martez must have known that he was running out of time. He threw a desperate glance over his shoulder, and froze, his eyes locked on the arrow that had formed on Deryn's drawn bow.

For tense seconds, neither of them moved, but then Martez relaxed, sliding back to the floor of the ravine. He faced Deryn and smiled defiantly. "Are you hoping I'm going to surrender?"

"No. I'm hoping you'll give me the excuse to shoot you."

"You like killing people?"

"Not normally. Just you."

"Yeah. You threw your knife at me before. Why?"

"It's too much to expect you'd remember me."

"Ah. You've got a grudge. Well, come on, you'll have to give me a few clues. I've lost count of the people who've sworn revenge on me." Martez paused, frowning thoughtfully. "Say, it wasn't that family, four years back in—"

"No."

"Just, you look a bit like—"

"It was a mining camp. Nine years ago. You'd found a demon wand of fireballs in some ruins."

"Oh, yes, there. My gang got wiped out. I didn't think we'd got any of your crew, though." Martez's manner was as if they were old friends, reminiscing.

"Just one. My lover. Her name was Shea."

Martez gave an exasperated sigh. "Why do people always want to tell me their names?"

"Because it's all you've left us with."

"Yeah, okay, Shea. You're pissed at me for killing her."

"I loved her."

"She wasn't just a quick fuck, then?"

Deryn's hand holding the bowstring was shaking. Her aim would not be good. At the close range, it would not need to be. She took sight, aligning the string with the side of the bow.

Martez clearly saw that he had pushed his taunting too far. He threw the Witch-Lord's sword onto the ground and raised his hands. "Go on then. Shoot me."

Deryn had never killed in cold blood. She tried to inject passion now, shuffling images in her head like a pack of cards—Shea riding her horse as if she was melded with the animal, her face in the lamplight as she climaxed, her body pale and lifeless as she lay in her grave. It did not work. She could not do it.

I'm sorry, Shea. Deryn lowered her bow, although she still kept her fingers hooked on the string. "Climb back up here."

"What you going to do about the sword?"

"I'll come back and get it, once you're secure in the wagon."

"You know the marshal will take it once you get to Oakan?"

"Yup."

"You'll get a few pissy little coins as a reward."

"Yup."

"So why not hang on to the weapons?"

"Because I don't want to become an outlaw, like you."

"Think about it. It's a great life."

"Weren't you the one who was complaining about being cold so much of the time?"

"You and I could—"

"I'm going to watch you hang, and remember Shea."

"Unless I can talk the marshal around. I know some things that might swing a deal."

"I wouldn't count on it." Deryn gestured with the bow. "Stop stalling and start climbing."

Martez pouted, as if debating with himself whether to obey Deryn, but then he crossed the gully floor and began to scramble up the rocky slope directly toward her. Now his hands were free, he could make better progress.

Deryn tried to shift a few steps back. She had no intention of letting him get within lunging range, although moving along the edge was not easy. Trees grew up to the rim of the gully. They even overhung in places, allowing little space for maneuver. Deryn found one patch of ground, just big enough for her foot, a bare four inches wide, but she was boxed in with no more room to retreat. She opened her mouth to tell Martez to climb up a few yards farther along the gully, when she felt the ground move beneath her foot. The lip of the gully had been hollowed out and was giving way under her weight. Deryn tried to shift to firmer ground, but she was out of time and space. The edge of the gully crumbled and she dropped over the edge.

Her feet landed awkwardly on the loose gravel and stones of the gully wall. The footing was unstable, especially given the steepness. Deryn stood no chance of recovering her balance. She tumbled and slid down the slope and ended up on her face at the bottom of the gully, with one foot in the icy water of the stream. Luckily she suffered no injury worse than mild bruises and grazing.

Immediately, Deryn scrambled to her knees. The bow had been ripped from her grip on the way down. She frantically cast around and spotted it halfway up the slope, lodged on a protruding tree root. At the same time, Martez was slithering down the gully wall, his goal obvious. The Witch-Lord's sword lay on the ground fifteen feet from where Deryn knelt—close, but not close enough. Martez was nearer and he was going to get to it before her. Even so, she had to try. Deryn launched herself forward, crawling, but already Martez was bending down, reaching for the sword.

Martez laughed softly as his fingers closed around the hilt. "What was the bit about being cold? What you said, back in the farmhouse? Oh yes, you said it would be warm in hell. I guess you are going to find out before me."

Deryn stayed kneeling, not bothering to stand. The ground around her was carpeted in powdery snow. Beneath it, Deryn could feel the imprint of loose rocks. Working by touch, she selected one, the size of her fist. Martez was arrogantly confident, his eyes fixed on the blade of the sword, not her, as he held it up to the light. His mouth opened, undoubtedly to deliver another taunting threat, but he never got the chance. The thrown rock smashed against his temple. Deryn's aim had always been good, with bow, knife, sling, or bare hand.

The blow thumped Martez back on his heels. He shook his head, as if hoping to clear it, but the motion only added to his daze. His balance was shaken and he stumbled to his knees. The second rock Deryn threw, bigger than the first, struck him square between the eyes. Martez landed flat on his back. Yet still his eyelids were open and his hand grasped the Witch-Lord's sword, feebly attempting to brandish it.

Deryn selected a rock, far larger and heavier than those she had thrown so far, halfway to being a small boulder. She stood up and raised the stone above her head, using both hands. It took all her strength to lob it the six feet that lay between them.

Martez's skull cracked open, like a coconut.

That one's for you, Shea.

❖

"The most powerful weapons demon magic can devise, and you killed him by throwing stones." Marshal Palemon shook his head, clearly torn between disbelief and admiration.

"Martez was careless and wasn't paying attention. He gave me a chance."

"Overconfidence let him down."

Deryn shrugged an agreement. To her mind, total self-belief was necessary for a warrior. In a fight, pessimism could so easily become a self-fulfilling prophecy. Martez's failing had been the blinkering that went with arrogance. *Observe closely, miss nothing, and focus on what's important.* This had been Brise's summing up of what it took to be a successful scout, the mantra she had instilled in Deryn.

Martez had been too pleased with himself to really notice what was going on around him. He had thought the world could be bullied into being what he wanted it to be. His focus had been wrong. He had been too enamored of the sword in his hand to pay attention to her. Had he looked, he could have ducked the first stone. If he had correctly identified what was important, the outcome might well have gone his way.

The marshal rifled through a stack of papers on his desk and pulled one out. Even with the page upside down, the lettering at the top was big enough for Deryn to read Martez's name there.

Palemon studied it briefly before continuing. "Regardless of how you did it, nailing Martez was a good job. There's a big price on his head." The corner of his mouth twitched into a fleeting ghost of a smile. "No matter what shape it's in. And I won't deny you your due, despite the difficulty it gives me."

As Martez had said, the reward paid in the king's name for turning over the Witch-Lord's weapons had been derisory in relationship to their value, little more than a month's pay to Deryn. However, the bounty for killing a wanted outlaw like Martez would be far more substantial.

Although disproportionate, it made some sort of sense. The king had no need to offer more than novelty value as a reward for handing over demon artifacts. Magic weapons were of no use to a law-abiding citizen. Even if Deryn held on to them, she dared not use them openly; otherwise she would be reported and arrested. Whereas a criminal would not hand over powerful weapons at any price. Furthermore, most commoners feared magic and would not want anything tainted by demons in their home. On the other hand, when it came to tackling an outlaw like Martez, honest citizens would need a real inducement to justify the risk. A large amount of money might also tempt a fellow criminal to betray him.

Deryn squinted, trying to make out the number printed below Martez's name. She looked to be in line to receive some serious money, enough to see her through that winter, and probably the next two as well—certainly enough to quit the job in Neupor and head down south to visit Brise.

"You're thinking you're going to be shorthanded back at the station?"

"Yes. I've lost Sergeant Nevin as well."

I'm not sure that lost *is the right word.* Deryn kept the thought to herself. "I might be induced to stay there for the winter."

Palemon frowned. "I'll happily give you Nevin's position, but I assume you're talking about more than a sergeant's salary."

"I'll take that as well, but I was thinking about the tomb. The king will want someone to investigate what else is there. If the money was right, I'd be willing to hang around in Neupor until spring as a guide for whoever he sends."

"How much?"

"A hundred dollars."

"Done." Palemon's eyes narrowed, possibly as he realized he had jumped at the offer a little too quickly. "You know you'll be getting ten times that for Martez?"

"Yes. But I was going to be staying in Neupor anyway. No harm adding to the bonus."

"Staying? Why?"

"There's somebody I want to stay with." Deryn grinned. "And if that's all, sir, I'd quite like to head off as soon as possible, so I can return to her before the snows arrive."

Palemon leaned back in his chair. His expression was halfway between amusement and disdain. "I suppose I shouldn't be surprised. We all know where Iron Wolves keep their brains."

Deryn did not challenge the implication. Let him think what he wanted. She gave a small dip of the head and turned to go, but as the door closed she caught part of the marshal's muttered parting shot.

"...a pulse and two legs."

The jibe should have irritated her, but instead Deryn smiled. True, she wanted Alana physically, far more than she had ever wanted anyone in her life, but the emotion ran so much deeper and harder. She felt the familiar ache in her cheeks from where her smile had gotten too broad.

So this is what falling in love is like.

Alana's cottage, Neupor, northern Galvonia
Two days later, diciembre 12, evening

The rich aroma of the lamb stew simmering over the hearth blended with that of fresh-baked bread and wood smoke. Amber firelight washed over the comfortable clutter filling the single room of the small cottage. The effect ought to have been cozy and reassuring, especially by contrast with the wind whistling over the thatched roof, but Alana could not relax.

A knot of disquiet had been tightening in her all afternoon. She fought the urge to open the door once again and peer out. She did not need to see how dark it was getting, or how the snow was coming down ever harder. She certainly did not want to get into the pointless game of estimating its depth and trying to judge whether the pass to Oakan would be blocked yet.

Why had Deryn not returned? Alana had expected her back by midday at the latest. Surely four full days was enough to complete the round trip. Had something gone wrong? Alana rubbed her forehead. She would not give in to panic. She would wait ten more minutes, then eat dinner and go to bed. Tomorrow she would go down to Neupor and see what news she could find. And then she would—

Alana slumped in her chair and rested her head in her hands. What would she do? What could she do? Supposing Deryn did not return. Alana closed her eyes at the thought, in part to hold back the silly tears. She should save them for when they were needed. All she was doing now was pointlessly upsetting herself.

The latch rattled. Alana was on her feet even before the door started to swing open.

Deryn stood in the doorway, a dusting of wet snow glittering on her hair and shoulders. More swirled wraithlike behind her in the fading light. Her lips were tinged with blue and the hint of darkness under her eyes revealed a lack of sleep, but she appeared unharmed and gave off no emotion other than joy.

Alana flung herself into Deryn's arms. "I was starting to worry."

"I'm sorry, it—"

The explanation could wait. Alana silenced the words with a kiss. Deryn's lips and skin were cold, but their touch flooded Alana with warmth.

Deryn's response was initially enthusiastic but short-lived. "Um."

Alana searched her face, anxiously. "What's wrong?"

"I'm cold."

"That's all? You're not hurt?"

"No."

"But what took you so long?"

Deryn laughed. "It's a bit of a story. Why don't you let me get inside and shut the door first?"

An icy gust carried with it a plume of snow, underlining the point. Even so, letting go of Deryn for the scant seconds it took to shut out the wintry dusk was an act of willpower. As soon as the door was closed Alana caught hold of Deryn's hand and drew her closer to the fire. Again she burrowed into the security of Deryn's embrace and nestled her forehead into the hollow of Deryn's neck.

"So what's the story? Did Nevin do something stupid?"

"Yes, very."

"Damn the man. What's wrong with him?"

"Quite a lot now. He's dead."

"What!"

"As I said, it's a bit of a story." Deryn took a deep breath, as if to launch into speech, but clearly became distracted and turned her face instead to the hearth. "Is that dinner cooking? I'm starved. How about we eat while I tell you?"

Now that the anxious knot inside her had loosened, Alana was aware that she also was more than a little hungry, but she still wanted another long kiss and a few minutes with her arms around Deryn before she did anything about serving the food.

While eating, they sat side by side, with legs pressed against each other, from ankle to thigh. It limited the elbow room, but was so comforting, especially when Deryn's tale reached its most dramatic parts. Alana could listen with the physical reassurance that all would work out well, even if she could not fully share Deryn's pleasure at the bounty for Martez. The reward seemed small in comparison to the danger involved, especially when considering just how much money the king's chief marshal had at her disposal.

Deryn seemed happy enough, though, at least in terms of the amount. "Sorting out the bounty claim was what took so long. I'd hoped to get away once I'd handed over the bodies, but Palemon had me giving sworn statements and signing claims and contracts all of yesterday. It was too late to set out by the time it was done, but since it's just me and Ross now, and I'm acting sergeant, we were able to leave Oakan before dawn. Just as well, because the way it's snowing, if we'd left it any later, we wouldn't have made it." Deryn smiled. "I think we might be snowed in up here now until spring."

Alana put down her empty bowl and wrapped her arm around Deryn's waist. "Snowed in for months with you doesn't sound too bad."

"It'll give us time to work out what we do next." Deryn's tone was devoid of emphasis as she delivered the words, but her emotions flared with doubt, verging on distress.

Alana looked sharply in her direction. "You're worried about something?"

Deryn was staring at the flames. "I don't know, it's…" She sighed and caught her lip in her teeth.

Was Deryn having second thoughts about their relationship? Alana's throat tightened, but she forced herself to ask, "What?"

"I'm sure Palemon would give me the sergeant's job here as a permanent thing, if I asked, but a place like Neupor, it's not where I thought I'd end up. And I don't know if I can…" She ended in an unhappy shrug.

Was that all? Alana smiled in relief. "If it makes it any easier for you, I don't particularly want to stay here either. And now I can control my talent, there's no reason why I should."

"You want to go back to your family in Ellaye?"

"Oh no." The mere thought made Alana cringe. "I'm well out of all that nonsense."

"Do you have any other plans?"

"No. Do you?"

"In the short term, money's no problem, thanks to the bounty, but eventually I'll need to work."

"And I've still got the gold chain I picked up at the tomb." Alana grinned. "The king's people don't know what was there, so they aren't going to miss it."

"If you help guide them to the tomb, maybe you could claim a reward as well."

"No. It would be safer if I'm nowhere in sight when they arrive. Orrin will probably want to visit the tomb in person, and I'd much prefer he doesn't see me."

"Does he know you're here?"

"Yes."

"Won't he want to talk to you?"

"Not as such. Tell him I started acting strange and then one day I vanished into the forest, and I haven't been seen since. You won't catch him shedding many tears. I'll hide out in Oakan. Once you've shown him where the tomb is, you can join me, and we can blow some of that money. As long as you don't mind sharing it with me."

"I'll have to think about it." Deryn mimicked seriousness, but then grinned. "We could have some fun."

"I'm sure of it."

"We could visit my foster mother. You say you don't want to stay with your family, but you could call in on them, maybe, without the king or Orrin knowing."

"I'd rather not."

"You don't like them?"

"It's not that. We're sort of fond of each other, some of the time, but if they knew I could control my talent, they'd want to use me, and I don't want to be used."

Deryn nodded, and turned back to staring at the fire. The concern in her had softened, but not faded completely.

Alana caught hold of Deryn's hand and raised it to her lips before asking. "So what do you think you'd want to do in the long term?"

"If it was just me, I'd go back to riding the Misery Trail. But I don't want to spend months away from you."

This was where the root of Deryn's unhappiness lay. Alana felt a smile grow on her lips, not that she liked her lover to be distressed, but it was nice to know just how much Deryn wanted to be with her. She pressed Deryn's hand against her cheek, partly to hide the smile, and partly because the contact felt so good.

"You don't get rid of me that easily, you know. Anyway, you might be tired of me after a few months, and welcome a break."

"Never." Deryn frowned as her doubts did a U-turn. "Do you think you'll get tired of me?"

"Stranger things have happened."

At the expression on Deryn's face, Alana could not restrain her laughter. Deryn really was very naive when it came to relationships. She met Deryn's eyes, hoping to show that the reservations were a result of her experience, not her intentions.

"I wish I could say I'm teasing you, but always, at the start of an affair, you feel certain it will last forever, and then the lust wears off, and you're left with someone you discover you don't like very much, and they develop lots of annoying habits and before long…"

Deryn's gaze was boring deeper and deeper into her soul, and with each word, the absurdity of what she was saying grew, until Alana could no longer go on. Was Deryn truly different from those who had gone before? Had Alana ever been so convinced that a lover was the only one for her? She looked down, regathering her thoughts. Were Deryn and she made for each other? Maybe in another thirty years or so, she would be able to answer that question, and regardless of how things turned out, she would be a fool not to give it her best shot now.

Alana lifted her head again. Her options were simple. "If you want to ride the Trail, I'll go with you."

"You don't have the training to be an Iron Wolf, and they don't take passengers on the Trail."

"But they have horses, and mules. Isn't there a need for someone to look after them? I'd be the best wrangler in the business." Alana grinned. "People would swear the animals could talk to me."

"As long as they don't really believe it, you'd do fine." Deryn started to smile, but then her expression faltered into dismay.

"What is it now?"

"The Misery Trail is dangerous. When I wanted to become an Iron Wolf, my foster mother tried to talk me out of it, because she was scared for me. I've just realized what she was feeling. I…I don't want you to be in danger. You'd be safer back here, waiting."

"I've just spent four days worrying about you. There is no way on earth I'm going to sit on my own for months, wondering if a windigo has bitten you in half and whether I'm going to see you again."

"But all the time we were on the Trail, I'd be worrying about you. I couldn't bear it if anything happened to you."

"Then it would be up to you to make sure you took good care of me. Isn't that part of your job, as scout, keeping the party safe?"

"Yes, but—"

"But nothing. I'm not letting you ride off without me. Anyway, I'd like to see the wilderness, and Sluey, even Nawlings."

Deryn frowned. The argument was not yet concluded, but Alana knew she would win in the end. For now she merely smiled and shifted around so she could rest her head on Deryn's shoulder. They sat for a while in silence, watching the flames and listening to the wind outside.

Deryn's arm tightened, pulling her close. "Do you really think you'll get tired of me?"

"I'm utterly convinced I won't. Right now, I want to spend the rest of my life with you, and can't imagine it changing. I don't know if I can trust my feelings, but all of that is for the future. We can wait and see how things go."

Alana turned so she could pull Deryn's head down into a kiss, deeper and more ardent than those that had gone before. Passion ignited inside her, a need to hold Deryn in her arms, a need to touch and be touched. She placed her hands on either side of Deryn's face and gently pushed her back so that she was again staring, years deep, into Deryn's eyes.

"For now, we need to go to bed." Alana could hear her own voice growing husky with desire.

"You want to sleep?"

"No. Do you?"

About the Author

Jane Fletcher is a GCLS award–winning writer and has also been short-listed for the Gaylactic Spectrum and Lambda Literary awards. She is author of two ongoing sets of fantasy/romance novels: the Celaeno series—*The Walls of Westernfort, Rangers at Roadsend, The Temple at Landfall, Dynasty of Rogues*, and *Shadow of the Knife*; and the Lyremouth Chronicles—*The Exile and The Sorcerer, The Traitor and The Chalice*, and *The Empress and The Acolyte*, and *The High Priest and the Idol.*

Her love of fantasy began at the age of seven when she encountered Greek mythology. This was compounded by a childhood spent clambering over every example of ancient masonry she could find (medieval castles, megalithic monuments, Roman villas). Her resolute ambition was to become an archaeologist when she grew up, so it was something of a surprise when she became a software engineer instead.

Born in Greenwich, London, in 1956, she now lives in southwest England, where she keeps herself busy writing both computer software and fiction, although generally not at the same time.

Visit her Web site—www.janefletcher.co.uk.

Books Available From Bold Strokes Books

Fierce Overture by Gun Brooke. Helena Forsythe is a hard-hitting CEO who gets what she wants by taking no prisoners when negotiating—until she meets a woman who convinces her that charm may be the way to win a battle, and a heart. (978-1-60282-156-9)

Trauma Alert by Radclyffe. Dr. Ali Torveau has no trouble saying no to romance until the day firefighter Beau Cross shows up in her ER and sets her carefully ordered world aflame. (978-1-60282-157-6)

Wolfsbane Winter by Jane Fletcher. Iron Wolf mercenary Deryn faces down demon magic and otherworldly foes with a smile, but she's defenseless when healer Alana wages war on her heart. (978-1-60282-158-3)

Little White Lie by Lea Santos. Emie Jaramillo knows relationships are for other people, and beautiful women like Gia Mendez don't belong anywhere near her boring world of academia—until Gia sets out to convince Emie she has not only brains, but beauty...and that she's the only woman Gia wants in her life. (978-1-60282-163-7)

Witch Wolf by Winter Pennington. In a world where vampires have charmed their way into modern society, where werewolves walk the streets with their beasts disguised by human skin, Investigator Kassandra Lyall has a secret of her own to protect. She's one of them. (978-1-60282-177-4)

Do Not Disturb by Carsen Taite. Ainsley Faraday, a high-powered executive, and rock music celebrity Greer Davis couldn't be less well suited for one another, and yet they soon discover passion has a way of designing its own future. (978-1-60282-153-8)

From This Moment On by PJ Trebelhorn. Devon Conway and Katherine Hunter both lost love and neither believes they will ever find it again—until the moment they meet and everything changes. (978-1-60282-154-5)

Vapor by Larkin Rose. When erotic romance writer Ashley Vaughn decides to take her research into the bedroom for a night of passion with Victoria Hadley, she discovers that fact is hotter than fiction. (978-1-60282-155-2)

Wind and Bones by Kristin Marra. Jill O'Hara, award-winning journalist, just wants to settle her deceased father's affairs and leave Prairie View, Montana, far, far behind—but an old girlfriend, a sexy sheriff, and a dangerous secret keep her down on the ranch. (978-1-60282-150-7)

Nightshade by Shea Godfrey. The story of a princess, betrothed as a political pawn, who falls for her intended husband's soldier sister, is a modern-day fairy tale to capture the heart. (978-1-60282-151-4)

Vieux Carré Voodoo by Greg Herren. Popular New Orleans detective Scotty Bradley just can't stay out of trouble—especially when an old flame turns up asking for help. (978-1-60282-152-1)

The Pleasure Set by Lisa Girolami. Laney DeGraff, a successful president of a family-owned bank on Rodeo Drive, finds her comfortable life taking a turn toward danger when Theresa Aguilar, a sleek, sexy lawyer, invites her to join an exclusive, secret group of powerful, alluring women. (978-1-60282-144-6)

A Perfect Match by Erin Dutton. The exciting world of pro golf forms the backdrop for a fast-paced, sexy romance. (978-1-60282-145-3)

Father Knows Best by Lynda Sandoval. High school juniors and best friends Lila Moreno, Meryl Morganstern, and Caressa Thibodoux plan to make the most of the summer before senior year. What they discover that amazing summer about girl power, growing up, and trusting friends and family more than prepares them to tackle that all-important senior year! (978-1-60282-147-7)

The Midnight Hunt by L.L. Raand. Medic Drake McKennan takes a chance and loses, and her life will never be the same—because when she wakes up after surviving a life-threatening illness, she is no longer human. (978-1-60282-140-8)

Long Shot by D. Jackson Leigh. Love isn't safe, which is exactly why equine veterinarian Tory Greyson wants no part of it—until Leah Montgomery and a horse that won't give up convince her otherwise. (978-1-60282-141-5)

In Medias Res by Yolanda Wallace. Sydney has forgotten her entire life, and the one woman who holds the key to her memory, and her heart, doesn't want to be found. (978-1-60282-142-2)

Awakening to Sunlight by Lindsey Stone. Neither Judith or Lizzy is looking for companionship, and certainly not love—but when their lives become entangled, they discover both. (978-1-60282-143-9)

Fever by VK Powell. Hired gun Zakaria Chambers is hired to provide a simple escort service to philanthropist Sara Ambrosini, but nothing is as simple as it seems, especially love. (978-1-60282-135-4)

Truths by Rebecca S. Buck. Two women separated by two hundred years are connected by fate and love. (978-1-60282-146-0)

High Risk by JLee Meyer. Can actress Kate Hoffman really risk all she's worked for to take a chance on love? Or is it already too late? (978-1-60282-136-1)

Missing Lynx by Kim Baldwin and Xenia Alexiou. On the trail of a notorious serial killer, Elite Operative Lynx's growing attraction to a mysterious mercenary could be her path to love—or to death. (978-1-60282-137-8)

Spanking New by Clifford Henderson. A poignant, hilarious, unforgettable look at life, love, gender, and the essence of what makes us who we are. (978-1-60282-138-5)

Magic of the Heart by C.J. Harte. CEO Susan Hettinger and wild, impulsive rock star M.J. Carson couldn't be more different if they tried—but opposites attract in ways neither woman can resist. (978-1-60282-131-6)

Ambereye by Gill McKnight. Jolie Garoul is falling in love with her assistant. The big problem is, Jolie is a werewolf. (978-1-60282-132-3)

Collision Course by C.P. Rowlands. Tragedy leaves Brie O'Malley and Jordan Carter fearful and alone. Can they find the courage to take a second chance on love? (978-1-60282-133-0)

Mephisto Aria by Justine Saracen. Opera singer Katherina Marov's destiny may be to repeat the mistakes of her father when she becomes involved in a dangerous love affair. (978-1-60282-134-7)

Battle Scars by Meghan O'Brien. Returning Iraq war veteran Ray McKenna struggles with the battle scars that can only be healed by love. (978-1-60282-129-3)

Chaps by Jove Belle. Eden Metcalf wants nothing more than to flee from her troubled past and travel the open road—until she runs into rancher Brandi Cornwell. (978-1-60282-127-9)

Lightbearer by John Caruso. Lucifer dares to question the premise of creation itself and reveals that sin may be all that stands between us and living hell. (978-1-60282-130-9)

The Seeker by Ronica Black. FBI profiler Kennedy Scott battles ghosts from her past, deadly obsession, and the evil that haunts her. (978-1-60282-128-6)

Power Play by Julie Cannon. Businesswomen Tate Monroe and Victoria Sosa are at odds in the boardroom, but not in the bedroom. (978-1-60282-125-5)

The Remarkable Journey of Miss Tranby Quirke by Elizabeth Ridley. When love enters Tranby's life in the form of a beautiful nineteen-year-old student, Lysette McDonald, she embarks on the most remarkable journey of all. (978-1-60282-126-2)

Returning Tides by Radclyffe. Insurance investigator Ashley Walker faces more than a dangerous opponent when she returns to the town, and the woman, she left behind. (978-1-60282-123-1)

Veritas by Anne Laughlin. When the hallowed halls of academia become the stage for murder, newly appointed Dean Beth Ellis's search for the truth leads her to unexpected discoveries about her own heart. (978-1-60282-124-8)

The Pleasure Planner by Larkin Rose. Pleasure purveyor Bree Hendricks treats love like a commodity until Logan Delaney makes Bree the client in her own game. (978-1-60282-121-7)

everafter by Nell Stark and Trinity Tam. Valentine Darrow is bitten by a vampire on her way to propose to her lover Alexa Newland, and their lives and love are placed in mortal jeopardy. (978-1-60282-119-4)

Beggar of Love by Lee Lynch. Jefferson is the lover every woman wants to be—or to have. A revealing saga of lesbian sexuality. (978-1-60282-122-4)

Summer Winds by Andrews & Austin. When Maggie Turner hires a ranch hand to help work her thousand acres, she never expects to be attracted to the very young, very female Cash Tate. (978-1-60282-120-0)

The Seduction of Moxie by Colette Moody. When 1930s Broadway actress Violet London meets speakeasy singer Moxie Valette, she is instantly attracted and her Hollywood trip takes an unexpected turn. (978-1-60282-114-9)

Goldenseal by Gill McKnight. When Amy Fortune returns to her childhood home, she discovers something sinister in the air—but is former lover Leone Garoul stalking her or protecting her? (978-1-60282-115-6)

Romantic Interludes 2: Secrets edited by Radclyffe and Stacia Seaman. An anthology of sensual lesbian love stories: passion, surprises, and secret desires. (978-1-60282-116-3)

Femme Noir by Clara Nipper. Nora Delaney meets her match in Max Abbott, a sex-crazed dame who may or may not have the information Nora needs to solve a murder—but can she contain her lust for Max long enough to find out? (978-1-60282-117-0)

The Reluctant Daughter by Lesléa Newman. Heartwarming, heartbreaking, and ultimately triumphant—the story every daughter recognizes of the lifelong struggle for our mothers to really see us. (978-1-60282-118-7)

Erosistible by Gill McKnight. When Win Martin arrives at a luxurious Greek hotel for a much-anticipated week of sun and sex with her new girlfriend, she is stunned to find her ex-girlfriend, Benny, is the proprietor. Aeros Ebook. (978-1-60282-134-7)

Looking Glass Lives by Felice Picano. Cousins Roger and Alistair become lifelong friends and discover their sexuality amidst the backdrop of twentieth-century gay culture. (978-1-60282-089-0)

Breaking the Ice by Kim Baldwin. Nothing is easy about life above the Arctic Circle—except, perhaps, falling in love. At least that's what pilot Bryson Faulkner hopes when she meets Karla Edwards. (978-1-60282-087-6)

It Should Be a Crime by Carsen Taite. Two women fulfill their mutual desire with a night of passion, neither expecting more until law professor Morgan Bradley and student Parker Casey meet again…in the classroom. (978-1-60282-086-9)

Rough Trade edited by Todd Gregory. Top male erotica writers pen their own hot, sexy versions of the term "rough trade," producing some of the hottest, nastiest, and most dangerous fiction ever published. (978-1-60282-092-0)

The High Priest and the Idol by Jane Fletcher. Jemeryl and Tevi's relationship is put to the test when the Guardian sends Jemeryl on a mission that puts her not only in harm's way, but back into the sights of a previous lover. (978-1-60282-085-2)

Point of Ignition by Erin Dutton. Amid a blaze that threatens to consume them both, firefighter Kate Chambers and property owner Alexi Clark redefine love and trust. (978-1-60282-084-5)

Secrets in the Stone by Radclyffe. Reclusive sculptor Rooke Tyler suddenly finds herself the object of two very different women's affections, and choosing between them will change her life forever. (978-1-60282-083-8)